MW00623073

ZODIAC ALIGNED

ZODIAC WOLVES
BOOK 4

ELIZABETH BRIGGS

ZODIAC ALIGNED (ZODIAC WOLVES #4)

Copyright © 2023 by Elizabeth Briggs

All rights reserved. This book or any portion thereof may not be reproduced or used in any manner whatsoever without the express written permission of the publisher except for the use of brief quotations in a book review.

This is a work of fiction. Names, characters, businesses, places, events and incidents are either the products of the author's imagination or used in a fictitious manner. Any resemblance to actual persons, living or dead, or actual events is purely coincidental.

Cover designed by Natasha Snow

Cover photo by Wander Aguiar

Models: Pat Tanski and Evan Keys

ISBN ebook: 978-1-948456-37-1

ISBN paperback: 978-1-948456-73-9

CHAPTER ONE

THE STARS TWINKLED ABOVE ME, cold and beautiful, and I couldn't help but wonder if my fate was written in their shimmering light. I stared at them, desperately hoping for a sign of some kind, or a hint of what my future held, but all I felt was lost, with no way to find the path I was meant to follow.

I turned my gaze back to what lay before me, but it did nothing to lift my spirits. The snow-covered clearing where the Convergence battle had happened the day before had been ravaged, torn up by both human feet and wolf claws. Some of the ground was scorched from the Sun Witch's flames, and the smell of death and smoke hung thick in the air.

On one side, a cluster of tents had been set up haphazardly in a ragged line for all the remaining shifters, many of whom were tending to the wounded and sleeping off the post-battle exhaustion. It was a temporary setup, but we all needed to recover before making any hard decisions about what to do next.

So many lives had been lost when the Sun Witches had taken control of the Zodiac Wolves and made them fight each other like mindless animals. Even more were injured, and some of the wounds were grave. I'd walked through some of the tents earlier to check on the other packs, but at one point I'd had to leave and get some air. The sight of so many shifters injured at one time broke my heart.

With the help of the Virgo and Ophiuchus healers, along with some rest and food, most of the injured shifters would be able to heal on their own over time. The others... I tried not to think about them. Especially since there was very little I could do for them now that I was no longer an Ophiuchus.

It could be worse, though. Yes, we'd been horribly defeated. We'd lost so much, and all our plans to stop the Sun Witches had failed. But we'd also revealed the true depths of the Sun Witches' powers for all the Zodiac Wolves to see, and when they'd mind-controlled all of the packs—except the Ophiuchus—we'd found a way to break free. Now no one would be able to deny that the Sun Witches had been lying to us for all these years, or pretend they were still our allies. We'd even managed to score a minor win of our own too.

Two shifters stood in front of one of the tents, guarding it. Although Evanora had escaped, along with the magical staff she used to mind control us, we'd managed to capture her daughter, Roxandra. We had her knocked out with

Ophiuchus poison for now, but we weren't taking any chances. She'd been put under heavy surveillance, and she'd be kept that way until we decided what to do with her. Roxandra was our best bet at finding a way to defeat the Sun Witches, and I couldn't wait until we could get her to a secure location and talk to her. She had information we needed, including how to break the false mate bonds. At this point, I was willing to try just about anything to get rid of the mating bond with Jordan.

Something caught my eye, drawing my gaze toward the edge of the clearing. The Aquarius pack moved as one, heads held high, though their faces were haggard and their eyes were wary as they disappeared into the snowy forest. I wasn't surprised to see them go. Many of the other packs had already left to return to their pack lands. The Scorpio, Aries, and Taurus packs had been the first to go, unsurprisingly. They'd been allied with the Leos and the Sun Witches, and none of us knew whose side they were on anymore. Would they ally with us now that they'd seen how the Sun Witches were controlling them? Could we trust them if they did?

For now, we'd let them go. Every other pack would be heading out in the morning too, returning to their pack lands to recover and regroup for the next fight. There would be a next fight, that much was clear, and we all needed to decide what we were going to do about it.

Something rustled in the bushes behind me, and I spun around quickly, already moving into a fighting position and drawing moon magic into my hands. I was still on edge from the fight, and half expected Evanora to loom out of the forest, staff in hand and ready to kill me for taking her daughter.

When I saw who it was, I still didn't relax. Kaden stood behind me, his dark hair unruly and his beard a bit too long. He moved with an alpha's grace and a masculine presence, though his steps were more hesitant as he neared me. When his eyes met mine, a rush of heat swept over me. I found myself drinking in the sight of him like I was parched for thirst and only he could sate me, but then I quickly looked away. I hated that he still could elicit that reaction from me with just a look.

"Is everything okay?" he asked. "I saw you go out here alone, and when you didn't return..."

I stiffened, torn between feeling pleased that he was worried for me, and annoyed that he wouldn't leave me alone. I'd been avoiding him as much as I could by leaving whenever he showed up or quickly excusing myself from conversations when he joined in. I knew that we'd have to talk at some point, but every time I faced him, all I felt was pain.

"I just needed some air," I said.

I still couldn't believe he'd kicked me out of the Ophiuchus pack. After everything I'd been through, he had to know how much that act would hurt me, and yet he'd still done it. It didn't matter that he'd apologized after the fact, or that he'd regretted what he had done. He had still turned his back on me and everything we'd built together, making me packless once more. I couldn't pretend like none of that had happened, or that I hadn't been destroyed by it.

He'd broken my trust. He'd broken *me*.

For that, I wasn't sure I could ever forgive him.

He knew it too. I could tell from the way his eyes shifted away from me, and from the heavy breath he took as he considered his next words.

"We have food at the Ophiuchus tent." He paused, waiting for me to answer. "You're welcome to join us."

I stared back at him for a few heartbeats, and my breath caught in my throat as I remembered the way his voice had sounded as he'd removed my Ophiuchus pack mark. I missed the other pack members more than I could express in words, and I desperately longed to share a meal with them now. Their scents would be warm, comforting, familiar—like home. Except it was a home that was no longer mine.

"I'm not hungry," I finally said. A lie and we both knew it.

Kaden stepped forward, his brows furrowing. "You're still one of us. Even if your pack mark is gone."

His voice went soft with another unspoken apology. It didn't have the effect he'd probably desired. Anger rose inside of me, and I turned to face him fully for the first time since he'd emerged from the bushes.

"You're the one who kicked me out." My hands clenched at my side and hot tears pricked my eyes. "You're the one who removed my pack mark. Now you act like I can still be one of you? Like it never happened? Like you didn't break my heart when you rejected me and made me packless?"

Kaden's face twisted with frustration and he jerked a

hand through his hair, his movements almost angry. Good. I didn't want to see his softness. I didn't want it to weaken me.

"Ayla," Kaden said. "That night... I wasn't thinking right, and I regret everything I did. I told you I made a mistake. What more do you want from me? Do you want me to grovel on my knees in front of you and beg for your forgiveness? I'll do it. I'll do whatever it takes."

"I don't want anything from you." Another lie. My heart ached, begging for that connection once more. I wanted to be a part of the pack I'd called home, and even more than that, I wanted to be his mate again, but there was no way I was going to tell him that.

"I can make you a part of the pack again," Kaden said, as if hearing my deepest desire anyway. "It was a mistake removing your pack mark. Let me make it right."

I shook my head, as the anger left me and turned back to despair. "All I ever wanted was a pack. A family. A mate. And right when I'd finally found all of that, you took it away from me." A single tear broke free and slid down my cheek as I forced the next words out. "You hurt me more than you could ever understand."

Kaden's eyes fixated on the tear on my cheek, his jaw tightening. "Ayla..."

I cut him off before he could say something that might make me break even more. I had to get the next words out, no matter how much they pained me. "I don't know if I belong with the Ophiuchus pack anymore." I drew in a shaky breath. "Or with you."

Kaden's eyes flashed with a reflection of my pain, and I

turned away before I could drown in it. Once I would have run into his arms and confessed my fears, knowing he was my safe place, the person I could turn to when I needed help. But he wasn't that person anymore. He had taken my love and dashed it against the wall, breaking it like a glass plate.

He called after me once, but I squared my shoulders and kept going.

I walked away from Kaden, and I didn't look back.

CHAPTER TWO

I WIPED my eyes as I headed back toward the tents. Wesley had been kind enough to loan me one, and I'd set it up near the Cancer and Libra packs, but still far enough away that it was clear I wasn't with them.

One other outcast tent sat beside mine. No one wanted to touch Jordan with a ten-foot pole in case they got mixed up in the politics surrounding him. Ethan, the Libra alpha, had loaned him the tent, always willing to play the peace-maker, and I appreciated his cool head more than I could ever express to him in words.

If only I could channel that cool head myself, I thought dryly, remembering my outburst of emotion with Kaden. I couldn't think straight when he was around. Every time he spoke to me, all the anger and pain filled me up until I burst, and I didn't know how to make that stop. The worst part was that I still loved Kaden, even after everything he'd done. My heart was broken, my mind was confused, but my soul still knew who my true mate was.

Jordan looked up as I stomped back over to the tent. His large frame was crouched in front of a makeshift fire pit, and he poked at the embers with a stick. His face was sour, and his body language screamed *leave me alone*.

"You look like you're in the same mood that I'm in," I said.

Jordan's scowl deepened, and he dropped the stick into the pit. It caught on fire after popping ominously a few times. "The Leo pack left without me."

That stopped me in my tracks. "What?"

"The beta took over, claiming he's the new alpha, and now they're gone. I have no idea where they went. I can't even follow them to try and reclaim my title as alpha." He sank to the ground and leaned back, stretching out his long legs. "It's like I'm packless now."

A bitter laugh escaped me as I sat next to him. "Welcome to the club."

"It's a shitty club to be in," he muttered.

"Tell me about it."

Jordan offered me a bag of chips, which I took with a nod of thanks. My stomach soured at the reminder that I could have had dinner with the Ophiuchus if things were different. This would have to do for now.

"You're still the alpha," I said while munching on a few chips. They weren't very good, but I ate a few more because I was hungry and I needed my strength. "You proved that during the Convergence when you used your alpha command to save your pack and stop them from fighting."

"I guess," he said, staring into the fire. This was a far cry from the cocky alpha I'd come to know, and I hated seeing him so out of sorts. He shook his head after a few moments and turned his gaze toward me. "What's gotten you in a bad mood tonight?"

"Kaden wants me back, but I'm still upset with him." I considered how much I should tell Jordan, before deciding he might as well know all of it. In an odd turn of events, Jordan understood me better than anyone at the moment. "I don't know where I belong anymore."

"Hmm." Jordan glanced over toward the tent where Roxandra was being held. "Maybe once the mate bond is removed, you'll know. Maybe we both will."

"I hope so," I said.

Jordan's eyes finally lit with the spark I was used to seeing there. "I can't wait until every bit of Sun Witch magic is removed from me." His hand drifted up to his neck, where he touched the moonstone pendant I'd given him. I'd let him keep it for now since it was the only thing stopping them from getting in his head. I couldn't imagine what it was like to have their magic in my mind all the time.

"How much did they control you?" I asked in a low voice.

"Too much. It went on for a long time." He opened his mouth like he wanted to say something else, but stopped himself and looked away.

"It's okay if you don't want to talk about it," I said. "But if you do, I'm here to listen. It might feel good to get it all out, you know?"

Jordan's mouth twisted, and I thought he would keep quiet, but eventually he started talking. "After the summer Convergence, the Sun Witches started living with the Leo pack. That's when they first got into my head."

He paused and I opened my mouth to tell him that he didn't have to share everything if it made him uncomfortable, but he continued before I could get the words out.

"It was subtle at first. So subtle I didn't even know they were there. They preyed on my emotions, my weaknesses, and my fears, turning them all against me. It wasn't until too late that I realized they were manipulating me. By then, they had me doing things that I'd never do in my right mind." Jordan looked back over at me, and a muscle in his jaw ticked. "Things like threatening to light kids on fire. I'm sorry for that."

I swallowed, remembering how he'd gotten me to leave the Ophiuchus pack with him. I'd hated him for that for a long time. Knowing that it wasn't him changed everything. I didn't think it was possible for me to hate the Sun Witches more than I already did, but hearing what Jordan had endured proved me wrong. I had the feeling he wasn't telling me everything either.

"What else did they do to you?" I asked, almost scared to hear the answer. How much of what I'd hated about Jordan hadn't been truly him at all?

Jordan stared into the fire as if he was remembering something. "After my father died and I became alpha, it got worse. They made me think I was in control until they wanted to prove a point. Like when they had me beat you when you tried to escape."

I remembered how Roxandra had whispered in Jordan's ear at that time. I hadn't thought anything of it back then, but now it made total, sickening sense. And if they'd made him do that...

"They made you try to force the mating with me too, didn't they?" I asked.

Jordan drew in a shuddering breath. "I still don't know how you can talk to me after that."

I swallowed hard, pushing back the memories of that night. "Even after it happened, even when I thought the worst of you, I saw there was some good in you too, deep down."

"You're wrong." Jordan shook his head. "Between my father's alpha commands and the Sun Witches whispering in my head, I don't know who I am anymore. But I know it isn't good."

I bumped my shoulder against his. "All of that is over now. No one's in your head anymore. You get to decide who you want to be now."

Jordan looked away again, but the frown on his face was more contemplative now. I hoped that my words would give him something to think about at least. Jordan had been a pawn in a long, awful game, but now he had a chance to start fresh and make some real changes. But it was up to him to make it happen. All I could do was be there for him and try to make sure he didn't stumble down a dark path again.

"Hey," Stella said, and I looked up in surprise as she approached, her boots crunching through the snow. She wore a big puffy coat, but her long dark hair was free and blew behind her in the wind. She gave Jordan a cold look and pointedly didn't greet him. "How are you doing, Ayla?"

"I'm fine. I mean, as fine as any of us can be." I couldn't keep the bitter note out of my voice.

"Somehow I don't believe that." She tilted her head and studied me with eyes that were too much like her brother's. "Kaden looked like hell when he got back to the tent, so I figured you two had another fight."

I sighed. "Things are complicated between us right now."

"That's the understatement of the year. I can't believe what my brother did to you. I gave him an earful about what an idiot he is, and how he needs to let you back into the pack right now. It's not right. You're one of us."

"Thanks," I said, warming a little at her words. "But we'll figure it out. Eventually."

"You know you can stay in my tent, right?"

"I appreciate that, but I think it's better that I stay away for now."

"Okay," Stella said, sounding like she was only agreeing to make me feel better. "But in my mind, you're one of us forever."

A lump formed in my throat at the sentiment, and I blinked rapidly, trying to stop myself from tearing up. "Thank you," I managed.

"I'll see you tomorrow," she said, before turning and walking away, without acknowledging Jordan even once.

I glanced at him to see if he was offended, only to find him staring at her with an intensity I hadn't seen in some time. His eyes followed her all the way to her tent, and he only looked back at me once she disappeared inside.

"Who was that?" he asked.

"Kaden's sister, Stella," I said. "Why?"

"Ah, so that's why she hates me." He nodded slowly, as if working something out in his head, but before I could ask him what it was, he rose to his feet. "I'm heading to bed. Night."

As he slipped inside his tent, I frowned after him, wondering what that was about. Freaking alphas and their mood swings. I shook my head and finished my chips before heading into my own tent, praying that tomorrow would bring some much-needed clarity.

CHAPTER THREE

WHEN MORNING CAME, I packed up my things and took down my tent, then went to say my goodbyes to Wesley. He looked up as I walked to the Cancer part of the camp and stood up to meet me. A few other Cancer pack shifters glanced at me, but they all stayed away as they packed up their belongings and prepared to depart.

"So this is goodbye for now?" he asked with a crooked smile, his eyes warm.

"I'm sure we'll speak again soon," I said, though I couldn't ignore the pang in my chest knowing he was leaving to head back to the Cancer pack lands. He was the only person here who still treated me the same after everything that had happened.

He cleared his throat. "You could come with us. I could make you a member of our pack again."

His words were kind, and I knew he was only trying to help me, but the thought of being a Cancer again made my gut twist. I'd suffered so much as one of them, and I wasn't sure they would ever accept me, even if my brother was alpha now. If anything, making me a member now, after I'd been cast out by another pack, might only cause problems for him. I couldn't allow anyone to question his leadership, not when things were already so dire. The Cancers—hell, the entire Zodiac Wolves—needed Wesley's leadership now more than ever.

"That's nice of you to offer, but I don't think that's a good idea." Even as I turned him down, I wondered if I was making a mistake. Wesley had always been my rock, the one person I could depend on when I was growing up. Though I'd hated living with the Cancer pack, it was tempting to go back to what was familiar, even if I knew in my heart it wasn't right. "I'm packless for now. Besides, I still have work to do." I jerked my head toward the tent the Ophiuchus pack members were guarding. "I'm going with the Libras to interrogate the Sun Witch and see if we can break the mating bonds."

"I understand," Wesley said. "But you'll always be welcome with the Cancer pack. I hope you know that." He lightly touched my arm. "Things are different now. You wouldn't be an outcast anymore."

I hugged him tightly. "You're the best thing that's ever happened to that pack. I hope you know that."

He chuckled low in his chest. "I'm not sure about that, but I'm doing my best."

I reluctantly pulled back from him. "Be safe."

"You too. Talk soon."

I walked away quickly, unsure of what I'd do if I stayed. There were so many emotions running through me still, and last night's sleep hadn't cleared them up. The desire to be a part of a pack again, or to be close to my family once more, was overwhelming sometimes.

I headed for the Libra pack next, searching out Ethan's familiar face among all the shifters. They'd already finished packing and it seemed like they were ready to go. He was talking to a few of the other Libra pack members when I found him. Though there was still snow on the ground, he wore no coat, only a button-down shirt with the sleeves pushed back, revealing his tattooed arms. Shifters always ran hot, but I got the feeling he was so busy he barely even noticed the cold.

"Oh, Ayla, good," he said, as he stepped away from the other shifters to speak alone with me. "I was just about to come and look for you. Do you think you'll be able to teleport all the Libra and Ophiuchus members back to the hotel in Toronto?"

"Both packs?" I asked, even though it was a stupid question. The Ophiuchus pack was still staying at the hotel in Toronto, after all. Of course they would be leaving at the same time as the Libras. But teleporting the Ophiuchus pack members meant teleporting Kaden too.

"Yes, along with Larkin and Jordan," Ethan continued. "They've both requested to come with us. And we'll also be bringing Roxandra, of course. Will that many people be a problem?"

"I'm not sure, but I can try." Both packs had only brought

their best warriors, and a few had been lost during the battle. I'd never teleported so many people before, but I'd grown strong in magic over the last few months. I didn't think the moon would fail me.

"Thank you for doing this," Ethan said, his voice low. "I know it must be hard for you."

I shifted on my feet, trying not to show just how uncomfortable I was. "I'm just eager to get out of here."

"I can understand that." He paused and studied me, his eyes seeing far too much. "I don't agree with what Kaden did, but I'm also not the person who can fix it. Just know that you're always welcome as a guest of the Libra pack. We'll help you with whatever you need."

"Thank you," I said, my chest tightening with emotion. "I really appreciate that. But right now all I want is to get some answers from Roxandra and to try to move forward."

"Of course."

The Ophiuchus arrived then, and my eyes were immediately drawn to Kaden, though I tried not to look at him. Being around him was like a punch to the gut, and it suddenly became hard to breathe. I tore my gaze away from him to count their numbers but seeing Stella and the other Ophiuchus members—including Harper, Dane, and Jack—giving me looks of pity only reminded me that I wasn't one of them anymore.

I was an outcast, someone who didn't belong anywhere. *Packless.*

I shook the thoughts away as Jordan joined the crowd, though everyone gave him a wide berth, and some even glared at him with outright hostility. He'd been our enemy for so long that no one truly believed he was on our side now. No one except me, anyway.

Jordan didn't seem bothered by it though. His cocky demeanor was back in full force, and he simply crossed his arms and ignored them all, like a king who couldn't be bothered with the disdain of his peasants. Typical Leo. Or so everyone assumed—but I knew better. I saw the slight crack in his facade, the flash of pain in his eyes before they turned hard again.

I wasn't sure what was worse: the other packs' pity or their anger. All I knew was that the tension had grown thick around us, and soon even Ethan's cool head wouldn't be enough to cut it if we kept standing around like this.

When the final member of our party joined us, I breathed a sigh of relief. Larkin's small frame rushed toward me, her long hair flowing behind her, almost as white as the snow under our feet. She smiled up at me as she approached, the sun shining down on her cute, freckled face. Though she looked like a fourteen-year-old kid, she was actually one of the oldest people here, though most of the shifters probably didn't realize that. As the lone witch among us, she was just as much of an outcast as I was.

"Sorry I'm late," she said, as she shivered and pulled the hood from her purple robe over her head. "I was casting a few purification spells on the area."

"We're all here now," Ethan said to me. "You may begin when you're ready."

I counted the numbers again, avoiding Kaden's gaze,

before turning to Larkin. "Do you think you could help me channel extra magic again? I've never teleported so many people at once."

She stood a little taller, her eyes flickering briefly to Ethan. "I'd be happy to help."

"Thank you."

I gave her a nod to show I was ready, and she gathered moon power inside her, her body glowing faintly with it. As she did, Ethan gestured for everyone to come closer, crowding around me in a way that made my heart beat faster. I drew upon my own moon magic too, filling myself up until I felt like I was about to burst, until it poured out of my eyes and hands with a soft white light. Then Larkin passed her magic to me, and for a moment it was too much, a bomb about to explode beneath my skin, a hurricane about to be unleashed upon the world—but then I let it out as I willed everyone to be in Toronto.

All at once, the magic Larkin had passed to me was sucked from my body, so quickly that I stumbled forward. Then my own magic rushed out behind it, and the area exploded with white light. Some of the shifters yelped or cried out, but then the light faded to spots in our eyes, and when our vision came back, we'd arrived in the lobby of Ethan's hotel in Toronto.

Relief spread through me, along with a deep, bone-aching exhaustion. My legs started to give out, but then someone caught me, and I sagged gratefully into their arms.

"Are you okay?" Kaden asked.

I should have known it would be him. Or maybe I had

known, and that's why I'd so easily fallen into his embrace, knowing he would keep me safe.

I gathered the last remaining dregs of my energy and got my feet back under me. "I'm fine. Put me down."

He looked like he might argue, but then he set me down and stepped back. My legs nearly gave out again. It was only sheer force of will, and the knowledge that Kaden was watching, that kept me upright.

Larkin rushed to my side, followed closely by Stella. "You look really pale," Larkin said. "I think you should lie down."

"I agree," Stella said, her brow furrowed with concern.

"I'm fine," I said. "I just overexerted myself moving that many people, I think. I should be back to normal soon." Hopefully.

While I caught my breath, I took in the sight of the hotel lobby, which had been done up in bright, golden lights while I'd been away. In one corner, an enormous white tree towered over us, topped with a glittering star. Suddenly the date hit me—December twenty-third. Only two days til Christmas. Somehow it had completely slipped my mind, with everything else that had been going on over the last few weeks.

"Happy holidays," I said faintly to Larkin and Stella, who were still looking at me with worried expressions.

Larkin smiled and patted me on the arm. "It's good to have you back."

Ethan came up to me. "Are you well?"

"Fine," I said, though it came out a bit more forceful

than I'd meant it to. If one more person asked if I was okay, I'd probably scream.

He nodded, wisely ignoring my tone. "I wanted to let you know that your old room is still ready for you. We've had it cleaned, but all your things are there. You should try to rest before we begin the interrogations."

"I think we could all use some time to get settled in," Stella said.

"Of course," Ethan said. "We'll meet up again in a few hours to discuss our next steps."

"I'll talk to you both later," I said to Stella and Larkin before they decided to carry me to my room. I started toward the elevator, but the line to get on it was long with so many shifters eager to return to their rooms.

Could I...? I searched out the magic inside myself, relieved to find it already filling back up, restoring itself. There was just enough there for me to make one more little teleport. I closed my eyes and imagined my room. There was a tug on the power, and the noise around me disappeared. I opened my eyes to see my old room, dark with the curtains already drawn.

Perfect. I kicked my shoes off and didn't bother to do anything else before I collapsed onto the bed. I was asleep before I could do so much as pull the blankets over myself.

I woke to a knock a few hours later. I stumbled blearily out of bed and pulled the door open without even checking who it was first. Big mistake.

All traces of sleep disappeared when I saw Kaden standing in front of me. He held out a small container of food, and it took a moment for my brain to realize he was offering it to me. Not just any food either, but my favorite meal from an Indian restaurant down the street. I inhaled the spicy smell of curry, and my traitorous stomach rumbled.

"I figured you probably hadn't eaten," he said.

I hesitated, torn between accepting the food and staying away from him. I wanted to act like I didn't need him anymore, like I didn't appreciate this gesture more than words could say, but I couldn't stop myself from reaching out and taking the container. Kaden knew that using magic drained me and that the fastest way for me to get back on my feet was with good food. But he also knew I probably wouldn't get it myself, so he'd gone and done it for me, even going so far as to get my favorite meal in Toronto. It was almost enough to make me melt. Almost.

"Thank you," I said, trying not to meet his eyes. *Stay strong*, I told myself. The curry was damn good, but it wasn't enough to make up for what he'd done.

His eyes lingered on me, his presence filling up the space between us. "We're going to meet in the conference room in an hour to start the interrogation."

"I'll be ready."

I closed the door before I could say something stupid like, "Come inside." He stood in front of the door for a few long moments. I didn't move, the container cradled against my chest, and waited with bated breath until his footsteps finally receded. Only then did I slump against the door, letting out a long breath, torn between relief that he'd finally left, and disappointment that he hadn't stayed.

CHAPTER FOUR

I ARRIVED in the conference room and found Kaden, Ethan, Larkin, and Jordan already waiting. The large table had been removed, and a lone chair sat on one side of the room with a camera and tripod pointed toward it. A few other chairs remained, but no one was seated, instead choosing to stand around like they were on alert.

Ethan was adjusting the video equipment when he turned and looked at me. "Good, we're all here now. We can get started."

"Where's Roxandra?" I asked.

"We have her locked up in our makeshift prison, the same one Jordan was held in. We plan to move her somewhere more secure once the interrogation is over, but for now, it's the best we can do."

"It's nice to be here as a guest and not a prisoner this time," Jordan said dryly.

Kaden growled, letting it rumble deep in his chest.

"Watch it, or you'll be back in that cell. How would you like it with Roxandra this time?"

Jordan's lips peeled back from his teeth in a snarl, and he tensed, clearly ready to fight. The two alphas had avoided each other back at the battleground, but now that they were out of danger, I had a feeling they'd be unable to keep their claws out of each other.

Ethan shot Kaden a less-than-amused look, before turning it on Jordan next. "Play nice, or you'll both be removed from the interrogation."

The two men scowled but looked away, temporarily mollified, and I couldn't help but roll my eyes at them. At least Ethan wasn't taking any of their shit today. I felt the exact same way.

"How are we planning to interrogate Roxandra?" I asked.

Larkin cleared her throat, drawing everyone's attention. "I can cast a truth spell on Roxandra to get her to talk."

"Why didn't you do that to Jordan when he was our prisoner?" Kaden snapped, which only made Jordan's sneer return.

"I did, but it didn't work on him," Larkin said, cocking her head. "Maybe because the Sun Witches already had so many spells on him. I'm not sure, but I'd like to try it again."

"If it doesn't work, we'll have to use other tactics to get her to talk." Jordan cracked his knuckles with a cruel smile, and I realized he meant torture. The thought turned my stomach, even if it was Roxandra we were talking about.

"Either way, we'll be recording the entire thing so we

can share it with the other alphas," Ethan said. If he was turned off by the idea of torture, he didn't show it. "They need to be kept in the loop so we can make decisions together. Larkin, would you like to run the interrogation?"

Her cheeks turned red and she shook her head quickly. "No, I'd prefer to not have much interaction with the Sun Witch. I'll cast the spell, but someone else can ask the questions."

This had to be hard for her. Her worst enemy in the same room as her? Larkin might be older than she looked, but she still was sheltered in a lot of ways. I rubbed her arm and gave her a warm smile, trying to show I was there for her. She shot me a grateful glance in response.

"Ayla should do it," Kaden said. "She has the most experience with both witches and wolves."

"Jordan has spent more time with the Sun Witches," I pointed out.

Kaden crossed his arms. "Yeah, but we can't trust him."

Jordan rolled his eyes, but then he said, "I agree, Ayla should take the lead on this."

Ethan arched an eyebrow. "I never thought I'd see the two of you agree on anything. Ayla, what do you think?"

"I'll do it." I chewed on my lip for a few seconds. "But I'm afraid I might forget something. If you have a question for her, feel free to jump in at any time."

"Great. If that's settled, then I'll have her brought in so we can start." Ethan grabbed his phone and made a quick call, then turned back to us. "Be ready for anything."

We glanced warily at each other as we spread out around the room, while my heart beat faster, knowing what we were about to do. Ethan had the camera begin recording, and soon a scuffling sound could be heard down the hall, just before two burly shifters dragged Roxandra into the room. She tried resisting them, but her movements were weak and ineffective. They kept their eyes forward as they shoved her into the chair, not looking at her if they could help it. She had chains around her wrists and ankles, and they used those to attach her to the chair so she couldn't get up.

Roxandra's red robe was torn and dirty, hardly the same color it had been in the battle, and her platinum hair was greasy and dull, like she hadn't showered in days. Her arms were covered in bite marks and bruises, courtesy of the Ophiuchus poison keeping her sedated. She also had a silver collar around her neck with phases of the moon etched into the metal. I almost felt bad for her, until I looked into her cold, colorless eyes and saw the hatred in them.

"You're bigger fools than I thought to bring me here," she snarled. "Let me go before my sisters destroy you all."

"The Sun Witches wouldn't dare attack the hotel with so many shifters in it," Ethan said, without a trace of concern in his voice. "No one is coming for you."

"You've seen what we can do. Do you really think you could stop us if we tried?" She let out a laugh. It sounded hoarse, like she'd spent some time screaming before this. "Your minds are far too easy to control."

Jordan growled, stepping forward, but Ethan raised a hand. Roxandra's lips curled up into a smile as her gaze landed on Jordan, and his anger visibly grew, his hands clenched at his side, his body tense as if it was taking all of his willpower to hold himself back.

"Larkin, cast the spell," Ethan said, as he moved in front of Jordan.

Larkin stepped forward, her movements hesitant, and Roxandra honed in on her with a predatory sneer.

"Little Moon Witch girl," Roxandra crooned. "What do you think you'll be able to do against me? The collar you put on me to block my powers won't last long, and then we'll see which of the two of us is stronger, hmm?"

Larkin didn't rise to the bait and instead began chanting softly in ancient Greek. Moonlight gathered around Roxandra, suffusing the room in a soft, luminous glow. Roxandra strained against the ropes, cursing as she felt the power of the moon touch her. She struggled a bit harder, making the chair scrape harshly against the floor, but Larkin's spell never faltered. If anything, her spine only grew straighter and her voice became stronger as the magic worked against her enemy.

Roxandra's voice suddenly raised above Larkin's in a desperate screech, also chanting something in ancient Greek, but it didn't seem to have any power. Instead, the silver collar around her neck pulsed with bright white light, and Roxandra made a wounded noise and fell silent. I didn't know if her comment about the collar possibly failing was true, but I hoped it lasted long enough to get us through this interrogation at least.

Larkin's brow furrowed in concentration, but she stood strong as the magic finished taking hold. The light pulsed brighter, and Roxandra made another sound like she was being hurt as the magic soaked into her skin. Larkin stopped chanting, and as the light faded, the room looked suddenly dull without the moonlight shining through it.

Larkin took a deep breath and turned toward me. "It worked. Roxandra will be forced to answer your questions now, and she won't be able to lie."

"Nice job," I said, giving her shoulder a squeeze. She'd stood strong as she'd cast the spell, even with Roxandra's taunting, and I was proud of her.

Larkin stepped carefully out of the way of the camera and leaned against the wall in the back of the room. I watched Ethan go to her and whisper something, which put a small smile on her face.

Now it was my turn. I took a deep breath and stepped forward. Roxandra's eyes turned to me, so full of hate that I almost took a step back.

No. This wasn't the time for weakness. I could do this. I needed answers, and I'd do whatever I had to do to get them. The Sun Witches had controlled and manipulated us for too long, but no more. It ended right here, right now, in this very room.

For a moment I simply took Roxandra in, studying her haggard appearance as I tried to decide which question to ask first. I had too many swirling around in my head, and they all seemed vitally important. I was finally going to get the answers I needed from the Sun Witches. But where to start?

One step at a time, I told myself. First, I would test out the truth spell to see how it worked and what its limitations were. I trusted Larkin's magic, but I didn't know the extent of it, and I wanted to make sure it was really working. I wouldn't put it past Roxandra to try to do something deceitful, if such a thing was possible.

I dragged a chair over so I could sit in front of Roxandra, while still leaving a clear line of sight for the camera to capture her answers and expressions. As I crossed my legs, the whole thing felt more like an interview than an interrogation. Maybe I'd lean into that feeling and see if it loosened her up a bit. Even if it just made her angry, that might get her to let something extra slip.

"Hello, Roxandra," I said, never dropping the smile. "Do you mind if I call you Roxie?"

"I'd rather you didn't," she said through gritted teeth, almost as if the words were being dragged out of her.

"Too bad. Let's try a few questions to test out how the spell is working." I leaned forward, never dropping eye contact. "What is your greatest fear?"

She squeezed her mouth tight as if trying to keep the answer inside, but the spell eventually made her blurt out the words. "Disappointing my mother and being replaced as her heir."

I sat back, absorbing her answer. "Interesting."

Roxandra's unnaturally pale eyes flashed as she watched

me, but she kept her lips sealed shut, confirming that she didn't have to respond to comments, only questions. But what about commands?

I decided to do another test, remembering the first time I'd felt those strange eyes on me. "Describe what you felt when you first saw me at the summer Convergence."

Roxandra shifted around a bit in her chair, as if the questioning made her physically uncomfortable. "I felt disgust and jealousy that a half-breed like you would be mated to Jordan, along with excitement knowing that the Leos were about to wipe out your pack."

Jealousy? I glanced back at Jordan, surprised by the words she'd used. He had his arms crossed, but his face was hard as he stared at Roxandra without blinking.

"Did you know Jordan was my brother?" I asked.

"No."

I nodded as she confirmed my suspicions. "How did I end up mated to him?"

Roxandra's answer was quicker this time, and her lips twitched a bit in a faint smile. "Your father made a deal with us. He wanted to send you to the Leos. He knew it would infuriate Dixon to have his son mated to a mutt."

I already knew the answer, but it still made my heart twist, just a tiny bit. "Looks like the truth spell is doing a good job. That little girl Moon Witch overpowered you after all, didn't she?" I grinned at the way Roxandra's face strained. "That was a rhetorical question, by the way. You don't have to answer it."

"Just wait until I'm free," she practically spat at me. "I'll enjoy making you suffer."

"I'm sure you will." I rubbed my hands together, eager to continue now that I knew how the truth spell worked. "Are you ready for the real questions now, Roxie?"

"No," Roxandra ground out.

A wicked smile touched my lips. "Too bad."

CHAPTER FIVE

I LEANED FORWARD as I prepared to ask Roxandra my next set of questions. I couldn't wait to finally get the answers I needed. "Since you confirmed that the mate bond with Jordan was fake, tell me... Are all the mate bonds fake?"

Roxandra panted as she resisted the truth spell, her shoulders shaking from the effort. Her face twisted with pain as if the spell was physically causing her distress.

"Really, it would be easier if you'd just give in," I said. "I promise I won't tell mommy that you were a bad girl."

"Screw you," Roxandra hissed out, which was a mistake. Once her mouth was open, the truth came pouring out. "Yes, most of them are fake."

It was chilling to hear the words directly from the source, even though I'd already known the answer. As the weight of the truth hung heavily in the room, I thought of Mira, heavily pregnant with her mate's child. She didn't want to know if her mate bond was fake, and I suspected other shifters would feel the same. But if we didn't know the truth, we could never be free.

"Why do you create fake mate bonds?" I asked, my smile gone. All the false levity had left me once we'd started this line of questioning.

"We do it to control you and to reshape the packs into what we want. We ensure you keep fighting with each other, which keeps you weak, and stops you from turning against us." She looked behind me as she spoke the next words. "And we do it to create alphas who will fall in line."

Multiple people growled behind me at that, and I glanced back to see Kaden clenching his hands. Even Ethan looked pissed off.

"How's that working out for you now?" I asked, shaking my head. Maybe the previous alphas had been willing to follow the Sun Witches, but more and more were standing up to them now. I had a feeling that after this video, we'd get everyone to turn against them. "Ignore that question. What I want to know is...why? Why can't you just let us be free?"

"We created the Zodiac Wolves. We are your masters. Like dogs, you can be bred and trained as we please." A cruel smile touched her lips. "And we can put you down if you disobey."

This time, there was only silence behind me. The Moon Witches had told me this was how the Sun Witches thought of us, but it made me sick hearing Roxandra speak the words out loud, as calmly as if she was talking about the weather. They really did believe they had every right to use us like pawns in whatever game they were playing.

I swallowed hard and tried to focus. I wasn't sure how long Larkin's truth spell would hold, and I needed to get as much information out of Roxandra as I could before then.

"How do you break the mate bonds?" I asked.

She gripped the arms of the chair tightly but kept her mouth shut. She really didn't want me to know this answer.

"Is there a spell?" I asked again, rising to my feet. "Tell me!"

Her body trembled with the effort of keeping the truth inside, her eyes bulging like she was in pain. "They can be broken," she finally gasped out. "But not easily."

A wave of relief went through me. Up until now, I wasn't sure that we could break them, and that I'd be tied to my brother for the rest of my life. Just hearing that it was possible took a huge weight off my chest.

"Explain," I said, loading the word with as much command as I could. I'd be damned if I wasn't going to wring this answer out of Roxandra. "And don't leave anything out. Tell me everything you know about breaking the mate bonds."

She glared at me with cold fury as she answered, and it sounded like she was fighting every single word, but couldn't stop them from slipping from her lips. "The mate bonds are part of the blessing we put on every shifter as a baby at the Convergence. The blessing locks away your wolves, along with your natural mate bonds, and allows us to create a new bond when we're ready. The same blessing spell also allows the Sun Witches to take control of you, just like we did at the last Convergence."

"What about the staff Evanora was holding?" Ethan asked. "Is that what controlled us?"

"No, the staff only amplifies the powers of whoever holds it. Evanora cast the spell to control you, and the staff made it spread to everyone there." She glared over at Kaden suddenly. "Except the Ophiuchus pack, who were immune because they were never blessed." Her glare returned to me. "And you, because you had the moonstone necklace on." Her eyes shot to where it rested around Jordan's neck. "It's a shame you gave it to Jordan."

I snapped my fingers, trying to get her attention back on me. "How do you break the blessing spell? I need an answer!"

"It's not that easy," she spat. "You can't just say some words and expect the blessings to vanish into thin air. It's a complicated process. The blessing spell needs to be completely unraveled, and I don't know anyone who has done it before. An elder Sun Witch might know how though, or there might be something in one of the old books..."

"If you figured out how to do it, could you teach Larkin?" I asked, growing impatient and frustrated with Roxandra's response.

"No," she said, looking Larkin up and down scathingly. "She doesn't have any sun magic. You need a Sun Witch to unravel the spell, and there's no truth spell in the world that will make me agree to do that for you. I'd rather die."

Before I could respond, Jordan leaped forward, snarling something unintelligible as he lunged for Roxandra's throat.

"You're going to break the spell if I have to make you do it myself."

She let out a gasp as he tightened his hand around her neck and shoved the chair so hard against the wall that it groaned. "Ooh, I love it when you're angry," she purred as if she was enjoying this.

Jordan went stiff, and let her go like touching her disgusted him. I looked back at Kaden and Ethan uneasily, unsure if I should continue the interrogation.

"You've always been my favorite shifter to control," Roxandra continued, as her gaze traveled down Jordan's body in a way that instantly set alarm bells ringing in my head. "Our perfect little alpha. So much fire in you. So much passion."

Jordan's control snapped and he lunged for her, his hands wringing her neck as she laughed. The sound died off as I watched, horrified, as Jordan continued choking her. The look on his face was almost inhuman. *He's going to kill her,* I thought.

I grabbed his arm and tried to haul him away, but he was too strong. I was only half shifter, after all, and he was an alpha. But then Ethan and Kaden joined me, and together we managed to pull Jordan off Roxandra before she could pass out.

"That's enough," Ethan said, as he wedged himself in front of Jordan.

Jordan was breathing hard, his face furious as he looked at Roxandra. She coughed, struggling to catch her breath, but even though Jordan had almost killed her, she was still grinning, her pale eyes pinned on him.

"I won't ever be controlled by you again," Jordan growled.

She rubbed her neck. "That's a pity. I loved fucking you."

Jordan let out a roar and launched himself forward again. Kaden jumped between them, shoving Jordan back against the wall and holding him there. But this time I was ready to strangle Roxandra myself after what she'd just said.

I stalked toward her with fury making my blood boil, but Ethan caught my arm before I could do anything. I shook him off as I faced Roxandra, nearly shaking with rage. "Did you make him sleep with you?"

"Oh yes." She had the audacity to laugh again, and my vision went red. "You've seen him naked, haven't you? Of course you have. All these shifters are always walking around with their cocks out. He's glorious, and I was hoping he would get me pregnant, but that didn't happen."

I physically recoiled at those words. Now all I wanted was for her to *stop* talking. The other shifters all looked at her with disgust and horror too.

"What the fuck?" Kaden muttered, from where he was still holding Jordan against the wall.

Jordan had stopped fighting, but he was breathing heavily, staring at the wall. I couldn't imagine what must be going through him, hearing her say such awful things.

"Why?" I asked through gritted teeth. I wanted to sink my canines into her neck for what she'd done to my brother, but I had a feeling this was important. "Why did you hope he would get you pregnant?"

Roxandra smiled, and this time it was dangerous. She carefully closed her mouth and stared at me, her eyes dancing with cruel amusement.

Anger surged through me, and I looked over at Larkin. "What happened?"

"The spell has worn off," Larkin said. "It only lasts for a short while. I'll need to cast it again."

"It's time for a break anyway," Ethan said, looking pointedly over at Jordan, who was still being held by Kaden against the wall. "We could all use one."

"Let me go," Jordan growled at Kaden.

"Why, so you can try to kill her again?" Kaden asked. "Actually, at this point, I might let you."

Jordan broke free of Kaden's hold, and I tensed, preparing for him to go after Roxandra again, but instead, he left the room without another word. I sighed and followed him out.

I found Jordan in the next conference room over, his hands clenched into fists as he stared blankly at a wall. His chest was heaving as if he'd just sprinted around the block, and he didn't seem to notice when I entered.

I walked over to the jug of water and poured some into a paper cup. "Drink this."

Jordan took the cup and glared down at it for a moment, before tossing it back as if he could take out all of his aggression on the water itself.

"I'm sorry," I said as he finished. "I know this must be difficult for you."

Jordan crushed the paper cup in his hand. "Why would it be difficult? Hearing how my entire life is a lie, and that I'm nothing but a Sun Witch fuckboy?"

He met my gaze and I saw the hurt and fear behind all that anger. He hadn't asked for this, and he desperately needed someone to help him. I stepped forward, moving slowly to not spook him, and wrapped my arms around him.

"I won't let them control you ever again." My voice grew stronger with each word. "And I'm going to find a way to break the mating bond too. I swear it."

Jordan went stiff for a few moments, although he let me hold him. I was about to pull away when he softened, wrapping one arm around me.

"Thank you," he said, his voice rough.

I pulled back, my own anger still simmering under the surface. "I had no idea she'd done all that to you."

He looked away, unable to meet my gaze. "It started after you escaped the Leo village with Kaden. The Sun Witches took full control of my pack then, and they sent the Taurus pack after you. That's when Roxandra..." He opened his mouth again, but nothing else came out.

I squeezed his hands tightly in mine, sympathy running through me. No one should have gone through what he had. "You don't have to say it. I understand."

He nodded, though he still wouldn't meet my eyes. "I wanted to tell you everything when you held me captive, but the Sun Witches had commanded me to not say anything about them. I couldn't disobey or break the magic, no matter how hard I tried. Not until the moonstone necklace was on me."

I thought back to the many times I'd visited him while he was being held in this hotel, and how it had sometimes seemed like he'd wanted to say something, but couldn't. Or how he'd always push me away whenever I got too close to the truth. Something twisted in my gut. If only I'd known sooner.

Someone cleared their throat behind me, and I turned to find Kaden leaning in the doorway. His arms were crossed over his chest, and he looked intently at Jordan.

How much did he hear? I wondered. I hadn't closed the door, so he'd probably heard everything.

As Ethan and Larkin came into the room next, Jordan squared his shoulders, tucking away the small bit of vulnerability he'd shown me. He looked every inch the Leo alpha once more.

"Thank you for your interrogation, Ayla," Ethan said. "You did an excellent job, and we learned a lot. Your questions were very...enlightening."

"It confirmed a lot of what we already knew," Kaden said.

"True, but a lot of the other alphas didn't believe it before. Now none of them will be able to deny that the Sun Witches have been manipulating and controlling us all this time. Not when they hear it directly from Roxandra's own mouth."

Kaden shrugged. "True, but Roxandra is right. We can't

keep her here for much longer. It's too risky. The Sun Witches could show up at any time and take control of the wolves again."

A collective silence passed over us as we remembered the bloodshed during the last time the Sun Witches had gained control.

"We could use some more of those moonstone necklaces," Ethan said, eyeing the one around Jordan's neck. He turned toward Larkin. "Is it possible to get more?"

Larkin flushed under the weight of Ethan's gaze. "I can try to get some from the Moon Witches."

Kaden shifted in my peripheral vision, and I couldn't help but look at him. His brow was furrowed, the look on his face troubled. I wished suddenly that I knew what was going on inside his head. I wanted to talk to him about everything we'd learned today, and my chest ached at the loss of what we'd once had.

Kaden's eyes lifted to mine as if he could feel my gaze upon him. We connected for the briefest moment, sharing a split second of our shared worries and fears, and then I looked away quickly, not wanting him to see how much I longed for more.

"We'll never get enough necklaces for everyone," Kaden said. "We need to find a Sun Witch who will help us."

I sighed, feeling deflated as I remembered how impossible it would be to break the mating bonds. "That's not going to happen. We were lucky to even get Roxandra."

"My mother might be able to help..." Jordan said, and

everyone turned toward him with their jaws dropped. "If we can find her, that is."

"Your mother?" I pictured Debra, the fierce, beautiful alpha female who had stopped Jordan from mating with me. "What does she have to do with the Sun Witches?"

"She's half Sun Witch," Jordan admitted.

Kaden growled low in his chest. "This would have been good information to know a month ago."

Jordan's hackles rose as he faced Kaden. "Didn't you hear? A month ago, I was still being controlled by the Sun Witches. I couldn't say anything." He shrugged. "Besides, I don't know how much help this information will be. I have no idea where she is. Or my younger brother, for that matter. They left the Leo pack after Ayla escaped, and I haven't heard from them since."

There was silence in the room, and even Kaden looked a bit mollified. He didn't stop glaring at Jordan though.

"Do you think she's hiding from the Sun Witches?" I asked.

"Probably," Jordan said. "If we can find the Leo pack, my cousin might know where she is. That's the only lead I have."

Ethan nodded. "I'll put out some feelers and see if the other packs have any idea where the Leos have gone."

"Sounds good," Jordan said. It was funny to see how much more easily he got along with Ethan than Kaden. Probably because Jordan and Kaden were more alike than either would want to admit—too headstrong and quick to anger, but fiercely protective of the people they cared about.

"I suggest we end the interrogation for the time being," Ethan said. "My people will get the video ready to send to the other alphas tonight. They need to know what we learned here. Then we'll resume the interrogation after Christmas."

"What about Roxandra?" Kaden asked.

"We'll increase her security for now. As soon as we finish the interrogation, we'll figure out what to do with her next."

None of us looked thrilled about that, but no one spoke up with any better ideas either.

"For now, I suggest we all get some rest," Ethan continued. "I'll keep you updated if anything changes."

He gave us all a nod and then left the room, and Jordan stormed out a few seconds later, like he was eager to get away from this place. I couldn't blame him.

Kaden lingered like he wanted to stay and talk to me, but I avoided looking at him until he finally got the hint and walked out, leaving only Larkin behind.

"Are you okay?" she asked, wringing her hands.

"I think so." I'd known that uncomfortable truths would be revealed while interrogating Roxandra, but she'd still somehow managed to shock me.

We paused as we listened to the shifters take Roxandra out of the other room, her cursing and fighting them the whole way until they disappeared down the elevator. I didn't want to face her again, at least not right now. My mind was heavy with everything I'd learned, and I suddenly felt like I'd been awake for days in a row.

"Are *you* okay?" I asked, noticing Larkin's face was paler than normal.

"I think so," she repeated back at me with a small smile.

"Good answer." I wrapped my arm around her and gave her a quick hug. The interrogation had been hard on all of us, for different reasons. I was grateful for a break from it for a few days.

CHAPTER SIX

AS I STEPPED into the hotel ballroom, I was immediately struck by the festive atmosphere, which instantly lifted my spirits. I'd completely forgotten about Christmas, but it was clear that the Libra and Ophiuchus pack members hadn't. The large space was decorated with twinkling lights and garland, giving it a warm and cozy feel, and the air carried the scent of pine from the tall tree covered in ornaments and tinsel. Everyone was dressed in their finest attire, and soft holiday music played in the background.

When I'd heard the Libras were throwing a party on Christmas Eve, I'd been surprised. But as I watched the other shifters smiling and laughing as they mingled and danced, it suddenly made sense. After everything we'd been through over the last few months, we all deserved something fun, at least for one night. A bit of levity after all the horrors we'd witnessed. Though we had many challenges ahead of us, for a few hours we could live in the moment and celebrate being together and alive.

I smoothed my hands down the skirt of the green cocktail dress I'd put on for the occasion. When I'd gone shopping with my friends a few months ago, I'd let them talk me into getting the dress. At the time it had felt silly and extravagant, especially because I'd never owned something so nice before, but now I was glad for it.

That trip seemed like an eternity ago, and I couldn't believe how much had changed in the time since then. The memory was fond, except for what happened after, when the Leos had attacked us in the park. We'd managed to subdue them, but then Kaden had killed them all while they were passed out and defenseless. It had been so unlike Kaden that I still could hardly believe he'd done it. That was when I realized that Kaden had turned into someone I didn't recognize anymore. A darker version of himself.

That had been the beginning of the end for us.

I found myself scanning the party, searching for a glimpse of him, but he wasn't there. Part of me was disappointed, but I told myself it was better if he didn't come. I didn't want to hear another hollow apology tonight, though I couldn't stop my heart from aching at his absence.

I noticed Jordan wasn't at the party either, but that didn't surprise me at all. He still wasn't welcome among most shifters here. They didn't know the truth about what had happened with Roxandra. Maybe that would change once more people saw the video of her interrogation.

I took a deep breath and made my way through the

crowd, smiling and greeting those I knew as I went. My plan was to make an appearance, pay my respects to Ethan, and then slink back to my room for the rest of the night. I was still an outcast, after all, and being here with the other pack members only made me feel that more keenly. I wasn't one of them, and might never be again.

I spotted the Ophiuchus beta, Clayton, standing near a table with cute little hors d'oeuvres. He wore a black suit that stretched tight across his broad shoulders and tall frame. Beside him, his mate, Grant, popped a canapé in his mouth. Clayton met my eyes and raised a hand, waving me over to them.

"Merry Christmas," I said, trying not to let my hesitation show. I hadn't seen Clayton or Grant since before Kaden had removed me from the pack. I had no idea how they would react to me now.

Clayton wrapped his burly arms around me. "It's good to see you again. I was worried."

"Gorgeous dress," Grant said, as he looked me up and down with approval. "That green is the perfect shade for your hair."

"Thanks," I said, relaxing immediately. It was nice to know I wouldn't be treated like a reject by everyone in the pack.

"I'm glad you're back." Clayton's voice lowered as he leaned in close like he was disclosing confidential knowledge. "Kaden has been...distraught without you."

Grant exchanged a glance with his mate. "We hope this is a sign you'll be rejoining our pack soon."

I gave them a stiff smile. I appreciated the support from the other Ophiuchus, but their words only brought the hurt back in full force. "I'm not sure."

The two of them shared another glance, this one more worried than before. Then Grant turned his charming grin back on me. "What you need is some eggnog. Or maybe a gingerbread martini."

My eyebrows rose. "Do they really have that?"

"Oh yes." He looped his arm through mine. "Come with us."

Clayton chuckled as Grant led me to the open bar, where the menu boasted a variety of holiday-themed cocktails. The two men convinced me to try the gingerbread cocktail, which was way too sweet but did put me in a better mood. Everyone else was enjoying themselves—why shouldn't I?

They tried to convince me to dance next, but that was where I had to draw the line. I watched them go as I sipped on my drink, and caught sight of Stella and Ethan out on the dance floor. They were both grinning as he twirled her around and dipped her to the upbeat music, and I couldn't deny that they looked good together. They were both gorgeous, smart, and sensible. Was I seeing a mate pair form in front of me?

When the song ended, Stella spotted me and ran over, throwing her arms around me. "Merry Christmas! What are you drinking? Whatever it is, I need one immediately."

As she dragged me back to the open bar, I laughed. "You seem like you're having fun tonight."

"I do love a good party," she said, before ordering a drink like mine.

I caught sight of Ethan on the dance floor again, now with a Libra woman I didn't recognize. "You looked good out there with Ethan." I nudged her. "Maybe he's your mate."

Stella grinned. "He's not, though I wouldn't complain if he was."

"Are you sure?" I asked.

"Pretty sure. I don't feel any sort of pull toward him. I just think he's hot. But who wouldn't?" She took a sip of her drink and tilted her head. "I think we're too similar to be mates anyway. Your mate should challenge you. Drive you a little crazy. Right?"

"Trust me, I know," I muttered, thinking about how Kaden had always gotten under my skin like no one else could.

"Exactly. Besides, it would break Larkin's heart if Ethan was my mate." She nudged me in the arm and I followed her gaze toward where Larkin stood on the edge of the ballroom, looking totally out of place and uncomfortable. Her eyes were stuck on Ethan as he danced with the Libra woman. "Poor thing has a huge crush on him, but he only sees her as a kid."

Sympathy for Larkin flooded me. I wished I could do something for her. She'd been accepted as a powerful ally to the shifters, but she would never truly be one of us. Being stuck in a fourteen-year-old's body didn't help either. She loved to read romance novels, but she'd once confessed to me that she'd never been in a relationship. As I watched her stare at Ethan, I hoped she wasn't setting herself up for heartbreak.

I was about to go over to her when Kaden entered the ballroom and everything just...stopped. My breath caught in my throat. My heart skipped a beat. My eyes ceased to blink. All that existed was Kaden standing in a black suit, his white shirt open at the collar just enough to show off a sliver of skin. Every instinct in my body screamed at me to go to him, and my hands actually trembled from the effort of holding myself back.

Stella followed my line of sight and quickly downed the rest of her drink. "Time for me to be somewhere else."

"What?" I asked, snapping out of my daze. "No, don't go."

She cupped a hand around her ear and shouted over the music, "Sorry, can't hear you."

She darted off to join Larkin on the side of the room, leaving me all alone while Kaden approached me. I had no choice but to face him.

"Ayla," he said, his gaze traveling down my body like a slow caress. "You look stunning tonight."

I flushed, remembering when I'd bought the dress. I'd only let the girls convince me to get it because I'd imagined Kaden taking it off me. If things were different, that might have been tonight. "Thank you. You look very handsome too."

"Can we talk somewhere quieter?" he asked.

I nodded and quickly finished my drink. I didn't know what Kaden wanted to talk about, but I didn't want to cause a scene and ruin anyone's night.

We made our way through the crowd toward a side door, and then we were out of the warm press of bodies and into the brisk night air. The garden twinkled with white lights, and a sprinkling of fresh snow only added to the Christmas wonderland feel. My hand itched to reach for Kaden's, wishing we could stroll through the night like lovers, but instead we stood an awkward distance apart, like neither of us was quite sure how to act.

"I got you a present," Kaden said, once we were alone.

My eyebrows darted up. "I didn't get you anything."

"I don't deserve anything."

I didn't reply. I couldn't argue with that.

Kaden removed a small present from inside his suit jacket and handed it to me. The wrapping was plain gold with a red bow, simple and elegant, and I opened it carefully. Inside was a soft leather camera strap that had been personalized with the words *little wolf* between a crescent moon and the Ophiuchus symbol. My chest tightened as I held it in my hands, rubbing my thumbs along the smooth leather. I hadn't received many gifts as a child, and getting them still made me emotional, especially when they were as perfect as this one.

"Thank you. It's lovely." I blinked back tears, trying not to show Kaden how much his gift meant to me. I was barely keeping it together, and if a single tear fell, I'd completely fall apart in front of him and become a sobbing mess. I sniffed and tried to cover up what a mess I was by saying, "But I'm not in the Ophiuchus pack anymore."

"You will be again," he said, his voice confident.

"How can you be so certain?"

Kaden reached up to touch my face, his rough fingertips lightly stroking my cheek. "Because I know we're meant to be together. I'll do anything to win you back. I made the biggest mistake of my life when I removed your pack mark, one I'm not sure I should ever be forgiven for."

I found myself leaning into his touch as I gazed into his eyes. "Kaden..."

"Every time I remember that moment, I still can't believe it was me. It was like something inside of me broke, and a darkness took hold of me. It whispered terrible things in my mind, and I couldn't shake it." His other hand came up to cup the other side of my face, as he gazed into my eyes. "But I'm working on it. I'm going to try to do better because I can't live without you. Even if the mate bond between you and Jordan is never broken, you're the only one I want as my alpha female."

Somehow we'd moved closer, as if our bodies couldn't help but be drawn together, and his thumb traced my lower lip. His eyes narrowed in on my mouth like he wanted nothing more in the world than to close the gap between us and press his lips to mine. I wanted that too, so much so that I found my own hands on his chest, gripping the front of his suit to draw him toward me. The pull between us was impossible to resist. At some point, I knew I would give in.

But something he'd said made me pause. I pressed my hand against his chest, lightly pushing him back as my head began to spin. The whispers in his mind, so subtle that he hadn't known they were there until it was too late... It sounded very familiar.

"What is it?" Kaden asked, his face flashing with vulnerability for the briefest moment as I pushed him away.

I bit my lip, not ready to share my theory yet. What if I was wrong? "I appreciate the gift, but I just... I need some time. Can you give me that?"

"Of course." He shoved his hands in his pockets, obviously disappointed, but he didn't push the matter. "I'll wait forever if I have to. Merry Christmas, Ayla."

He walked away, slipping back into the party, and I decided not to follow. I'd made my appearance, and now it was time for me to head back to my room, alone—though I had a feeling I wouldn't be able to sleep much tonight either.

Was it possible the Sun Witches had gotten into Kaden's mind too?

CHAPTER SEVEN

"THIS IS A TERRIBLE IDEA," Jordan said, scowling at me.

"Probably, but we're doing it anyway." I grabbed his hand and thought of the island where I'd spent many of my summers on vacation with my family. In the blink of an eye, we left the hotel lobby and arrived on the cold shore of the Cancer pack's hideout, our shoes sinking into the sand.

Jordan's mouth twisted. "I hate when you do that."

I couldn't help but laugh at his sour face. "I thought you'd be used to it by now."

"Nope. It always makes me want to throw up." He shook off the feeling and stood a bit straighter. He wore a dark red shirt and jeans, his meager effort at being festive. "Let's get this over with."

We headed up the steps of the closest house, which was pale blue with a white wrap-around porch and an old slate-gray roof. I knocked lightly on the door as a chilling sea breeze whipped at my hair and tugged on my green dress. It was the same dress I'd worn the previous night because I figured Jordan and Wesley hadn't seen it, so why not get some more use out of it? I'd covered it up a little with a black cardigan, although now I wished I'd worn something heavier.

When Wesley opened the door, I cracked a huge smile. "Merry Christmas!"

"Ayla! I'm so happy to see you." Wesley's face lit up as he grabbed me in a hug, but then it dropped to a frown as he caught sight of Jordan beside me. "He, on the other hand, is not welcome here."

"Told you," Jordan said.

"What were you thinking, bringing him here?" Wesley asked me while glaring at Jordan. "The whole reason we came here was so that the Leos wouldn't be able to find us. Now you brought their alpha right to my front door."

"I teleported us here, so he has no idea where we are or how to get here," I said. "But Jordan's not the enemy either. You have to trust me on this."

"You should have left me back at the hotel," Jordan muttered.

"Agreed," Wesley said, crossing his arms.

"No way." I gave each of them a stern look. "It's Christmas, and I want to spend it with my brothers. *Both* of them. I don't care that you two don't get along, or that your packs have hated each other for as long as we can remember. You can suck it up for a few hours and at least be civil. That's all I want for Christmas. Okay?"

"I can be civil," Jordan said, jutting out his chin. "Can he?"

Wesley's jaw clenched. "I'm not the one who helped slaughter the Cancer pack."

Jordan's posture went from neutral to defensive in an instant. "That was my father's doing, not mine."

"You weren't exactly an innocent bystander though, were you?" Wesley growled.

"Enough!" I held up my hands, stopping this from going any further. "We all had shit dads. Here's your chance to prove that you're better than them and that we can put this stupid blood feud behind us, at least for a single day."

"Fine," Wesley said, stepping back. "Get inside before anyone else in the pack sees you. I don't need any blood stains on my front porch."

"Don't worry, I already promised Ayla I wouldn't kill anyone today," Jordan said.

"It's not them I'm worried about," Wesley muttered, as he led us into the living room.

Last time I'd been here, the house had been packed full of people, mostly teens who'd lost their parents at the Convergence. I was relieved to see none of them were here now since they probably wouldn't think too highly of the Leo alpha either.

A warm fire crackled on one side of the room, and a small, sparsely decorated Christmas tree stood in the corner like it had been an afterthought, but at least Wesley remembered to put one up. I settled in on one of the white sofas, trying to get past the initial awkwardness and tension. I'd known this meeting would be a difficult one, but if we were going to be a real family, and perhaps more importantly, end the war between the Cancers and the Leos, we had to start somewhere.

"You'll be happy to know I'm no longer the Leo alpha anyway," Jordan said to Wesley, as he took a seat. "Your secret hiding place is safe with me."

Wesley shook his head. "I'm not sure what's worse—you leading the Leos, or some other asshole I don't even know."

"For you? Definitely the latter. The new alpha was our former beta and my Dad's closest ally. I don't think he'd hesitate before wiping out your pack. For good this time."

"That's only temporary," I said, waving a hand. "You're the true alpha of the Leos. I know it, and so does everyone else. You'll get your pack back, and once you do, you can lead them in a new direction." I leaned forward, glancing between my two brothers. "Together you can turn the Leo and Cancer packs into what they were meant to be. Allies."

Jordan let out a groan. "Okay, we get it. We're going to be best friends by the end of the night. Happy now, Ayla?"

"Very," I said, pulling my legs up onto the couch and settling in. He was being sarcastic, but I could already feel the tension easing between the two men. This might actually work.

Wesley raised an eyebrow. "Well, this conversation got a lot deeper than I expected for a Christmas afternoon. Let me grab some eggnog before we keep going."

"Please tell me it's spiked," Jordan said.

Wesley snorted. "There's no point in eggnog unless it makes the room spin."

Jordan grinned. "Finally, we can agree on something."

After Wesley returned with three mugs and passed them out between us, the awkwardness quickly faded. At first, the conversation was stilted, but soon Wesley was making us all laugh by telling embarrassing stories about me until I threw a pillow from the couch at him in response. Then Jordan told us about how he'd once set his Christmas tree on fire as a kid, nearly burning down his entire house, but he made it so funny we were all soon howling with laughter. The very alcoholic eggnog didn't hurt either.

Eventually, the conversation turned more serious again, and Jordan surprised me by asking Wesley how the Cancer pack was doing these days. Wesley looked stunned by the question, but then set his mug down and gave Jordan an overview. After that, they couldn't stop talking. About our dads. About our packs. About what they wanted to do as alphas.

At one point, I excused myself to use the restroom, and then I lingered in the doorway, watching them. My two brothers, finally talking to each other. They looked nothing alike, except for their matching blue eyes, but they were more similar than they'd ever admit. With some effort, they might even be friends one day. And if they could get along? Maybe the other alphas could too.

I decided to give them a few minutes to bond without me there, so I slipped out onto the back porch and headed down to the beach. The sun was starting to set, casting brilliant orange and pink light across the water, and the sea breeze caressed my face. I breathed in deep, letting the familiar ocean scent fill me. Even though I'd always been an outcast in the Cancer pack, I still loved the ocean. How many times had I gone to this very spot to escape from my dad and my stepmom?

Heavy footsteps in the sand made the hairs on the back of my neck stand up. Some instinct told me I was in danger, and when I spun around, a quick bolt of fear shot through me at the sight of my old tormentors, the beta's son, Brad, and his girlfriend, Lori. The pair had taken special pleasure in torturing me back when I'd been completely at their mercy as an outcast half-human shifter. Along with their friends, they'd given me many of the scars on my body now. But I wasn't that frightened, defenseless girl anymore—and I refused to be scared of them ever again.

"I thought I smelled something," Lori said, pinching her nose as they approached. "Turns out it was a packless mutt."

I rolled my eyes. "You'd think that after so many years of bullying me, you'd come up with some better insults."

"You must really want a beating," Brad growled. "Turning up here again? You have a serious death wish."

"Try it," I told them, wishing they'd either get on with it already or leave me alone. "Or fuck off, if you're not going to make my night interesting."

"Run away, little mutt," Lori said, flicking her pink nails at me. "Before we teach you another lesson."

Brad prowled closer. "You don't have your snake boyfriend to protect you this time. Or your brother."

Brad suddenly lunged for me, his hands changing to claws. Before, this would have left me scrambling backward, trying to get away from his superior strength and speed, but now I held my ground. Using the tricks Kaden had taught me, I swerved out of the way at the last second, then used Brad's momentum to make him flip onto his back. He landed with a thud on the sand, while I stood over him.

"I don't need anyone to protect me," I said. "I can do that myself now."

Lori charged me next, but I blasted her back with a wave of moon magic. It wasn't even a strong one, but it knocked her down on her ass in the water, soaking her white pants. I couldn't help but grin at the sight.

Brad's eyes burned with hatred as he stood up again. "You're so dead, mutt."

The two of them shifted into their wolf forms and came for me. A year ago, this would have meant I was in serious trouble. I'd had no wolf and no Cancer powers to protect me, only my smart mouth, which, to be honest, usually caused me more trouble. Things were a lot different now.

I shifted without even thinking about it, my body changing as fast as any alpha's. My white paws hit the sand and my tail flicked behind me as I faced my two biggest bullies. They attacked me with their teeth and claws, but I was too fast for them, and I'd been taught by the best. My skills had been honed in real battles, while theirs had only been used to bully weaker opponents. And even though I didn't have the Ophiuchus poison bite anymore, my canines were still plenty sharp. Within seconds, I had them both bleeding, but they still didn't stop. It was like they simply couldn't believe that I was better than them.

Time to teach them a lesson, I thought, as I opened my jaw wide. Pure white moon magic spewed out of my mouth, like fire from a dragon. They donned their Cancer armor, but it did little to block the torrent of moonlight that hit them, knocking them back into the waves. They were lucky I didn't put any more power into it. Unlike them, I had no desire to kill anyone on Christmas.

They sputtered and yelped as they got out of the water, and then they dashed across the beach, running away with their tails between their legs. I watched them go with a smile spreading across my face. Something told me I wouldn't be hearing from them anymore.

Someone started clapping behind me and I spun around, ready to fight again, but it was only Wesley and Jordan. How long had they been there? Had they been watching the entire time?

I shifted back and searched for my clothes to cover myself up a little. My green dress was torn but not completely unwearable. My underwear was a lost cause though, along with my cardigan. "What are you two doing out here?"

Wesley grinned. "We heard a commotion and came to check it out, but by the time we got here, you had it under control. Nice work, by the way."

"Very impressive," Jordan agreed. "Kaden really is a fool. You would have made a killer alpha female."

"You're a true alpha even without a pack." Wesley

stepped forward and squeezed my shoulder. "I'm proud to be your brother."

I opened my mouth to deny it but stopped myself. He was right. I didn't need a pack or a mate to be a powerful alpha. I was a Zodiac Wolf and a Moon Witch, and no one could ever take that away from me. I had everything I needed inside of me.

I always had.

CHAPTER EIGHT

PALE MOON MAGIC lit the conference room and soaked into Roxandra's skin. She let out a sound like she was in pain but didn't stop fighting, twisting her hands in their bonds and trying to tip the chair backward.

Larkin finally let out a breath and stepped back, allowing the light to fade away. "The spell is in place."

The camera was already recording, the red light blinking, with a miniature version of Roxandra reflected in the small screen. Ethan gave me a tight nod, signaling I should begin. Behind him, Kaden leaned in the doorway with his arms crossed, while Jordan leaned against the other wall, also with his arms crossed. The looks on their faces were almost identical, and I would have laughed if it hadn't been such a tense situation.

My nerves were strung even tighter today than they had been the last time. I had some very important questions to ask Roxandra, and I wanted to make sure I got to them before the truth spell wore off.

I took my seat in front of her. "Time for another chat, Roxie."

Roxandra glared at me, her lips pressed shut as if she was afraid she'd start spilling every single Sun Witch secret if she started talking.

"First question. Is the Moon Curse a lie?" I planned to start with a few questions that I already knew the answer to but wanted to get recorded on camera for the other alphas. It was a good way to make sure that the spell had taken hold.

"Yes," she said, her voice almost bored. "The Moon Curse hasn't been active for many years."

"Why did you let the Leo Pack attack us at the Convergence?" I asked next, watching her closely.

"To set off a pack war that would weaken both packs, allowing us to more easily take control," Roxandra spat out. "Why are you asking me questions you already know the answers to?"

I gave her my sweetest, most saccharine smile. "It makes me happy to watch you squirm."

Next, I went through a list of questions that Ethan had prepared for me from the other alphas, mostly confirming things we already knew, and Roxandra answered each with the same spiteful look in her eyes. I had a feeling that if her hands were free, she'd wrap them around my throat and laugh as she squeezed the life out of me.

Once I finished the list of questions, Larkin cast the

truth spell again, to make sure it didn't run out before we finished the interrogation. Roxandra glared at me in silence once it was done, mulishly setting her chin, but then her eyes fell on Jordan. The sight of her looking at him made me angry all over again. From where he leaned against the wall, he appeared completely at ease, but I could see how tense his shoulders were, and how tightly he had his jaw clenched. On the other side of the room, Kaden looked equally agitated.

I'll figure this out for you both, I thought. *You and everyone else who was hurt by the Sun Witches.*

I squared my shoulders and looked back at Roxandra. "Where is Jordan's mother?"

Roxandra's eyebrows creased into a frown, and I wasn't sure if it was from resisting the truth spell or from confusion. "I don't know."

Frustration welled up inside me, but I pushed it down and asked my next question. "Where are the Leos now?"

"I don't know," she said again.

"Is—" I bit back the words. I'd been about to ask, *is there anything you do know?* But I didn't really want to leave that question up to Roxandra's interpretation. "Where are the Sun Witches now?"

Roxandra let out a pained noise, trying to keep her mouth shut. She shook her head once, then twice, but eventually, the truth spell won out. "They're likely in Solundra."

"What is Solundra?" I asked.

"The realm of Helios," Roxandra spat out, like I was an idiot.

Of course. I should have realized there would be a realm

for Helios, just like Selene had Lunatera. "Can you take us there?"

Her eyes narrowed. "Can? Yes. Will? No."

I stared back at her without flinching, but we both knew no one could force her to do anything except answer our questions. Unless we resorted to torture, but I had a feeling that wouldn't work very well on her. She had nerves of steel, and wouldn't betray her people, or her mother, easily.

I'd finished with the questions we had planned, and now it was time to ask the ones I'd been mulling over for the last few nights. The ones I was truly scared to ask, but needed to know more than anything else. My eyes darted to Kaden once, as I steeled myself for what we might learn.

"I have a few more questions, Roxie."

"Lucky me," she snapped.

"Can the Sun Witches control people's minds without the blessing spell?" I asked.

A slow smile spread across her lips, as if she knew where I was headed with this and delighted in the prospect of my suffering. "Yes. The blessing spell allows us to take the wolves over completely, but we can use our mind magic on anyone."

My hands clenched in my lap as a sinking feeling spread through my gut. "Have the Sun Witches used any of that mind magic on anyone in this room, other than Jordan?"

"Yes," Roxandra said, cocking her head, her smile growing wider. "I wondered how long it would take you to figure out. I had so much fun putting dark thoughts in his head."

"Who?" I asked. I needed her to say it.

"The Ophiuchus alpha."

"What?" Kaden asked, though it sounded more like a shout. He strode toward us like a warrior charging on the battlefield. "What are you talking about?"

Roxandra let out a laugh, her head falling back onto the chair. "I'm so pleased that you didn't know we were messing with your head. My mother said I would have to be especially subtle for you. It was hard, but it was so worth it."

"How?" Kaden demanded. "How did you put the thoughts into my head?"

"When we killed you, our magic wormed its way inside a little. Just enough to let us in easier." Her shoulders rolled in a casual shrug. "An unexpected side effect, but one that made you very useful to us. It was hard at first though, especially with all the wards you set up around the hotel. We could have breached them, of course, but that would have alerted you to our presence. Instead, I got into your head every time you left the hotel and whispered things in your mind. We encouraged the dark thoughts you already had, pushing harder and harder, until you snapped."

The tension inside of Kaden finally broke at her last word, and he rushed Roxandra. Ethan was on him in an instant, dragging him down to the floor and trying to pin him, but Kaden wrenched him off and tossed him aside as if he weighed nothing. Ethan's back hit the wall, and he let out a grunt of pain but shook it off. He crouched, ready to strike again, but Jordan had taken his place. He stood in front of Kaden, his hands out.

"Don't," he said, his voice low, deadly, and infused with a bit of command.

Kaden bared his teeth. "Move."

"No," Jordan said simply, meeting Kaden's anger with unshakable calm. He'd been in the same situation days ago. He knew exactly what it felt like. Kaden had stopped him from killing Roxandra then, and now Jordan seemed to be returning the favor. They stared at each other for a long moment, and an understanding passed between them. For the first time, they seemed to be on the same wavelength.

Kaden's stance changed as he backed down. "This isn't over."

"No, it isn't," Jordan agreed. "We won't let her get away with it."

"I have a few more questions," I said, and both men turned to me. My voice dropped to a whisper. "We have to know."

"Ask them before the spell wears off," Kaden said, through gritted teeth. Like me, he had to be torn between wanting to know everything and wanting to bury his head in the sand and forget any of this had ever happened.

I gripped the arms of my chair as I turned back to Roxandra. "Did you make Kaden kill the Leos who attacked me and my friends?"

"Yes." At this point, she'd given up trying to fight the truth spell. "I had to make sure they wouldn't reveal the Sun Witches' secrets. It wasn't hard though. He wanted to do it anyway."

"If you were here, why not just command Kaden to let Jordan go?" Ethan asked.

"I wanted to, but my mother wouldn't let me. She believed that having Jordan as your prisoner would cause more conflict." Her eyes flickered between Jordan and Kaden, and then back to me. "Instead, we got into Kaden's head to sow discord, dripping a little more poison into his mind every time he left the hotel. We hoped it would destroy his relationship with Ayla, cause fighting within the packs, and make everyone turn against him. It was easy because he was already in a dark place. All we had to do was amplify those feelings." She gave me a haughty look. "Seems like it worked too."

I felt sick to my stomach. It all made perfect, horrifying sense. I should have known something was wrong with Kaden. No, I had known, deep down. I'd sensed something wasn't right with him. But I never could have imagined all of this.

"I'm going to kill you," Kaden said to Roxandra, his voice deadly calm.

Jordan let out a snort. "Get in line."

But before either of them could act, a sudden ear-splitting sound pierced the air, making us all jump. The hotel alarm.

Shit, I thought. *This can't be good.*

CHAPTER NINE

AS THE ALARM continued to blare throughout the conference room, everyone snapped into action around me, preparing for battle. The two burly guards ran back in, and I whipped around to Roxandra, wondering if she'd done something to cause this, but she looked just as surprised as I felt.

"That's the alarm," Ethan said, as he pulled out his phone and started sending a message. "We must be under attack."

"Is it the Sun Witches?" I asked. Had they arrived to try to free Roxandra? Damn, I'd hoped we would have more time before they made a move.

"The wards are still intact around the hotel," Larkin said, after frowning in concentration. "It doesn't make any sense."

"Maybe it's not the Sun Witches," Kaden said.

Larkin's eyes grew wide. "Who else would it be?"

Jordan swore under his breath. "Whoever it is, they must be here for *her*. We can't let them get her."

Ethan snapped his fingers at the guards. "Take her back to her cell while we deal with this. Don't let anyone get near her. I'll send more reinforcements down too."

The two guards nodded and began to extract Roxandra from the chair. Her surprise had melted to amusement, as she watched us panic.

"I told you they'd come for me," she said in an awful singsong voice. "I can't wait to watch you all die."

"Kaden, bite her before I rip her fucking head off," Jordan growled.

"With pleasure." Kaden grabbed one of Roxandra's arms, and though she fought him, she wasn't nearly strong enough to stop his poison fangs from sinking into her skin. She looked at him with absolute loathing for another second before her eyes closed and her body slumped down in her chair.

"Let's go," Ethan said, rushing out of the conference room.

Everyone followed him without question, and we raced down the stairs instead of waiting for the elevator. My heart beat faster as I tried to keep up with the alphas, while Larkin came up last behind us. We burst into the lobby, and I was instantly overwhelmed by the strong scent of blood. I choked on the smell for a few seconds, blinking as I took in what was happening in front of me.

It was absolute chaos, with shifters fighting all around

us, and many already dead on the ground. A huge chandelier had somehow crashed to the floor, spilling shards of crystal everywhere, and they were covered in blood. The Christmas tree in the corner had been completely shredded too, the decorations scattered or destroyed in the fight. Wolves snarled and fought, and at first, I couldn't tell who or what they were fighting. Not Sun Witches, that was obvious. But not other shifters either.

Impossibly fast men and women in black clothes clashed with our wolves, slashing with razor-sharp nails and tearing at throats with their fangs. My own wolf woke inside me with a vengeance, my instincts urging me to *kill, kill, kill,* like it recognized on some primal level that these creatures were our natural enemies, and there was only room for one of our kinds on this Earth. I'd felt this same urge only once before when I'd first met Killian, the vampire who lived with the Moon Witches.

"Vampires," I yelled, loud enough to be heard over the sounds of combat.

The alphas instantly shifted, flowing into their wolves and charging into battle without hesitation. Jordan let loose his Leo roar, which sent both the shifters and vampires near us scurrying away in a panic. Kaden and Ethan leaped over a tangle of fighting shifters and vampires in tandem, and then I lost sight of them in the mayhem.

A dark brown wolf was sprawled out close to me, bleeding from a gash in her side. She whimpered, turning her brown eyes toward me, but then one of the vampires rushed over. The vampire was painfully beautiful, with golden hair that curled perfectly at the ends, and her eyes met mine as she latched her fangs onto the wolf's neck. I gathered moon magic inside me and blasted her with it. It knocked the vampire back, my magic stunning her momentarily, but then she shook it off and came straight for me. She moved much faster than any shifter I'd seen, and I began furiously throwing balls of moon magic at her. I managed to stop her from advancing but wasn't doing much more damage than that.

"How do we hurt them?" I asked Larkin, who'd been fighting behind me.

Larkin created a bolt of moonlight shaped into something like a shard of ice, and launched it toward the female vampire, spearing her through the chest. The vampire slumped down, finally dead.

"They're vampires," Larkin said. "You need to stab them in the heart, or cut off their heads."

It seemed so obvious when she put it like that, but I'd never faced vampires before in combat, so how was I to know how much of the lore was true? A lot of the things that people believed about werewolves were a bunch of nonsense, after all.

"Aim for their heads or their hearts," I yelled as loud as I could, hoping the shifters closest to me would spread the word to their other pack members through their telepathic bond.

More vampires charged toward us, and I copied Larkin and managed to take one of them down, but they moved so quickly it was hard to aim the moonlight spears to hit their chests in the right spot. A black-haired male vampire rushed at me, supernaturally fast, and I missed his heart, hitting the wall behind him with my magic, and my pulse raced as he got closer and closer.

But then Kaden was there, his huge black wolf protecting me with his body, and he swiped one massive claw across the vampire's chest. Fangs snapped at Kaden's throat, but he bit back, nearly as fast, tearing out the vampire's neck. He managed to rip the vampire's entire head off, making blood spurt wildly in a horrific display. It seemed he'd gotten the message about how to kill them.

And he wasn't the only one. I spotted Jordan across the room, back in his human form, actually reach inside a vampire's chest to rip its heart out. Ethan's gray wolf stood beside another vampire who looked like he'd been completely dismembered and turned to little more than bloody pulp.

More shifters, all Ophiuchus, emerged from the elevator to join the fight. Kaden let out a short howl, and the other Ophiuchus warriors fell into formation around him, changing their attacks to focus on beheading the vampires or destroying their hearts. It was like they'd trained for years to fight the vampires, and the few Libras in the lobby began to copy their movements too.

Damn, Kaden is a good alpha, I thought, with a pang in my chest. But even though I was packless, I could still help them in the fight.

Larkin seemed to have the magic situation under control, so I shifted and joined the other wolves in the fray.

The first instant that my teeth met vampire flesh, my inner wolf practically cheered, as if she'd been waiting for this moment her entire life. I brushed up against Kaden's side after I helped him take another vampire down, and he nuzzled me with his bloody snout. I found myself nuzzling him back, relieved he was alive, and secretly thrilled to be fighting alongside him once more.

Within minutes, we got the upper hand as more and more vampires fell around us. My fangs snapped at the heel of a ginger-haired vampire, but he fled outside in a blur of movement, into the sun-lit gardens behind the hotel. By the time I'd chased after him, he was already long gone.

The fighting ended suddenly, going from absolute chaos to nothing at all as the remaining vampires escaped with their incredible speed. Blood splatter stained nearly every surface of the lobby, and the entire space had been destroyed, as though a wrecking crew had come through. Many wolves were dead or injured, covered in bite and scratch marks, and those that lived looked completely shell-shocked. There were dead vampires too, but their bodies were a lot less recognizable after the shifters had finished tearing them apart.

Kaden and I shifted back and he rested his hands on my upper arms, silently making sure I was okay. I nodded at him, unable to find any words to express the horror of what we'd just been through. I was just so relieved Kaden was unharmed, and I found myself pressing my forehead against his as I caught my breath.

Once the initial shock passed, I spun around and

looked for the others. Jordan stood to the side, rolling his shoulder and wincing a little. Larkin's shirt was torn and she was bleeding from a small cut on her shoulder, but it didn't look too bad. I assumed she wouldn't turn into a vampire just from that, but what did I know? Not enough about vampires, obviously. I'd have to do something about that.

Ethan looked grim as he surveyed the damage to his hotel and the carnage all around us. His gaze snagged on a dead shifter a few yards away, the Libra he'd danced with at the Christmas party, and a muscle twitched in his jaw.

"I thought vampires were a myth," he said, his voice low.

We once thought that about the Ophiuchus pack too, I thought, though I didn't say it out loud.

"They're real." Larkin wiped her hands on her jeans, but all that did was smear blood all over them. "Although these vampires were out during the day, which shouldn't be possible with the Sun Curse."

"What were they doing in my hotel?" Ethan growled. I'd never heard him sound so pissed off before.

"They're working with the Sun Witches," Jordan said.

"How do you know this?" Kaden asked, as he crouched by one of his fallen warriors. Most of the fighters had been Ophiuchus, since we were the ones living in the hotel, and I could see how much it hurt him to see even more of his pack members dead or injured. It hurt me too.

Jordan shrugged and then winced. I had a feeling he'd be a bit sore for a few hours until his enhanced healing took care of it. "One came to visit the Leo pack when the Sun

Witches were controlling me. I've never seen them in action though. I didn't know they'd be so...deadly."

In wolf form, Jack rushed in from outside, along with Harper and Dane. They must have tried to follow the vampires as they'd escaped. Jack shifted back and shook his head. "They're gone."

"Why did they leave so suddenly?" Ethan asked.

At the time, I'd thought they were running because we were overpowering them, but now it did seem odd how quickly they'd broken off their attack.

It hit me like a kick to the chest. "Roxandra!"

"Shit," Jordan muttered. "It was a distraction."

We bolted back up the stairs, not even bothering to redress as we raced to the conference room, but we were too late. The two guards were dead in the hallway, still in human form with huge gashes in their chests, their throats ripped out by vampire fangs. Two other shifters, who must have been sent to help guard Roxandra, had also been killed.

"Fuck!" Kaden yelled.

Ethan went into the conference room, though he must have known it was pointless. Roxandra's chair was empty, the camera tripod knocked over. Her bonds had been cut clean through, likely with a vampire's nails, and her moon collar was on the ground, broken in half. Ethan swore and kicked the collar across the room.

I bent down and grabbed the camera, worried the footage might have been lost or wiped clean, but when I rewound it, it was still there. Thank the goddess. At least we had Roxandra's confession recorded so that the other alphas could see it.

Back in the hallway, a nearby window was broken, clearly from the inside. Jordan stalked over to it and looked out. He shook his head, confirming what we already knew.

Roxandra was gone.

CHAPTER TEN

WE ALL HELPED CLEAN up the lobby, needing to do *something* after Roxandra had slipped out of our grasp. This gave us somewhere to focus all the energy left over from the fight, though the mood was a lot more subdued now. Bodies had to be moved, and the wounded had to be tended to before they could return to their rooms to rest. Piles of debris had to be swept up, and blood had to be scrubbed off the walls and the marble floors.

Almost every inch of me was covered in dried blood by the time I teleported back to my room. I took a long, hot shower, and used the time to go over everything that had happened in the last few hours. I practically had whiplash trying to keep up with it all. Not just the vampire attack, but everything that had come before it, including all the revelations about what the Sun Witches had done to Kaden.

Roxandra had admitted that they'd tried to drive a wedge between us, to ruin our relationship, and they'd succeeded. Kaden and I needed to get past this somehow if we were going to be allies. The Zodiac Wolves needed both of us, that much was clear, and we had to work together if we were going to defeat the Sun Witches. I couldn't dent it any longer—I needed Kaden's help, and he needed mine. And maybe someday we'd be able to become more than allies again too.

I had to talk to him—and Larkin had given me the perfect excuse.

I took the elevator to give myself a bit of extra time to think about what I would say. Kaden was still staying in the penthouse suite, which had once been mine too before our relationship had fallen apart.

When I reached the door, I hesitated for a few seconds before knocking. There was a brief pause during which I considered going back to my room, but then Kaden opened the door. He'd also showered, and the ends of his hair were still wet. He wasn't wearing a shirt either. *Typical.*

He leaned against the doorway, causing my eyes to take in a large expanse of his perfect, muscular chest. "Hello, Ayla."

"Hi," I said, suddenly overcome with awkwardness as I fumbled for my next words and tried not to stare at his naked skin. "I think we should talk."

"Come inside."

He stepped back and gestured for me to join him. I stepped into the living room, and when he shut the door, tension raised between us. I swallowed as I remembered all our time in this penthouse together, like when he'd made breakfast for me in the kitchen, or how we'd gazed out at the city together, or how he'd bent me over the couch and taken me from behind...

I licked my lips, my mouth suddenly dry, my blood suddenly warm. Kaden looked down at my mouth like he was also having similar thoughts.

I cleared my throat. "I brought something for you."

Kaden raised an eyebrow. "I hope it's not a belated Christmas present."

"Not exactly." I reached into my pocket and pulled out the moonstone necklace Larkin had given me earlier today when we'd had a moment alone. It was similar to the one Jordan wore, but not quite as large or as powerful. "Larkin got this from my mother when she visited at Christmas. I think she originally planned to give it to Ethan, but this afternoon she suggested I pass it along to you."

He rubbed the back of his neck. "If it's for Ethan, I don't want to take it."

"We decided you need it more. It'll stop the Sun Witches from getting into your head again. Unless you'd rather I take it back..."

"No." Kaden took the necklace and put it on. He let out a deep breath, as if something heavy had been lifted from his shoulders. "Thank you. Please give Larkin my thanks too when you see her."

"I will." The tension in my body relaxed too, knowing that he was protected. "Maybe I can take you to see my mother sometime. She can teach you to shield your mind."

Kaden gave me a wry smile, but there was a hint of

sadness in his eyes. "I'm surprised you'd want to introduce me to your mother after what happened between us."

My heart ached at the reminder of our past, but I knew this was why I had come to see him. "I know now that it was the Sun Witches who did all that, not you."

He let out a heavy sigh and sat on the sofa, looking defeated. "That's not entirely true. It wasn't all the magic. Some of it was me."

I perched on the other end of it, watching him gather his thoughts and wishing I knew how to make things better. My chest hurt with everything I wanted to say, but I had to keep control of my emotions, or I might blow up again...or fall apart completely.

"Ayla, what I'm going to say... It's hard for me, but I need you to know," Kaden said, his voice heavy with emotion. "When I died, it broke me. I couldn't protect you and I felt powerless."

"That wasn't your fault."

"That didn't matter. The feeling only got worse when the members of my pack betrayed me. Then they came back to me dead, and the other alphas refused to do anything about it. And then you sided with Jordan over me..."

I let out a short noise of protest. "That wasn't fair. You never should have made me try to choose."

"I know," Kaden said, sounding frustrated. "Trust me, I know. I knew it then too. But I couldn't stop."

"I wasn't really choosing Jordan over you anyway. I was choosing to not let you kill Jordan. There's a difference." I'd told him as much when we'd been fighting, but he'd been so blinded by his rage that he hadn't been willing to listen to me. "Not just because he's my brother, but because I saw the rage and jealousy in your eyes, and it scared me. If you'd killed him, you would have gone to a very dark place, one you wouldn't have been able to come back from...and I couldn't bear the thought of losing you both."

"I was already in that dark place. The Sun Witches might have pulled the strings, but I'm not sure I would have done anything differently without their poison in my mind."

I shook my head, unwilling to believe what he was saying. "No, I should have known it wasn't you. You weren't acting like yourself. Not the Kaden I knew, at least. It was like you became a different person."

"Trust me, it would be easier to blame it all on the Sun Witches. Don't you think I want to do that, knowing that might help you forgive me?" He let out a sharp, pained laugh. "It's tempting, but I'm done lying to myself, or to you. The Sun Witches were able to control me so easily because I had all of that darkness inside me already. The anger and jealousy, those were mine. All they did was give me a nudge."

"It sounded like a lot more than a nudge," I muttered, though I appreciated that he was finally being honest with us both. But as part of being honest, he had to admit to himself that the Sun Witches had been controlling him too.

"Maybe it was. I don't know. It's hard to tell how much was me, and how much was them. My memories of that time are...jumbled. But I know it wasn't all them, and I'm sorry for everything I did." When he spoke again, his voice was rough. "I lost my way. I lost myself. And worst of all, I lost you."

I reached for his hand, feeling the warmth of his skin against mine. "You haven't lost me. I'm here, aren't I?"

Something in my words changed his demeanor, like they gave him hope when previously he had none. "Then I swear I won't ever let you go again. I'm going to spend the rest of my life trying to be the man you deserve. I love you more than anything, Ayla."

My heart swelled with love and sadness at the same time as tears filled my eyes. I quickly blinked them back, not wanting to show how much this was hurting me. "I love you too, Kaden. I'm sorry for my part in all of this, and for not seeing the truth earlier. And I forgive you..."

"But..." Kaden said, as if he knew what was coming next.

"But we both need time to recover from all of this. We're still so freshly hurt from everything that happened over the last few weeks and all the new things we learned, and I think you need to work through some things on your own too. We both do."

Kaden nodded slowly, his eyes filled with pain and understanding. "Yeah, you're probably right. It's terrible not being able to trust my own mind. I've started questioning everything I've said and done over the last few months. So much of it was me, I freely admit that, but how much? Even worse, how would I know if they were in my head again? How would I stop them if they were?"

I could see the turmoil on his face, and I wanted to take his pain away, but I knew that wasn't something I could do.

"The moonstone necklace will protect you as long as you're wearing it," I said, hoping that would bring him some peace, but I sensed it wouldn't be enough. A necklace was too easy to remove or overpower. I couldn't imagine how awful it would be knowing that the Sun Witches had gotten in my head or that they could do it again so easily. A trip to visit my mother was definitely in our future—she'd taught me how to shield my mind, and I knew she could help Kaden too.

But until then... I chewed on my lip for a few seconds, wondering what would happen if I told Kaden what I was thinking. We were being honest with each other though, and if Kaden was willing to really make an effort to change, maybe he would listen to me.

"There's one other person we know who is going through the same thing as you," I said slowly. "Maybe you should talk to him."

Kaden's back stiffened the moment he realized who I meant. "No."

"Just think about it," I said quickly before he could shut me down. "You two have both gone through a terrible ordeal, and though I'm always willing to listen, I'll never be able to fully understand what it was like for you. What it's like now, knowing the truth. But Jordan can."

"I can barely stand to be in the same room as that cocky Leo," Kaden growled.

I sighed, unable to hide my disappointment. "Don't forget you're on the same side now. If you actually talked to each other, you might finally see who the real enemy is."

Kaden grunted, his expression stubborn. "I'm not actively trying to kill Jordan anymore. That's the best I can do."

"I guess that's better than nothing." Maybe Kaden would change his mind later, once he'd thought about the situation more. I couldn't expect him to change overnight, especially when he'd only learned about all of this earlier today. But that was also why we couldn't be together, at least, not yet. Until he got past his anger, hatred, and jealousy, there wouldn't be enough room in his heart for me.

"I should probably get to bed," I said, as I rose to my feet. "It's been a long day, and we all have a lot to think about."

Kaden trailed me to the door, but he stopped me before I could open it. "Ayla, wait."

"What is it?" I asked, noticing the concern in his voice.

"The full moon is in a week or so, and you're packless. You'll go into heat again."

Oh shit. With everything else going on, I hadn't really had time to think about the implications of being packless for the next full moon. The memories of my first full moon with Kaden hit me so hard it made me gasp, while desire raced through my blood. It was doused almost instantly by terror at the thought of being near Jordan during the full moon instead.

"Fuck," I whispered.

"Exactly. If you won't join the Ophiuchus pack again, you should have Wesley give you the Cancer pack mark. Or hell, get Jordan to give you the Leo one. They don't go into heat 'til much later in the year. You'd be safe until we find a way to break the mate bonds."

He must be really worried, if he was suggesting I become a Leo, of all things. But joining one of those packs wasn't an option. I was an Ophiuchus in my heart, but letting Kaden put the pack mark back on me felt too much like forgetting that he'd been the one who had taken it away. And if he made me an Ophiuchus again, did that make me his alpha female again too? Did I even want that?

I closed my eyes and swallowed hard. "I'll figure something out."

"I know you will." He rested one hand on my shoulder. "But I'm here if you need me."

I found myself staring up at him, thinking of how he'd helped me the last time I was in heat. He hadn't let any other male get close to me then, and I knew he would be even more possessive now. "You would help me again?"

His hands settled around my waist and he pulled me closer. "Would I make sure no other man touched you? Would I fuck you all night to ease the need inside you? Would I make you come so many times you never had a single doubt in your mind that you were mine?" His lips brushed my ear. "Yes. A thousand times, yes."

Then his mouth was on mine, and mine was on his. I wasn't sure who'd started the kiss, only that we'd both succumbed to it without hesitation, and once it had started, it wasn't a thing that could easily be stopped. My body had ached for his touch for so long, and his familiar scent and taste made me melt against him. With a satisfied noise, his hands slid to my back, up to my shoulders, and my neck. He dug his hands into my hair, winding it around his fingers as he deepened the kiss even more.

The pleasure shocked me out of whatever spell I'd been put under, and I pulled away with a gasp. We stared at each other, our pulses racing at the same speed, and I touched my lips, still tasting him on them. I wanted to walk away, and I wanted to stay, and I was so torn between the two options that I couldn't move at all.

Kaden surprised me by opening the door for me. "Like I said, I'm here if you need me. Sleep well, Ayla."

CHAPTER ELEVEN

ETHAN DECIDED to call a meeting outside, even though temperatures had dropped below freezing and it threatened to snow at any moment. None of us wanted to be in a conference room again anytime soon though. Instead, we sat at a long wooden table with heat lamps all around us and tried to figure out what to do next.

"We lost too many of our own in that attack," said Kaden, his eyes dark with anger. "We need to come up with a plan to prevent something like this from happening again."

"The vampires caught us off guard," Ethan said, his tone sharp. He'd taken it personally that they'd attacked his territory, and that we'd never seen them coming. "It won't happen again."

Jordan leaned back and crossed his arms. "We need to increase patrols and set up better warning systems, especially since the wards failed."

Larkin bristled at that. "They didn't *fail*. They were set

up to block any Sun Witches from entering the hotel. But everyone else—shifters, humans, and even vampires it seems—can come and go. We can't do much else, since we're in the middle of Toronto."

"That sounds like a fail to me," Jordan said.

I shot him a look. Everyone's nerves were on edge, but he wasn't making this any easier. It had been a couple of days since the vampire attack, and we'd all had a hard time recovering from it.

"Maybe it's time we move the Ophiuchus pack again," Clayton said, though he sounded hesitant to suggest it. I wasn't sure why Kaden had asked him to join the meeting this time, but perhaps he still didn't trust himself and wanted his beta's opinion too.

"But where?" I asked, my stomach twisting at the thought of the Ophiuchus leaving. Would they go before the full moon? I couldn't imagine Kaden would abandon me. Or maybe he expected me to go with them?

"I could ask if the Moon Witches would allow you to hide in Lunatera for a while," Larkin said.

"No. We're done hiding." Kaden rubbed his beard as he considered. "I think you're right, Clayton. We've stayed with the Libras for too long. We need to prepare to head back to Coronis soon."

My eyes widened at the idea of them returning to the Ophiuchus pack lands in Manitoba. "Is that safe?"

Kaden's eyes met mine. "Nowhere is safe, but at least we would be home."

Home. The word hit me hard, and I looked away. Where exactly was my home now?

"You're welcome to stay as long as you need," Ethan said. "All of you."

I thought he was speaking directly to me, but then I noticed he was looking at Jordan. If the Ophiuchus left this hotel, Jordan would be on his own too.

"Have we gotten any leads on where the Leos are now?" I asked.

"Not yet," Ethan said, his brow furrowed. "And nothing on the vampires or Sun Witches either."

Larkin sighed. "The Sun Witches are likely in their realm, which we won't be able to get to. They might have the vampires with them too."

"Another dead end," Jordan muttered.

"What about the other alphas?" I asked. "Have you received any responses to the latest video yet?"

"Yes, there was an outpour of shock, horror, and disbelief," Ethan said. "We'll need to call another Zoom meeting soon with all of them to discuss our next steps."

That was something at least. Ethan had asked Kaden if he wanted the part about his mind control removed from the recording, but Kaden had told him to leave it in. He wanted the other alphas to know everything, even if it painted him in a bad light.

"I'm going to head back to Lunatera," Larkin said, as she slowly rose to her feet. "I'll try to get some more moonstone necklaces made, and I'll ask my vampire friend if he knows anything that will help us, although I'm not sure how much help he will be. He's been living in Lunatera for a long time."

"Any help you can give us would be appreciated," Ethan said.

I stood up and gave her a hug. "Tell my mother I miss her."

"I will."

She headed back inside, just as a Libra woman I'd seen in the lobby came toward us. She had dark skin, short brown hair, and wore a suit. "Pardon me for interrupting, but we received something I think you might want to see."

"We're almost done here anyway," Ethan said. "What is it?"

She handed him a red envelope. "It looks like a Christmas card."

Ethan frowned down at it, while the woman disappeared back into the hotel. "It's addressed to Jordan."

Jordan grabbed the envelope from Ethan's hand and began tearing it open. "And everyone knows that's suspicious because no one in their right mind would send me a card." The card had a picture of a wolf with a Santa hat on the front. Jordan quickly scanned the inside. "It's from the Scorpio alpha. He says the Leos are staying in their pack lands in New Mexico. They want to join us as allies, but need some help ousting the Leo pack first."

"Do you think it's a trick?" Kaden asked.

"No, I think it's real." Jordan passed Kaden the card so he could look it over himself. "The Leo beta is mated to a Scorpio, and they've been our allies for many years. Now that he's pretending to be alpha, he probably thought he could hide with them for a while."

"Sounds like they're not too happy about it," I said. If we could find the Leos, there was a chance we could find Jordan's mother. Maybe even in time for the full moon. Of course, once we found her there was no guarantee she'd be able to break the spells on us.

"How would you like to handle this?" Ethan asked Jordan.

"Get me inside the Scorpio pack lands, and I'll challenge the beta for the position of alpha—and I won't lose."

"And if you win?" Kaden asked.

Jordan shot Kaden a scathing look at the word 'if.' "Once I'm alpha again, I'll get the Leos to leave peacefully and go back to our village."

"It's a risky move," Ethan said. "It could be a trap, and even if it's not, we might fail. But if we win, we would gain two new allies—the Scorpios and the Leos."

"If this works, I might be able to get the Taurus and Aries packs to turn against the Sun Witches too," Jordan said.

Kaden scoffed. "All the Zodiac Wolves united? Seems impossible."

"We'll make it happen," I jumped in, before Jordan could quip something else to Kaden. I didn't need them to start arguing again. "We need to get all the packs working together if we're going to free ourselves from the Sun Witches, especially if they have the vampires on their side now."

"The Libra pack will help you with whatever you need," Ethan said. "But I think I should personally stay out of this fight."

"Probably a good idea," Jordan said with a nod.

"I'm going with you," I told Jordan. I couldn't imagine losing him so soon after finally reaching a place where we were getting along. He was my brother, and despite our rocky path, I wanted him safe. I would do whatever I could to make sure he got out of this alive. "I can teleport us out quickly if something goes wrong."

"I'm coming too," Kaden said, and everyone turned to him in shock, including me.

"Why, so you can cheer on my opponent?" Jordan asked.

Kaden rolled his eyes. "With my invisibility, I can help you get in without anyone noticing. After that, it's all on you."

I was beyond surprised that he would offer to help Jordan with anything, even if he was only going because I was. Maybe he really was changing. Something inside of me softened a little. Another piece of my heart fit back together again.

"With Kaden's invisibility and my teleportation, we would only need a small attack force to infiltrate the Scorpios," I said.

Jordan shook his head. "Sneaking inside isn't an option. The Scorpios live in underground caverns, which are difficult to navigate if you're not familiar with them. I've only been there a few times with my dad, and I'm not sure I could guide us through."

"What do you suggest?" Kaden asked.

"We bang on their door and demand an audience." Jordan flashed a cocky grin. "I am the Leo alpha, after all. How could they deny me?"

We spent the next few hours making plans while Ethan's assistant brought us sandwiches. Clayton would begin getting the Ophiuchus pack ready to return to Coronis, while Ethan worked on setting up more defenses in case of another vampire attack. The rest of us would lead a small group of warriors to the Scorpio pack lands in New Mexico to reclaim Jordan's throne.

I just hoped it wasn't a trap. If it was, I wasn't sure how we would bounce back. Every time we lost a battle, it was harder to regroup. Watching friends and family die without a way to retaliate was demoralizing for everyone. I didn't blame the others for feeling lost, tired, and on edge. I was right there with them.

These thoughts weighed heavily on my mind as I headed back to my room. I could have teleported, but instead, I found myself in the elevator with Kaden. Alone.

Had I done it on purpose? Maybe.

We stood facing each other in the elevator, the mirrored walls reflecting our expressions back at us. Kaden's masculine presence filled up the space, and we stared at each other without reservation. For the first time in weeks, it was like I was truly seeing him. All his strengths and weaknesses. All his desires and fears. Everything.

"I'm glad you're coming with us," I said, as the elevator kept rising. My heart raced as I looked into his eyes, feeling a pull toward him that I couldn't ignore. "Thank you for helping Jordan."

"I'm not doing it for him," Kaden said, his voice low and intense.

"I know, but I appreciate it anyway."

"I would do anything for you, Ayla. *Anything*. Even things I never thought I would do, like supporting the son of the man who killed my parents." He took a step toward me, his eyes smoldering. "There's no one controlling my strings anymore. I make all my own decisions now, and they all lead back to you."

The elevator door opened to my floor, and I stepped out, waiting for him to follow. "But the Ophiuchus will be leaving soon..."

"Yes. With you." Kaden exited the elevator, moving close to me. "I already told you I'm not letting you go again."

I began walking down the hallway toward my room, with Kaden by my side. "What if I don't want to go with you?"

"We both know you do."

I felt a flutter in my stomach as a wave of desire and fear washed over me. When we reached my door, I paused. "I don't know what I want."

"I do." He pinned me with his dark gaze. "Let me in and I'll show you."

CHAPTER TWELVE

HUNGER BREWED in his eyes like a storm, and it woke something in me, an answering call that felt as natural as breathing. I swallowed and told myself I'd insist that he leave at any second now. I really would.

But then I found myself stepping into my hotel room and opening the door wide, silently inviting him to follow me inside. As I waited to see if he would join me, I shrugged off my jacket and stared out the window, wondering what I was thinking. I'd invited the wolf into my nest—would he bite me in return?

Was it terrible that a part of me hoped he would?

Kaden shut the door and approached me from behind, resting his hands on my shoulders. They were warm and possessive, and my body stiffened in response.

"You seem tense." He slowly moved my red hair to one side, then lowered his lips to my neck. "I can help you with that."

Kaden's mouth met my skin and I sank into his touch, eyes fluttering shut as I remembered how good it felt to be *his*. His breath was hot against my neck, sending shivers down my spine, and each soft, slow kiss felt like atonement. He kneaded the muscles in my shoulders and back, massaging out the stress there, and I found myself letting out a soft moan in response.

Without thinking, I turned in his arms and dragged his mouth to mine. I'd been thinking way too much lately. All I wanted was to *feel*.

Kaden groaned and pressed against me, deepening the kiss. It was like taking a drink of water after a long hike, satiating a part of myself I hadn't realized was so thirsty. His hands scoured down my body and my back hit the wall as a desperate need took over both of us.

But then I remembered the last time I'd felt like this, and how he'd used my lust to manipulate me. That might have been the Sun Witches, but how could I be sure?

I turned my face to the side, gasping for air. "Kaden, I don't know if I can do this."

He pressed his face against my hair. "You don't have to do anything. Let me take care of you."

I wanted that so badly, but my brain still thought of when he'd fucked me in the snow and then left me to cry. "But last time..."

"This won't be anything like last time," Kaden said, and it sounded like a promise. "This time will be all about you."

His low voice sent desire pooling into my core. I was rapidly losing the ability to make decisions based on logic.

Everything inside me was screaming to let him do whatever he wanted to me.

"Trust me." He took my chin and turned my face back to him. "The real me. The one you fell in love with. The one begging for a second chance now."

I searched his eyes and saw only desire and a need for redemption. This moment would change everything between us. Did I let him in again? Or did I keep pushing him away?

"I trust you," I whispered, as all my walls came down.

A slow, beautiful smile spread across his lips as my cocky alpha returned. He slowly and very deliberately kneeled in front of me, his eyes never once leaving mine. "As an alpha, I kneel for no one but you. I'll get down on my knees every single night if that's what it takes to win you back."

Pleasure flared inside me at his words and at seeing him in front of me like this. "I like you on your knees."

"You'll like what I have planned for you even more."

He took my boots off first, almost reverently, neatly setting them to the side. Then his hands slid up my calves and along my thighs, under my long-sleeve dress and up to my waist, where he pulled my leggings down. I arched against the wall to help him get them off, and my panties went with them.

He paused, eyes still on my face, as his hands circled my ankles. Compared to other things he'd done to me, it was nothing, yet somehow it felt more provocative than anything else. My heart beat wildly and my breath caught in my throat as I waited for what he would do next.

Kaden guided my feet wider, and then his hands caressed up my naked legs as I spread easily for him. He trailed his fingertips up the sensitive skin of my inner knee, before pressing harder into my thighs, and I gasped at the slight pressure. He kept his eyes on me as his hands slid under my dress, and I had to lean back against the wall as my body melted into his touch. I closed my eyes briefly, wondering what I'd agreed to, but then Kaden was moving his hands higher, and all thought left me completely.

He teased at the skin of my inner thighs for a few heartbeats, and when I opened my eyes, he was looking up at me like he'd never seen anything more beautiful. "I'm going to take care of you. Now and every other night you'll have me, for as long as we live."

He gripped my dress and shoved it up, and then his eyes finally broke contact as his head dipped between my thighs. His breath teased me first, and I shuddered in anticipation. Then his mouth, that perfect, sensual mouth, finally found its way home.

I cried out at the sharp pleasure of his tongue moving against my most sensitive skin, and of the feel of it sliding against me and then inside. He stroked me slowly, like he was savoring every taste, while his hands gripped my hips to hold me in place. All I could do was lean back against the wall and try not to let my legs give out from under me.

Kaden turned his attention to my swollen clit, and I let out a shuddering breath. He ran his tongue around it a few times, teasing me, and I curled my hands into his hair, my fingers needing to grab onto something, anything. Then he flicked the tip of his tongue against me, before sucking my clit into his mouth.

"Kaden—" I wasn't sure what I was saying. Just that I had to say his name, even if I couldn't form any other words after that. I rocked my hips toward his mouth and let out a whimper, needing more, but unable to express exactly what. Now I was the one begging, even though he was on his knees. "Please."

He released my hips and hooked one of my legs over his shoulder, giving him a better angle to fully eat me out. He kept one hand on my thigh, holding me in place, while his other hand gripped my ass, giving it a hard squeeze. Then he slid one big finger inside my pussy, while still sucking and licking my clit.

"Yes," I cried out. He knew exactly how to get the most pleasure out of me, and though he could have made me come fast, he seemed to want to drag this out as long as possible. He slipped another finger into me and fucked me slowly with them. He was in no rush this time, like he wanted to savor every single second.

He let me grind my hips down on his face, taking my pleasure as I wanted, and he hummed as if it felt just as good to him as it did for me. I let my head fall back against the wall as I rubbed my pussy against his mouth. Kaden gave and gave and gave, using his tongue and his fingers to keep me right on the brink for what felt like an eternity.

"Kaden!" I finally shouted, knowing I would die if he didn't make me come right this minute.

He chuckled against me, and then his other hand slid down my ass, to my other hole. I gasped as he circled it once and then slowly worked his way inside. Fucking me from two different angles, while he sucked hard on my clit. I absolutely exploded with pleasure, coming hard against his mouth and around his fingers, crying and begging for him to stop and keep going all at once. I was pretty sure my legs gave out at one point, unable to hold me through the orgasm rushing through me, but Kaden somehow kept me in place.

He didn't stop though. Not until he'd dragged every single drop of pleasure out of me. Only then did he release me.

His eyes found mine again as he slowly stood up, catching me in his arms as I nearly melted all over the floor. He picked me up and carried me to the bed, which wasn't far since this hotel room wasn't anywhere near as large as the penthouse. I was still in a daze as he kissed me on the lips softly and pulled a blanket over me.

"Feeling better?" he asked.

"Much," I managed.

"Good." He pressed a kiss to my forehead. "Get some rest, little wolf."

I gazed up at him, surprised he wasn't removing his clothing or climbing into bed with me, but he headed for the door instead. True to his word, he'd kept it all about me. He gave everything and took nothing in return. Which, naturally, only made me crave even more.

"Stay," I said.

Kaden paused, took one long breath, and turned back to me. He climbed on top of the covers, propped up a pillow behind him, and grabbed the TV remote. "Let's watch some of that cheesy baking show you like. Then we can order something for dinner. Chinese? Indian? What do you think?"

"I'd like that."

As he turned on the show, he wrapped his arm around me and I snuggled up against him.

It felt like coming home.

It felt like *fate*.

CHAPTER THIRTEEN

I BREATHED in the brisk New Mexico air and studied the cave opening Jordan had told us was the main entrance. The Scorpio pack lived underground in tunnels and caverns, an interconnected system that was a maze to anyone who wasn't familiar with them. I couldn't teleport us inside, since I'd never been there before. We only had Jordan's memory to rely on, and he hadn't been to visit the Scorpios in a few years, so we were mostly going in blind.

"I spot two guards," Kaden said, using his hand to shield his eyes from the sun. He was keeping us all invisible while we made a plan since there was nowhere to hide here. There was nothing around for miles except rocks and shrubs. "Shouldn't be a problem."

Stella rubbed her arms. "I thought it would be warmer here. Isn't New Mexico supposed to be hot?"

"Not in January," Jordan said. "It's still a hell of a lot warmer than Toronto."

"Yeah, but I'd rather be back in Toronto," she snapped.

Jordan arched an eyebrow. "Why *are* you here then?"

She huffed. "I'll take any excuse to sink my teeth into a Leo."

A cocky grin spread across Jordan's face. "I'm into that if you are."

"What?" Stella's eyes widened, and then her lips curled in disgust. "Ugh!"

She stomped away to the other side of our group, moving beside Jack. Jordan shrugged and turned back to studying the cave entrance with Kaden and me. I gave him a sharp look. The two of them had been driving me crazy the entire way here. I'd been surprised when Stella had volunteered to come with us, but grateful since her invisibility might be useful. She'd avoided Jordan as much as possible though, as if she couldn't stand to be near him. Naturally, this had turned into a challenge for Jordan, who seemed determined to get close to her as much as possible.

"What?" Jordan asked, his face the picture of innocence.

"Don't antagonize her."

He shrugged again. "She brought that on herself."

"Enough," Kaden said, clearly annoyed with all of us. "Let's get ready to move."

It had been a long flight, followed by a long drive to the caverns, and everyone was tired and anxious about what we were about to do. No wonder we were all cranky. But at Kaden's command, we pulled ourselves together and grew serious once more.

Jack signaled for the three other Ophiuchus warriors to

fall into position with him and Stella, fanning out behind the two alphas and myself. We'd brought the warriors mainly for show since, if all went well, only Jordan would be doing any fighting. It never hurt to be cautious though, and we were prepared to fight—or escape—if necessary.

I wished Harper and Dane could have come with us, but Kaden had decided they should stay behind to guard the hotel in case the vampires or Sun Witches attacked again. It was for the best, since this would be the perfect opportunity for an ambush while we were gone.

"Ready?" Kaden asked.

Jordan nodded, his eyes fixed on the guards in front of us, his back straight and determined. Leo confidence and bravery radiated from him like sunlight. I pitied anyone who tried to deny him his right to be alpha today. "Ready."

Kaden let our invisibility drop. For a second, I marveled at how his magic—along with Stella's—had grown over the last few months, all thanks to Larkin's training. Before, he'd had to touch me to keep us both invisible, and I hadn't been able to see myself or him. Now he could conceal multiple people from a distance, and we were able to see each other the entire time.

The Scorpio guards spotted us immediately. We approached the cave entrance slowly, trying to show we were not there to fight, with me on one side of Jordan, and Kaden on the other. More Scorpio guards arrived, but we kept walking forward without hesitation, though I prayed we weren't heading into an ambush.

"State your purpose here," one of the Scorpios said. He

was a tall, muscular man with wavy black hair and striking cheekbones, who seemed to command some authority. The beta, I suspected.

"I'm Jordan Marsten, alpha of the Leo pack, and I demand an audience."

A few of the guards exchanged uneasy looks, but the one in charge nodded. "Come with us."

We were led inside, with the guards moving in front and behind us, caging us in. My shifter eyes adjusted quickly to the dim light inside the cave, and I was greeted by the musty smell of damp earth and the sound of dripping water. The cave narrowed to a thin tunnel, forcing us to walk one at a time through it. I ran my fingers over the rough, jagged walls, feeling the cool, gritty texture. I couldn't imagine living down here, though I couldn't deny that it did offer the Scorpio pack a lot of protection from attacks. It was also the perfect place for the Leos to hide, though I wondered if they missed the sun.

The narrow tunnel twisted sharply, and I had to watch my step to avoid tripping on the uneven ground. When it widened again, we encountered more guards, who were protecting an elevator built right into the rock. The Scorpio beta used his handprint and a code to open the elevator, which was huge, able to hold a large number of people or lots of heavy freight. We all clambered inside, and he used his handprint again to take us down, deep into the earth.

When the elevator door opened, I gasped. The Scorpio village was nestled in a large natural chamber, and dozens of holes in the ceiling let in beams of sunlight to light the space.

Homes and structures had been carved into the cavern walls, creating a network of terraced levels with elevated walkways, staircases, and elevators connecting them. Pools of water broke up the various spaces, along with natural rock formations that hung from the ceiling or grew from the ground. In the middle of it all was a large, flat space with a huge Scorpio symbol on the ground, and that was where the beta led us now.

I didn't see anyone other than the guards who stood around us. There was not a single shifter out on the walkways or in front of their houses. Had the Scorpios and Leos been warned to stay inside? Were we being led into a trap?

As we reached the center, four Sun Witches appeared in front of us. I barely had time to recognize their orange robes before they were hissing something in ancient Greek, while the Scorpios ducked to the side. I threw up a shield as fast as I could, encompassing our entire group in just a heartbeat. Blazing hot balls of sun magic bounced off it and fizzled out, and the Sun Witches looked surprised. They tried a different spell, and I felt their control wrap around me, trying to bend me to their will, but my mother had taught me how to combat such magic. Moonlight blazed from my eyes as I fought them off. Everyone else in our group was immune, since they were in the Ophiuchus pack, or, in Jordan's case, wearing a moonstone necklace.

Jordan let out his lion roar, not even bothering to shift into his wolf form, and the Sun Witches cowered in fear, sent into a panic by his Leo pack power. It would only give us a few seconds, but that would be enough.

"Take them down," Kaden commanded, just before he shifted into his huge black wolf. The other Ophiuchus warriors shifted too and then they all went invisible, thanks to Stella and Kaden's Moon Touched gifts. I teleported myself and Jordan to a ledge overlooking the village center, and we watched as invisible claws and fangs took down the four women in orange robes. The Sun Witches tried to fight back, but it was over quickly. Only one of them managed to escape, disappearing into a cloud of smoke, likely heading back to Solundra to report what she'd seen. That wasn't ideal, but there was nothing we could do about it either.

When it was done, Jordan walked back down to the village center and called out, "A trap? Really? I thought better of you."

"It's good to see you again, Jordan." An older man emerged from behind a rock formation. His coppery skin was wrinkled and he had long black hair streaked with gray, but he had a magnetism about him that was both alluring and intimidating. I recognized him as the Scorpio alpha, though we'd never formally met. The other Scorpio warriors gathered around him, obviously prepared to defend their leader if we attacked.

"Did you send me the card, Dasan?" Jordan growled. "Were you hoping to lure me to my death?"

"I sent the card, yes, but it was not a trap. Everything I said in it was true. I simply left out the fact that the Sun Witches also had their swords at our throats." The older man spread his hands with a cryptic smile. "But I knew you could handle that problem for us. We thank you for your help."

"How convenient," Kaden muttered.

"Where is the Leo pack?" I asked.

Dasan raised a hand, and shifters from both packs began to emerge from inside dark caves and from behind closed doors. Only their coloring alone told me which pack was which—the Leos tended to have fairer skin and hair than the Scorpios. The shifters gathered around the village center like they were preparing to watch a show, while Jordan stood tall as he gazed among them.

There was a ripple somewhere at the back of the crowd, and a large shifter I recognized from the winter Convergence stepped forward. He had sandy blond hair shaved into a buzz cut and muscles that stretched his t-shirt to the limits. He was older, about the same age as Jordan's dad would have been, but that only made him look tougher, like he'd seen some battles and lived to tell the tale. It was obvious from the way he carried himself that he was the Leo beta, Austin Bates.

"You have some nerve coming back here when you're no longer the alpha," he shouted at Jordan, as he pushed his way through the crowd. "Now I'll take your Leo mark away and you'll be packless like your bitch mate."

With a shock, I realized he was talking about me. I never thought of myself as Jordan's mate anymore, only his sister.

Jordan growled next to me, deep in his chest. "I'm the true alpha of the Leos. If you want the position, you'll have to fight me for it."

"You're nothing but the bastard child of a pansy Cancer

and a half-witch whore," Bates spat. "You call yourself alpha? You're barely even a Leo."

If the words hurt Jordan, he didn't show it. He stood his ground as Bates got right up in his face. "Sounds like you're scared to fight me. What do you think, Ayla?"

I gave Bates a scathing head-to-toe look. "I think he's barely holding onto this position and he knows it."

His eyes flashed with hatred. "The fuck do you know, you—"

Kaden grabbed the beta's throat. "Call her one more thing, and I'll rip your fucking throat out right now and save Jordan the trouble."

Bates shoved Kaden off. "Don't touch me, you fucking snake."

"What will it be?" The Scorpio alpha asked, his eyes dancing with dark amusement. "Will you fight for the role of alpha?"

"Only if it's a fight to the death," Bates snarled.

Jordan didn't even hesitate. "Fine with me."

Dasan nodded. "You each have five minutes to prepare, and then we will begin."

The Leo and Scorpio shifters formed a fighting circle right over the Scorpio symbol on the ground, with Jordan on one side and Bates on the other. Ripples of excitement and fear rolled through the crowd, and I wondered who they hoped would come out of this alive.

"Are you sure you can win?" I asked Jordan in a low voice, as I watched Bates tear off his shirt. "He's bigger than I remember."

Jordan gave me an incredulous look. "Are you seriously doubting me right now?"

"No." I bit my lip. "I believe in you, but you're my brother, and I worry about you too. If there's any doubt, we can walk away right now."

"I have to do this. The Leo pack needs me to step up and lead them." He rested a hand on my shoulder. "Don't worry. I won't lose."

Kaden moved close to Jordan, then spoke so quietly that I barely heard him. "Watch your left side. That's where you leave openings when you fight."

"Thanks." Jordan gave him a slight nod, though his raised eyebrows showed he was just as surprised by Kaden's words as I was. Kaden walked away after that, joining the Ophiuchus warriors on the sidelines.

Jordan's gaze landed on Stella and he grinned. "A kiss for luck?"

"How about a punch to the face?" she replied.

"Whatever gets you going..."

She let out an annoyed huff and crossed her arms, but didn't turn away. Jordan kept his eyes on her as he removed his shirt and then shucked his jeans and briefs, like he was daring her to look away...or look down. Her eyes never left his face as she glared at him, until he tossed me his clothes and headed for the ring. Once his back was to us, she finally let out the breath she'd been holding. I arched an eyebrow at her, but she ignored me and went to stand with her brother.

When both men stood naked in the center of the ring, Dasan stepped forward and raised his voice so he could be heard over the crowd. "A challenge has been issued and accepted. Today, under the supervision of the Scorpio pack, Jordan Marsten and Austin Bates will fight for the position of Leo alpha. To the death."

Both men bowed their heads in acknowledgment, and then the Scorpio alpha moved out of the ring. The fight had officially begun.

CHAPTER FOURTEEN

THE TWO LEOS prowled around the ring as they sized each other up, their eyes locked in a fierce stare-down. As packmates, they'd probably trained together before, but it was a different thing entirely to be fighting each other and to the death. Bates was older, larger, and more experienced, but Jordan had speed and youth on his side, along with a strong dash of defiance.

Bates broke the rising tension by making the first move, darting in and giving an experimental swipe of his fist toward Jordan's face. My brother dodged with ease, raking his claws down Bates's side. The beta let out a growl, and then two began to fight in earnest, both of them moving with shifter strength and speed.

Bates began shifting into a large reddish-brown wolf, but Jordan shifted faster and smoother. My brother's fur shone like gold in the patches of sunlight filtering through the cave, and I almost thought I felt Helios's touch upon him, though I was probably just imagining things. What did I know of the sun god, after all?

The wolves circled each other, snarling and snapping as they looked for an opening to attack, or a moment of weakness they could exploit. Their fur stood on end as they both charged, becoming a blur of razor-sharp claws and teeth. They fought with a single-minded determination, each one convinced they would come out victorious, and I held my breath, unable to tear my eyes away.

The audience was completely silent, as if everyone was holding their breath like I was, and the sound of snarling and growling filled the cavern as the two Leos battled. The fight was intense and brutal, with both wolves landing several blows on each other. Every strike that hit Jordan made me tenser, and I was glad to be holding his clothes. It gave me something to do with my hands.

Jordan's eyes practically glowed with intense, animalistic fury as he pinned Bates down, and I thought it would be over. But then Jordan paused, distracted by something he saw, his wolf ears standing straight up. I followed his gaze and saw a flash of platinum and red, disappearing behind a large stalagmite.

Roxandra.

The moment of distraction was enough for Bates to scramble away from Jordan, and the beta shook himself out, before leaping into another attack. Jordan narrowly dodged it, obviously rattled by what he'd seen.

Shit. I couldn't let Roxandra mess this up for Jordan. I dropped Jordan's clothes and darted after the Sun Witch to stop her before she could do anything to my brother.

I slowly came up behind her as she peered around the rock formation to watch the fight. "Found you."

I grabbed her shoulder and instantly teleported us away to a ledge I'd seen on my way in. Roxandra spun around, but the teleportation disoriented her, and she took a moment to recover. Roxandra started to blast me with sun magic, but I threw up my own moon magic, and the impact of the two sent us both flying backward. I landed in a shallow pool, water spraying all over me, while Roxandra slammed back against the cave wall, sending tiny rocks falling around her.

Before either of us could get to our feet, I teleported back to her and threw myself on top of her with a guttural roar. I grabbed her robes as rage made my vision red.

"I won't let you hurt them again!" I slammed her back against the wall, and I was about one second from ripping her throat out.

"You idiot," she said, as she fought to get me off her. "I'm not going to hurt Jordan. I want him alive!"

Her robes suddenly caught fire and I jerked back, my body reacting instinctively. We glared at each other, preparing to attack again, waiting to see who would make the next move.

"What are you doing here?" I asked.

"Making sure Jordan doesn't lose."

"He doesn't need your help!"

I spotted her preparing another attack and I lunged toward her, turning my hands to claws. I scraped across one side of her face, drawing blood, and she screamed and vanished into a puff of smoke.

I hope that hurt, I thought, as I sheathed my claws. Then I heard a howl that I recognized as Jordan's and panic shot through me. I reached out for the mate bond, which was so muted now I barely even noticed it anymore, and felt him there. Injured, but alive.

I rushed to the edge of the ledge. Below me, the two Leos bit and clawed at each other, tearing chunks of fur and flesh from each other's bodies. The ground was slick with blood, and both wolves were bleeding from deep gashes, but they showed no sign of backing down. They were slowing down though. Jordan was limping, favoring his left leg, and Bates had a wound in his side that seemed to be causing him problems.

I put my hand against the nearest rock formation as a wave of worry made my knees weak. *Come on, Jordan. You can do this. Be the better Leo.*

The two wolves clashed and then danced back again. Jordan paused under a patch of sunlight, and visibly took a moment to regain his strength as the sun's rays illuminated his fur. He was a child of the sun, through and through, and when he darted toward Bates again, he moved with lightning speed. He bowled Bates over and clamped his jaws around the beta's throat. Bates struggled uselessly against Jordan's superior strength and power, but my brother never showed any mercy. It was to the death, after all.

Bates slumped to the ground. Jordan shifted back to human form and stood over the defeated wolf. His naked body was covered in blood, but he stood tall and gazed around at all the shifters watching him. He let out a triumphant roar, his victory echoing through the cavern, and chills ran down my spine. All around Jordan, the Leos fell to one knee, their heads bowed, showing submission to their alpha. There could be no doubt now that he truly deserved the title.

I rejoined Kaden and Stella as the Leos began to cheer for their alpha. They surrounded Jordan, and the Ophiuchus and Scorpios stayed back, letting the other pack have their moment.

"What was that?" Kaden asked, jerking his chin to the ledge where I'd fought Roxandra.

"Nothing I couldn't handle." I grabbed some water from my pack and chugged it. "I'm just glad that's over."

"Were you worried?" Kaden shrugged. "I never doubted he would win. He's the strongest shifter I've ever fought."

"Don't let him hear you say that," Stella piped up from my other side. Her eyes were glued to Jordan, and this time she was definitely taking him in. *All* of him. "His ego is already big enough."

I raised my eyebrows at her, and she quickly looked away, her cheeks flushed. Was she thinking about his ego being big...or something else?

It took some time for the excitement to die down. Kaden and the other Ophiuchus walked away to discuss plans to head back to Toronto, but I stood to the side of the crowd, waiting for my brother. Making sure a certain Sun Witch didn't return.

Eventually, the Leo shifters began to head back to the caves, and someone covered up the beta's body. Jordan sauntered over to me, using a towel to wipe off some of the blood. He flashed me a cocky smile. "Told you I'd win."

"I'm glad you're not dead." I eyed the way he stood, like one of his legs was bothering him. "Are you okay?"

He shrugged. "Nothing I can't heal."

"I could ask one of the Ophiuchus to help."

"The only one I'd let lick me is Stella, and somehow I think she'd rather I bleed to death."

I wasn't so sure after seeing the way she'd been staring at him, but I didn't think it was my place to mention it. Something was going on between the two of them, but we had bigger problems to worry about right now.

Jordan stepped closer to take his clothes from my hands. "Was Roxandra here, or was I going mad from blood loss?"

"She was here. I took care of it."

He closed his eyes for a second as if he was in pain. "I'll never be free of her, will I?"

I wished I had an answer for him, but we both knew he was right. The only way he'd be rid of her was to kill her. "What does she want with you?"

"Besides the obvious?" He gestured at his naked body, his grin returning. The pain was still there, but the humor probably made it easier to cope with.

I raised my eyes to the ceiling. "Ugh."

The Scorpio alpha joined us then, interrupting us before we could speculate more. "Congratulations on your win," he told Jordan. "My beta will take you to a small, private hot spring where you can wash your wounds and rest your bones. Then we will talk." Dasan turned to me next. "I've had rooms prepared for your people as well. The Scorpio pack would be honored if you would stay the night and join me for a feast tonight."

I nearly told him that I didn't speak for the Ophiuchus anymore, but he was being so polite that all I said was, "Thank you for your hospitality."

"No, thank you for solving this problem for us." He bowed his head slightly. "We Scorpios keep our promises. We will join you against the Sun Witches."

A huge sense of relief flooded through me. Today we'd won not only the Leos but the Scorpios too. An alliance between all the packs suddenly seemed not just possible but within our grasp.

THE SCORPIO FEAST was an intimate affair, with only a select few members of their pack invited, along with some trusted Leos that Jordan had hand-picked, plus the Ophiuchus we'd brought. Dasan and his alpha female, a gorgeous woman with eyes that missed nothing, hosted us in a dark and mysterious cave, with dim lighting and soft music playing around us. They served Southwestern food full of flavors and textures that were new to me, along with a selection of fine wines and strong tequilas. A sense of mystery and intrigue surrounded the Scorpios, while the Leos were busy celebrating their alpha's win, and the Ophiuchus just looked out of place. Dasan kept encouraging everyone to eat and drink though, and soon everyone began to relax and let down their inhibitions.

We were all a little wild, after that. Maybe it was the full moon approaching, or maybe it was the feeling of victory after a battle, but after we'd eaten our fill, other hungers awoke in us. A few people paired off into the darkness together, including a Scorpio woman who led Jack away with a coy smile. It seemed Dasan wanted us to be pleased in every way possible.

To my surprise, Stella excused herself early and went to her room alone. Jordan had many offers from Leos and Scorpios alike, but he brushed them off with a cocky grin and a flirty word. And me? I found myself alone with Kaden once more, after being dragged away from the party by his firm hand.

He cornered me in a dark part of the cave, where no light touched, and kneeled in front of me once more. As his mouth pressed against my warm skin and his tongue circled my clit, I cried out his name like a blessing. Once again, he gave me everything and asked for nothing in return. Then he carried me to my bed, and I asked him to stay. We fell asleep in each other's arms only minutes later, exhausted from everything that had happened that day.

Needless to say, I was very refreshed in the morning.

And Jordan? He was like a different man. He'd picked another beta and charged him with leading the pack back to their village outside Phoenix. He'd also spoken with his cousin and had a lead on where his mother was hiding—in Nevada.

Our next destination.

CHAPTER FIFTEEN

WE DROVE DOWN A LONG, winding dirt road that led off the main highway and into the middle of nowhere. Jordan was in the driver's seat, his face taut with concentration, as the car bumped along the uneven ground and kicked up dust that made it hard to see. Not that there was much to see, anyway. The landscape around us was rugged and barren, with nothing but rocky hills, shrubs, and gnarled, spiky trees for miles.

"Are you sure this is the right way?" Kaden asked.

"Nope," Jordan said. "Do you have a better idea of where to go? I'd love to hear it."

Kaden growled and slumped back in his seat. It had been like this the entire trip, which had only made it feel even longer. I was the only one here to mediate between the alphas too. Stella, Jack, and the other Ophiuchus had opted to return to Toronto instead of going on this wild quest with us. I was beginning to think they were the smart ones.

So far, we'd gotten lost twice. We'd been driving for hours, and it was starting to feel like we'd never find this place. I scrubbed my hands over my eyes, ready to call it, but when I looked out my window again I spotted the distant silhouette of houses in the distance.

I sat up straighter and pointed. "There. Do you think that's it?"

"Let's find out," Jordan said.

He put his foot on the gas and I held on to the inside of the car as we zoomed along the rocky road. We were soon greeted by a large fence with a gate that marked the entrance to the property, and we stopped the car to get out. The gate was made of sturdy, weathered wood and was adorned with a sign too faded to read. Beyond it, a long driveway led up to the ranch house and a few other structures, which were surrounded by vast open desert and distant mountains.

Jordan studied the ranch house, a large, rustic wooden structure with a wide porch and two rocking chairs. "This place is familiar. I think my mom brought me here once when I was a kid."

"It looks abandoned," I said. The only sounds I heard were the wind whistling through the shrubs, the occasional bird call, and the tinkle of a half-tangled wind chime on the porch.

Kaden lifted his face toward the sun and breathed in. "It's not."

We climbed over the gate, and as we did, I felt something invisible *snap* around us, with a flicker of magic brushing against my skin. A ward.

The door of the main house burst open and two older women walked out, wearing jeans and bearing shotguns. I'd never seen them before, but the hairs stood up on the back of my neck at the feel of their magic. Now that we'd breached the wards, I sensed it everywhere.

"Sun Witches," I muttered. "If they attack, I'll teleport us out of here."

"They won't," Jordan said.

His mother, Debra, emerged from the house next, along with a teenage boy I vaguely recognized, though I'd never formally met him. Before anyone could attack us, the boy ran down the porch and raced across the driveway. "Jordan!" he yelled.

"Hey, Griffin." Jordan's face lit up just before the boy slammed into him, and the two threw their arms around each other. Side by side, it was impossible not to recognize that the boys were brothers. They both carried the golden hair of the Leos and the sea-blue eyes of their Cancer father.

Debra's own golden hair whipped in the wind as she grabbed Jordan in a tight hug, closing her eyes as she held him close. "I'm so glad you're okay." Her eyes snapped open and landed on Kaden and me. "Though I'm not sure about the company you keep."

"Ayla is family," Jordan said. "And she's Griffin's sister too. He has a right to know her."

Griffin looked over at me, surprised. "I have a sister?"

Debra didn't look very happy about Jordan revealing that secret. "They don't belong here."

Jordan glanced back at us. "I wouldn't be here without them."

Debra pursed her lips as she gave us another harsh once-over, but then she turned toward one of the women holding shotguns. The older woman nodded, and both Sun Witches lowered their weapons.

"Brea?" Jordan asked, looking at the older woman, as if he wasn't sure it was her.

She reached out an arm and he stepped into her embrace. "Yes, child. It's good to see you. It's been too long."

"I guess you'd better come in." Debra motioned for all of us to follow her. "Griffin, go help Margaret with the horses while I speak with your brother."

Griffin groaned, casting an exasperated look toward his brother, but then he headed off to the stables while the rest of us went inside the main house. Our steps creaked against the old hardwood floor as we were led into a living room with a huge stone fireplace. Comfortable leather sofas and armchairs were arranged around a large wooden coffee table. The woman named Brea came in with us, while the other witch waited just outside, still on guard.

"What are you doing here?" Jordan asked his mother, as we spread out around the space and tried to get comfortable. I was ready to teleport us away immediately if they looked like they might attack us. Even though they were related to Jordan, they were still Sun Witches, after all.

Debra sighed and sat beside her son. "My life was in danger after I stopped the Sun Witches from forcing you and Ayla to mate. After Ayla escaped, I took Griffin and ran here."

"Why didn't you tell me?" Jordan asked, something tight in his voice. "Or take me with you?"

Debra gazed at him, her eyes sad. She looked much older than her years at that moment. "I tried, but the Sun Witches had their claws in you too deeply. I couldn't get you free. I hated leaving you behind, but I had to get Griffin out of there before they did the same to him."

Jordan's fingers went to the moonstone necklace around his neck. "Ayla helped free me."

"Is that so?" She looked at me then, giving me another appraisal. "Your magic has grown. That much is clear."

"It's good to see you again," I said. Though she'd always been rude to me, she'd also helped me a few times, in her own way. I gestured toward Kaden. "This is Kaden, alpha of the Ophiuchus pack."

"We know who he is," Brea said. She'd put the shotgun down, but had her arms crossed as she eyed us from the side of the room. I couldn't tell how old she was. Like Evanora and Celeste, who were practically immortal thanks to living in timeless realms, she had eyes that looked ancient. But unlike them, her skin was tanned and leathery from the desert sun, and her hair was gray and wispy, like clouds on a hot summer day.

"This is my aunt, Brea," Debra said, gesturing to the woman. "She defected from the Sun Witches many years ago, along with a few other women, who all live here now."

"I had no idea there were any Sun Witches who didn't follow Evanora," I said, my eyes widening in surprise.

"There are very few of us who are still alive," Brea said with a bitter tone.

"Why did you defect?" Kaden asked. He'd been quiet up until now, but his eyes missed nothing, and his body was tense, as though he was ready to fight at the slightest provocation.

Brea scowled at him as if she might not answer, but then she looked at Jordan and uncrossed her arms. "I suppose Jordan should know about his family history, grim though it may be." She moved to the window and looked out at the setting sun on the horizon. "The Sun Witches were once very patriarchal. Helios and the sun have male energy, after all. But Evanora's father, the High Priest, abused this power. He raped, beat, and controlled the female witches, and many of the other male Sun Witches followed his patterns of abuse."

I'd heard a little about this before from my mother, who'd been the product of one of his attacks. It sickened me, knowing I'd come from such a man. I couldn't even imagine the trauma and pain that my grandmother and so many others had endured.

Brea turned back to us. "Evanora was his favorite daughter, but that didn't mean he was any easier on her. Quite the opposite in fact. Eventually, something snapped inside her and she decided he had to be stopped. She gathered together many of the women who had been ill-treated by the male Sun Witches and concocted a plan. Even back then, her magic was incredibly strong, but it was her mind that was truly dangerous. She was the most cunning woman I'd ever met, and I became her greatest supporter and closest friend. Together, we wiped out the male leaders, including Evanora's father, and she declared herself High Priestess." Brea looked down at her hands, stretching the long, veiny digits out as if remembering what they'd done. "But she didn't stop there. She ordered us to kill all the male Sun Witches. Every last one of them."

That explained why I had never seen a male Sun Witch before. I swallowed hard, and everyone's eyes were glued to Brea as she continued her story.

"We tried to stop her—me and a few other Sun Witches. Not all of the men were bad, of course. There were husbands, fathers, sons... But Evanora said they were all tainted. She spared no one. Not even her own husband."

My stomach twisted as I thought about Evanora killing so many people. Logically I knew she was capable of it, but it was another thing entirely to hear about all the horrible things she'd done, even to her own people. Her capacity for cruelty somehow never failed to surprise me.

"What happened after that?" Jordan asked, perched on the edge of his seat.

Brea put her hand on his shoulder in a tender gesture. "Helios did not approve of what she did. He cursed the Sun Witches, and not just Evanora, but every single one of us who survived. Now we're unable to have male sons anymore, and so the Sun Witch blood is dying out and growing weaker. Soon, we'll be completely gone. That's why Evanora is in a panic." Brea paused before adding, "The only one who's succeeded in having sons in all these years is Debra."

"How?" I asked.

Brea finally sat on the couch across from us. "My sister, Eleanora, fell in love with a wolf, the Leo alpha at the time—Marshall, Jordan's grandfather. It was forbidden, but she didn't care. She'd always been a rebellious one." Brea glanced at Jordan's mother. "When she had Debra, the Sun Witches cast them both out. Eventually, I gathered the strength to leave Solundra too, along with the other witches who disagreed with Evanora's leadership. We've been hiding here ever since."

"The Sun Witches considered me an abomination for having wolf blood," Debra explained. "I was never considered one of them. Until I bore two sons. Then they suddenly took interest."

I knew all about being an outcast, a half-breed, and for the first time, I felt a pang of sympathy and understanding for what Debra had been through.

"That's why Roxandra..." Jordan began, but his voice trailed off and his eyes flashed with pain.

Somehow I knew exactly what he was thinking, maybe because of the mate bond, or because of some understanding we shared. He was remembering when Roxandra said she'd hoped to get pregnant with his child—all because she wanted another male with Sun Witch blood. I rested my hand over Jordan's, silently giving him my support.

"Why she did what?" Debra asked.

Kaden's eyes passed between us, and I sensed that he understood too. Like Jordan, he'd been a victim of the Sun Witches himself. He cleared his throat, distracting Debra from her question. "Does that mean that Jordan has Sun Witch magic?"

Jordan snorted. "If I did, wouldn't I have used it on you by now?"

"Good point." Kaden shrugged, and I flashed him a grateful smile for the way he'd so deftly changed the subject.

"We've searched for any trace of magic within Jordan, but found none," Brea said. "We think that as part of Helios's curse, both Jordan and Griffin are unable to use any Sun Magic."

Debra waved a hand. "Who can say? It's been so long since a male Sun Witch has been born, and you're both part shifter as well."

"How do we break Helios's curse?" Jordan asked.

"We don't know for sure," Brea said. "My suspicion is that it will only end once Evanora is removed from power...or dead."

"Evanora has other ideas though." Debra eyed me again. "Once they learned that Ayla was half Moon Witch, they were even more determined to have Jordan mate with her. Evanora wants a baby with Sun, Moon, and wolf blood. One that she can control. Can you imagine how powerful it would be?"

Jordan's face twisted with disgust. "Thank god that didn't happen."

I shuddered. The thought was terrifying, and not just because it involved me having a baby with my brother.

"Why did you come here?" Brea asked, bringing me back to the present.

"We need your help." I took a deep breath and glanced at Jordan. "The fake mate bond between us must be broken. Roxandra told us it was tied to the blessing spell put on us as babies, and said there might be a way to remove it. Do you know how?"

"Such a thing has never been done, but it might be possible," Brea said slowly. "Only the oldest and wisest of Sun Witches would even know how to attempt such a thing."

"Good thing we came to you then," Jordan said with a grin.

"Yes, good thing." Brea smiled back at him, her eyes bright with centuries of knowledge. "I might be able to help you."

Hope and relief flooded me so quickly that I gasped and found myself clutching Kaden's hand. "Really?"

She held up a hand, her face stern. "Yes, but I'll need some time to read through my old books and prepare the spell. Besides, the sun is setting, and a spell like this needs to be done during the day."

"Of course." I bowed my head, thankful for even a chance.

"Thank you," Jordan said, sounding as relieved as I felt.

We locked eyes briefly, both of us excited and hopeful

for the first time in ages, and then I turned to Kaden. His hand tightened around mine, and my heart raced knowing that soon the false mate bond might be broken and I could finally discover who I truly was—and who I was meant to be with.

CHAPTER SIXTEEN

THE SUN BEAT down on us intently as we walked outside, as if it knew we were about to call upon it for something big. Dry, desolate land stretched for miles in every direction, with hardly any greenery to disturb it, until it reached the mountains in the distance. Tumbleweeds blew across the ground in the breeze, and the sky above was a vast expanse of blue, with only a few wispy clouds drifting by.

Brea stopped outside a gated fence that led to nothing but more sunbaked land. "Behold, the way we Sun Witches once used our magic for life instead of death."

She opened the gate and said a word in ancient Greek, and suddenly everything in front of me changed. The barren land turned to lush, green fields stretching all the way to the mountains, growing wheat, potatoes, and many other things I didn't recognize. I even spotted fruit trees, strawberries, tomatoes, and other things that I'd never expected could survive here.

"The Sun Witches had something like this in the Leo village, but on a smaller scale," Jordan said, and I remembered the magical garden with the gazebo and all the things that had transpired there. They were not fond memories. Kaden grunted, and I was sure he was thinking of the place too, probably remembering when he'd destroyed it with a combination of moon magic and shifter might.

But this place was different. It was clear the Sun Witches had grown and nurtured it with great care, which allowed them to be self-sufficient out here, so far from civilization. For so long I'd only thought of the Sun Witches as villains who used their powers to burn and destroy, but now I was seeing a different side of their magic.

"How do you keep it hidden?" I asked.

"Evanora's family is strong in mind magic, but ours is strong in illusion magic," Debra said with pride, from where she stood beside Jordan.

"We bend light to only show what we wish to be seen." Brea uttered another word in ancient Greek, and the desert appeared in front of us once more, like a curtain falling in front of a scene.

"Incredible," I said.

She let the illusion drop again and led us into a flat field of grass, where a few cows were grazing on one side. In the distance, I spotted Griffin on one of the horses near a small river and saw a Sun Witch I didn't recognize picking raspberries and putting them in a basket.

Brea stopped in the middle of the field. "This is where we will attempt the spell."

"Do you think you can do it?" Jordan asked.

"I believe so, but I've spent much of the night poring through my old books, and never found any mention of something like this being done before. Nevertheless, I think I've found a way to unravel the blessing spell, though it might take a few attempts. I will warn you though, it won't feel good."

"We'll do anything to remove the mate bond," I said, my voice a little more desperate than I intended. There was an urgency in my bones, but it had nothing to do with the spell. Tonight was the full moon and I remained both mated and packless, which meant I would go into heat again if I didn't do something to stop it—like beg Kaden to let me back into the Ophiuchus pack. That was the smart, obvious choice, but I stubbornly refused to do it except as a last resort. Kaden had taken my pack mark, and if I got it back, I wanted it to be because I was truly one of them, not because I had no other choice.

"Let's just get it over with," Jordan said, his voice equally strained. I hadn't mentioned the full moon to him, but he wasn't an idiot. He knew what would happen. The mate bond would make us both wild tonight, even if we managed to stay apart. Last time, he'd felt me fucking Kaden through the mate bond. I was sure he wanted to avoid a repeat of that tonight.

"Cast the spell on Ayla first," Debra said. "If the spell backfires, we don't want it to hurt Jordan."

"Ouch," I muttered. I got it though. Her priority was her son, and I was nothing to her. But I shrugged it off and stepped forward. "I'm fine with being the first one. The sooner the better."

"Very well." Brea looked me up and down. "I will warn you again. This won't be pleasant."

I lifted my chin. "I can take it."

I'd lived through pain before. I could deal with this too.

Brea looked up at the sun and then began chanting, softly at first, and I couldn't help the instinctive tightening of my muscles at the sound. Every other time a Sun Witch had chanted in ancient Greek around me, bad things had happened. I forced myself to relax. Brea was different. She was helping us. Or so I hoped. What if this was all a trick? No, she wouldn't hurt Jordan. And if they did turn on us, Kaden was right there, ready to take Brea down if necessary. I forced myself to stay calm.

The sun's warmth soaked into my bones as Brea's chanting grew louder and her eyes glowed with bright light. When her hands began to glow too, the sun seemed to get brighter, and I squinted my eyes against it. Sweat dripped down my back and beaded on my forehead as the heat intensified. Sun magic hummed in the air all around us, flowing through Brea toward me, and fear made me sweat even more. It took everything in my power to stand there doing nothing as a Sun Witch cast a spell over me.

As the heat became almost overwhelming, Brea started moving her hands in slow, purposeful movements. Trails of sun magic followed her, hanging in the air for a few seconds after her hands left the spot. She continued chanting, walking around me as she weaved the magic like a net. I felt it on me, sinking into my skin, but I forced myself to not fight it.

She's helping, I told myself over and over again as she continued. The magic wrapped itself around me and started tugging, like barbs stuck in my skin, trying to pull something out that refused to budge. Each tug sent pain coursing through me, and I gritted my teeth and clenched my fists. The pain would only be temporary, and well worth it if this worked.

I closed my eyes and sucked in a gasp as the torture continued, turning my vision red, making my limbs tremble. *Hold on,* I told myself. *Surely it will be over soon.* But the pain kept growing, and an anguished cry escaped my lips as I fell to my knees.

"Stop!" Kaden yelled. "You'll kill her!"

My face hit the dirt moments later, and then the pain stopped. Kaden gathered me in his arms as I floated back to reality, and I blinked away the stars in my eyes.

"Ayla," Kaden said. "Ayla!"

I sucked in a long breath. The pain was completely gone, and I felt fine again. Just a little shaken. "I'm okay."

"You're not," Kaden growled. Jordan looked concerned too from where he stood behind Kaden, but he knew better than to get in the middle of this.

"I'm not injured. It was just...a lot." I was able to stand, and I brushed myself off. "Let's try again."

"No way," Kaden said. "You're done."

I growled back at him. "I'm done when I say I'm done. If you can't handle it, then leave."

He looked surprised by that and wisely kept his mouth shut. He didn't know what it was like, being bound to my own brother, forced to desire him even though the thought made me sick. Besides, I was stronger than he knew, and I was tired of him underestimating me. Kaden needed to learn to trust me too, if he wanted our relationship to work.

"I'm sorry," Brea said, her voice sincere. "I'll give you a moment, and then I'll try something else."

"We don't have time to waste," I said. "Do it now. I'll survive."

Brea looked skeptical but turned to Debra, who shrugged. "Very well. I'm going to adjust the spell slightly and see if it works better."

She cast the spell again, but this time she gathered the sun's energy within herself first, until she was practically bursting with it. She didn't do any hand movements, and when she was ready, she held her palms out toward me and released the magic in one blast. It hit me hard, sending me flying back, and for a moment all I saw was bright white light as pain took over my world.

When I came back, I was lying on the grass, staring up at the sky. I reached for the mate bond and felt Jordan there, worried, anxious, stressed. Lust flared across me at the connection, intensified by the impending the full moon, and I quickly tamped it down, locking the mate bond behind walls once more. I sighed, knowing the spell had failed again.

The two men helped me to my feet but didn't comment,

though they both looked miserable for different reasons. I nodded for Brea to try again.

Brea consulted one of the books she'd brought, and then chanted something different, moving her hands in a new pattern like a dance. This time, the magic sparked all around me like little fireflies flitting across my skin. While the first spell had pulled hard on the blessing, and the second one had tried to push against it, this felt more like it was trying to coax the magic from my skin, slowly unraveling it piece by piece. It took the longest and hurt the least, and I grew hopeful that it was working finally.

When the spell was completed, Brea scanned me with weary eyes. "Do you feel any different?"

As the magic faded, that sick, powerful pull toward Jordan slammed into me, along with the itch of my upcoming heat already taking root under my skin. If anything, the spells had only made the mate bond stronger, like it was fighting against the magic, trying to wrap tighter around our souls.

I shook my head, as all my hope slipped away, and defeat dragged me down.

"That should have worked," Brea said, her brows furrowed. "I'm sorry. That was my last idea."

"Fuck," Jordan yelled, turning away like he couldn't stand to look at me anymore. I knew he was doing it to stop himself from running to me like the mate bond wanted. A lesser man wouldn't have been able to fight it, that was how strong it had become.

I pressed my hands to my eyes, feeling that same burn

inside me, and the same agony knowing we'd failed. We'd come so far, and after all this time, there was still nothing we could do to break the mate bond. Kaden reached for me, but I shoved him away, unable to accept his comfort when need pulsed inside me for the wrong man.

"Please," I begged Brea, as tears slipped down my cheeks. "There must be something else we can try."

She sighed and began looking through her books again, but I could see in her eyes that she didn't think she would find anything. We were out of options.

Debra glanced between me and Jordan, her lips set in a thin line. I knew she didn't want this mate bond any more than we did. "Do you think it could be her moon magic preventing the spell from working?"

"No," Brea said, as she flipped another page. "If anything, her moon magic should be helping me. It has always fought against the blessing spell. It's the only reason she's been able to resist Jordan so long." She paused then and stared off into the distance. "Moon magic..."

Debra sucked in a breath. "You think?"

Brea slammed the book shut and handed it to Debra. "Yes. A mixture of sun and moon magic. Like the witches of old used to do. It might work."

My head jerked up, but I was scared to hope again. Still, it was worth a try. "What do I have to do?"

For the next thirty minutes, Brea taught me how to do the spell, while Kaden took Jordan for a walk. It was a lot easier for me to think without him nearby, and I picked up on the ancient Greek quickly after all my time spent studying it with the Moon Witches. Then Brea moved me through a series of hand flicks and twists, repeating it slower and then faster, while Debra barked out her critique of my movements. I'd never done magic like this before, where it was more like learning a dance than a spell, but Brea eventually decided I was ready, and Debra reluctantly agreed.

We summoned the men back, and then it was time. I met Jordan's eyes and swallowed hard. This was our last chance. If this didn't work... I couldn't bear to think about it.

Brea began chanting and gathering her sun magic, channeling it toward me, and I repeated her words and movements, calling upon the moon. I expected the magic to clash, like when I'd fought Roxandra, but there was no explosion as the opposing forces met. Instead, the sun and moon magic twined together in a weave of light that settled over me like a balm. The magic spread inside me, making me glow with a mix of gold and silver, hot and cold, male and female. Tiny little needles of light seemed to burrow into me, pricking something deep inside of me, not just in my body, but in my very soul. There was a sharp gasp of pain and a bright burst of light, and then I felt something *release*. The magic that held me tight suddenly let go, and I fell to my knees as the weight of it left me in a rush.

Kaden and Jordan hurried to my side, checking to see if I was okay, and I blinked and tried to focus on them. Their handsome faces were both taut with concern, and they kept asking if I was all right.

I sucked in a breath as my senses came back to me, and then I looked at Jordan and felt...nothing. Love, yes, but the kind that a sibling feels, and nothing more. No lust. No pull. No mate bond.

I wept with relief. "It's gone. It's really gone."

Jordan let out a strangled sound in his throat, and then he grabbed me in his arms and we cried together, the relief so overwhelming it was like a dam had burst in both of us. It was over. We were free.

I pulled back, wiped my eyes, and turned toward Kaden. He watched me with hope in his eyes, but it was the kind of hope that you're afraid to feel because it means too much, and you know you'll be crushed if it turns out to be false. I understood completely. Would we be mates now? Like him, I was scared to hope.

A sharp pain ignited on my chest, above my heart, and I gasped and pressed a hand there. It felt like something had burned me. A stray bit of sun magic? A side effect of the spell? It faded quickly, but when I moved my hand, I couldn't believe what I saw.

A pack mark.

I unbuttoned my shirt a little to get a better look, marveling at what I saw. An Ophiuchus symbol, as clear as day, sitting right over my heart. The spot where it would be if I was an alpha female.

"Did you do this?" I asked, glancing up at Kaden.

His jaw was practically on the ground and it took him a second to reply. "No."

"How?" I asked.

It was Jordan who answered. "Because you were meant to be an Ophiuchus all along. Just like your mother said."

I pressed my hand over the mark and closed my eyes, feeling whole and completely me for the first time in my life. I was an Ophiuchus by right. I didn't need Kaden to give me a pack mark. I'd earned it all on my own, and this one would never be taken away from me.

"I knew it," Kaden said, his voice barely above a whisper. He stared at the pack mark above my heart, and then he dragged his eyes up to mine. Something stirred inside me, a call I couldn't ignore, and my wolf howled inside me, aching to be freed.

"Tonight," I told him. True mate bonds were activated when both shifters were in wolf form, or so I'd been told. Tonight, we would find out if we were truly meant to be together.

He nodded, knowing what I meant, and the hope in his eyes changed to something else. Something like hunger.

I turned toward the two Sun Witches, who watched the entire thing with interest. "Thank you," I told them before my throat closed up with emotion. I wanted to say more, but it was too much. I could only hope they read it on my face.

"You're welcome," Brea said, bowing her head slightly. "I'm pleased it worked. I finally feel like I'm undoing some of Evanora's evil."

"It's a start," Jordan said.

"Are you feeling all right?" Debra asked him, as if he'd been the one who'd just had a spell cast on him.

"I'm fine. Better than fine." He ran a hand through his golden hair. "Although I'd be a lot better if the blessing spell on me was gone too. Are you up for it, Ayla?"

"Of course." I grabbed a bottle of water and chugged it down, feeling parched. That spell had really taken it out of me, but this wouldn't be finished until Jordan was completely free too.

And then we'd figure out how to free the rest of the Zodiac Wolves.

CHAPTER SEVENTEEN

A MIX of anticipation and excitement raced through my blood as I stepped outside. The sun had just set, painting the endless sky over the ranch in brilliant red and pink, with a swath of dark blue at the top that faded to black. Soon the full moon would rise, but for the first time in days, I wasn't afraid of what that meant.

Now that I was no longer mated and packless, I wouldn't go into heat tonight, but every wolf felt the call of the full moon, and it tended to make us a little wild. The difference was that this time I would embrace it as a free wolf.

I walked toward the fruit trees I'd seen earlier. It wasn't a forest, but it was the closest I could find, and it would provide some cover and privacy tonight. My breath caught and my pulse quickened as I thought about what was coming.

Tonight would change everything.

As the moon breached the horizon, I quickly removed my clothes and set them under one of the trees, before allowing my wolf to run free. The shift was smooth and quick, without even a trace of the Sun Witch spell inside me to slow me down. I shook my white fur out and stretched my paws, before taking off in a sprint.

I dashed between the fruit trees, breathing in scents that were new to me. This place was so different from the forests I knew so well, and though I missed my home, I was excited to explore somewhere new. I put my speed to the test, running as fast as I could, weaving through the foliage. My heart sang with joy, reveling in the feeling that I was finally free.

The moon rose higher in the sky, her soft light shining bright upon me like a blessing. I raised my snout and let out a short howl, singing my praises to Selene. An answering howl sounded behind me, making my ears perk up.

Kaden.

His scent came to me on the breeze and something primal took hold of me, knowing he was coming for me. I began to run, and there was no doubt in my mind that he would follow. Just like I wanted him to.

I raced through the trees, my powerful legs propelling me forward with each bound. Crisp night air whipped through my fur, and the only sounds were my panting and the rustle of fallen leaves beneath my paws. A thrill went through me as I heard a growl behind me, and then I felt Kaden's hot breath on my heels.

You can run, little wolf, his voice said in my mind. *But*

I'll always catch you. And when I do... I'm not letting you go.

I stumbled, shocked to hear him in my head, but then remembered that I was an Ophiuchus again. His words awoke some feral instinct inside of me and I suddenly darted to the left, determined to prolong the game. The black wolf followed, as I knew he would. We were drawn together, a magnetic attraction that was impossible to ignore. My heart pounded faster, fully aware that I would never be able to outrun my alpha. He was getting closer and soon he would catch me...and claim me.

I turned down another row of trees, breathing in the scent of oranges, but then I felt a nip at my tail. It was the only warning I had before Kaden tackled me to the ground. We tumbled in a flurry of fur and teeth, and I growled at the bigger wolf as I managed to break free. But before I could take two steps, Kaden was on me again, pinning me to the ground. I whimpered softly as I submitted to him, though I felt no fear, only intense need and love.

He let out a growl as he nuzzled into my neck. *Mate*, he said. *Mine.*

Our eyes met and the mate bond slid into place with an intensity that shocked us both. Suddenly, everything felt more intense, more real, especially the wolf on top of me. I felt my mate's presence inside of me, as if we were one being instead of two. All the pieces of my life suddenly clicked into place, and I saw that every step had been leading me to my true mate. To Kaden.

Mate, I repeated back to him. *Mine.*

This bond was nothing like the one I'd had with Jordan.

That bond had been oppressive and almost painful in its intensity and urgency. This felt like coming home, like smiling at a fond memory, like taking a bite of my favorite food. Like I'd known all along, from the very first moment I'd met Kaden, that we were destined to be together, and now the moment was finally here.

We shifted back at the same time, both naked and in each other's arms, still nuzzling each other, which then turned to soft kisses across each other's skin. The kisses grew more intense as need spread through us, the mating bond begging to be completed in the most primal way. But it didn't force us. It gave us the final choice.

"I always knew it was you," Kaden murmured against my neck. "I knew it the moment we met at the waterfall, even though your wolf was still locked away. I knew it even when you were mated to the son of my enemy. I knew it even when the Sun Witches tried to turn me against you. You are my mate. My alpha female. My destiny."

"I knew it too," I said, as I wrapped my legs around him. "I was just scared to believe it."

His cock was hard and wedged between us, so close to where I needed him, but he didn't move, even though he must have felt the same overwhelming desire to join with me. I could barely think straight. All I wanted was to feel him inside of me, and to have the mate bond sealed.

"Do you want this?" he asked, and I understood everything he meant in those words. It was one thing to want him because of the mate bond, and it was another thing entirely to want him of my own free will. After everything that had happened between us, he wanted to be sure. He wanted me to choose him.

"Yes." I took his face in my hands and met his eyes. "I love you."

He sucked in a breath. "I love you too, little wolf."

Then he claimed my lips in a searing kiss, and I clung to him as his cock slid into me in one long movement. We both sighed as we joined together, as he filled me up so completely that I felt every single hard inch of him. More than that, I sensed him on a new level, now as my mate. I felt his love and his desire and his sense of how right this was, and I knew he felt all of the same things from me.

Kaden looked down at me like I was a revelation. As he traced my bottom lip with his thumb, his wonder and awe hit me through our bond. I felt it too, but need pulsed through me even stronger, and I tightened my legs around him, begging him to move.

"Hurry up and fuck me," I said, as my hands gripped his broad shoulders, my nails digging into his skin.

He grinned. "We have the rest of our lives. We don't need to hurry."

"Kaden," I cried out, howling his name to the stars. I had no idea how he could hold himself so still while his cock pulsed inside me.

"Anything for you, Ayla."

Then Kaden growled and grabbed hold of my hips as he let the beast inside of him awaken once more. He pulled out of me and then slammed back home, forcing my hips down into the cool, soft ground. *Yes,* my body screamed. *Yes.* This

was what I'd been wanting, what I'd been missing and needing. Later, there would be time to take it slow, to marvel at
each other's bodies, but right now I needed him to claim me
as his mate.

He pulled me up, so he was on his knees and I was
wrapped around him, riding him under the bright moonlight. He kissed me hard as we moved together, his hands
stroking my breasts, my hips, my ass. He fucked me on his
knees like he was worshiping me, making sure that every
thrust brought me greater pleasure. He claimed me like a
god, and I cried his name to the stars as he made me his
goddess.

The climax swept through us both at the same time,
pulsing through the mate bond, and all we could do was ride
through it together. I'd never felt anything so intense before
—a mixture of my pleasure with his, a love that had no end
and no beginning.

When it was over, we stared at each other as we gasped
for breath, while the mate bond settled between us. The
intensity of it faded until it was simply there, comfortable
and familiar, as if we had always been bound together like
this.

"Mine." Kaden pressed his forehead against mine. "I said
it before, but now there is no doubt. Every inch of you is
mine."

"Show me."

With a wicked grin, Kaden set me down on my back in
between the fruit trees, and then he moved down my body
with his mouth. He kissed me everywhere, leaving no inch

of skin untouched, from my nipples to the curve of my hips. He took his time on my breasts, running his tongue around my nipples before taking one into his mouth and brushing his teeth across it, knowing it would make my back arch and my voice cry out. He took just as much time on my clit, teasing it until I was practically sobbing for release, though he wasn't ready to let me come again.

Then he flipped me over and did the same thing on my back, trailing his mouth across my naked flesh. When his teeth brushed the curve of my butt, I gasped. Then he parted my ass to slide his finger inside my back hole.

"Every single inch," he growled, and then slid another finger inside, stretching me wider. Preparing me for what was to come. He'd warned me once that he would take me here one day, and my heart pounded faster in anticipation.

"Show me," I repeated. I wanted to belong to him in every way possible, and I wanted him to know that I trusted him completely.

He pulled my hips up and rubbed his cock against my pussy, sliding between my folds just enough to coat himself in my slick. I moaned at the feel, trying to angle my body to get more, my hands pressed into the dirt. But just when I thought he might make me come like that, his cock pulled back and positioned itself at my back door, seeking entrance.

His cock was so much bigger than his fingers, and I stopped breathing as he slowly made his way inside. He stretched me until I thought I couldn't possibly take any more, and I arched my back against the bright spots of pain mixed in with the pleasure. When he bottomed out inside me, I nearly wept with relief, and then the real claiming began.

With one hand, he gripped my hip, holding me in place as his cock slid in and out of my ass. With the other, he touched my clit, his fingers inside my pussy. I'd never felt anything like it before, and all I could do was succumb to what he was doing to me.

"Please," I cried. "More."

Kaden pushed me down, my face pressed against the dirt, and my fingers dug into it uselessly as he thrust harder, rutting me from behind like the animals we really were. I reveled in the feel of it all, the stretch around his cock, the slap of skin against skin, and the sound of his heavy breathing above me.

As his fingers increased their pressure, I knew I wouldn't last much longer, and I sensed Kaden was close too. He growled and leaned over me, his teeth brushing against my shoulder, and I closed my eyes and shuddered as pleasure washed through me. Kaden threw back his head and howled his release to the moon while his cock surged.

My limbs gave out and Kaden followed me down, tumbling us into the earth in a tangle of naked skin. I nestled up against my mate as soft moonlight fell upon us, like Selene's hand reaching down to cradle us. No words were needed, and none were spoken, as we held each other and simply felt the mate bond thrumming between us, tying us together for the rest of our lives.

We were truly mates now, and nothing would change that.

CHAPTER EIGHTEEN

IN THE MORNING, Brea and I removed the blessing from Griffin and Debra, and with his wolf freed, Griffin shifted for the first time. The rest of us laughed as his lanky reddish wolf dashed across the ranch, scaring the cows and the chickens. Then we returned to the house for some lunch, and afterward, I found myself taking a nap in one of the comfortable old armchairs. Using all that magic drained me, especially after Kaden kept me up far too late. Not that I regretted a single second of it.

When I woke, I found myself alone, and the sun much lower in the sky. I yawned and stepped out onto the porch, sensing Kaden was there through our bond, and heard his voice on the wind.

"You know what it was like," he said to someone, from around the side of the house.

"I do," Jordan replied. It was strange, not feeling him

there anymore. I'd gotten so used to his constant presence in the back of my mind. But it was a relief too.

I hesitated, knowing I could stay and listen, but something about their conversation felt private. Maybe Kaden had finally taken my advice to talk to Jordan about what they'd been through. I went back inside, giving them some space.

Debra and Griffin were in the kitchen, cutting up some vegetables and preparing dinner. As they worked, they moved around each other with the ease of two people who had lived in each other's space for a long time. Griffin smiled at me, while Debra didn't try to bite my head off, so I figured I was welcome.

"We're making a roast for dinner," Griffin said, holding up the knife he was using to chop carrots.

"That sounds delicious," I said with a smile. He seemed like a sweet kid, and I'd never had a younger brother before. I was excited to get to know him more.

I hope I can, I thought with a pang. Maybe once all of this was over, I'd take him out for some ice cream and ask him what his favorite subject in school was. Or whatever it was that cool older sisters did.

I sat at the kitchen island, watching them work, while Griffin launched into a replay of what it was like when he first shifted. Debra and I indulged him, laughing and asking questions, but I found myself yawning again. Doing that spell multiple times must have taken more out of me than I'd thought.

That was a problem. There were hundreds, maybe thousands, of shifters who needed the blessing spell removed. How could Brea and I possibly free all of them? We'd never be able to do it one by one, as we'd been doing here. That would take an eternity. No, we'd have to find a way to cast the spell on multiple shifters at once.

We needed Evanora's staff or something like it. Her staff had amplified her power to allow her to control all of the shifters in the area. Could something similar be done to break the blessing spell on a mass scale? Would it even work with my Moon Witch magic?

I excused myself for a moment and went to find Brea to ask her if she had any ideas. She was in a neat, tidy study that smelled of old books, but she stood at the window, gazing out toward the mountains.

"You'll be leaving us soon, I imagine," Brea said, as she turned toward me. "Can I trust you to keep this place a secret once you're gone?"

"Of course," I said, a little hurt that she'd think otherwise, though I understood where she was coming from. She'd only survived this long by being very careful and a little paranoid. "I owe you a great debt, after all. And if you have any doubts, remember that Griffin is my brother, and I'd never do anything to put him in danger. Or his mother."

If what the Sun Witches had done to Jordan was any indication, they'd do anything to get their hands on Griffin soon too. He was safer here than anywhere else at the moment, especially now that he was free of all Sun Witch magic that could control him.

"Is there something you wanted to ask me in return?" Brea asked, her ancient eyes missing nothing.

"We need your help to free the other Zodiac Wolves," I said. "The spell requires both sun and moon magic."

"Yes, it does." She cocked her head. "Lucky for you, you contain both."

"Me?" I asked, blinking in surprise.

"You are the daughter of Celeste, are you not? Did she tell you that she is Evanora's sister?"

My cheeks flushed. "Yes, but my mother said there is no sun magic in me."

"She lied. Or perhaps she couldn't sense it. But I do, especially now that the blessing is removed."

I shook my head, finding it hard to believe. "I don't feel anything."

"It's there, a tiny spark inside you, which might turn to a flame if properly coaxed." She picked up an old, leather-bound journal from on top of her desk and held it out to me. "This is one of the books we give to apprentices, to help them learn sun magic. You can read ancient Greek, yes?"

"Yes," I said, as I gingerly took the book, almost afraid to touch it.

"If you choose to learn, you'll find everything you need in there. I've also written down the spell we used to break the Sun Witch blessing in the back. With some practice, you should be able to do it on your own."

"Thank you,'" I finally managed to get out, past the lump in my throat. If I could do it on my own... That would be huge.

Brea nodded. "Celeste might be able to help you also. She's the only other witch I've met who could use both sun and moon magic."

"How did you know she was my mother?" I asked.

She shrugged. "It seems obvious to me. Which means that Evanora must know as well. Be careful."

"I will," I said, clutching the book to my chest. "But even if I can learn to do the spell on my own, it won't be enough. I need Evanora's staff."

Brea moved to stand behind her desk, her eyes narrowing. "What are you asking me?"

I sucked in a breath, already knowing the answer, but needing to ask anyway. "Could you take us to Solundra?"

"It has been many decades since I've crossed into that realm." She touched her wrinkled face as evidence. "No, I can't take you there. Going to Solundra would be suicide for all of us."

"But—"

She held up a hand. "You wouldn't stand a chance there, no matter how many shifters you had on your side. The Sun Witches are even more powerful there than they are on Earth, and you wouldn't be able to use your moon magic in Solundra. With the blessing spell still active, Evanora could easily take over the wolves again too."

I sighed, disappointed even though I'd known it was a long shot. "Then I'll have to find some other way to get her staff."

"Perhaps the Moon Witches have something similar," Brea said with a wave of her hand.

"I'll check next time I visit them, though they're reluctant to help us."

"It's hard to fight when hiding seems much safer," she said, gazing outside once more. "I understand this all too well."

"Would you fight?" I asked her. "If we stand against Evanora and her witches, would you help us?"

"We're old ladies," she said with a soft chuckle. "We won't be of much help to you."

"We both know that's not true." I took a step forward. "I've felt your magic. You're as powerful as Evanora is, and you know she needs to be stopped. Just like you know she will find this place someday. You won't be safe until she is gone—and it might free you from Helios's curse too."

Brea sighed, brushing back her wispy silver hair. We heard the sound of Griffin laughing from the kitchen, and Brea closed her eyes for a moment. When she opened them, they were filled with resolve. "Yes, we will fight. When the time comes, and you make your stand, we will be there."

"Thank you," I said, getting choked up once more. I'd never in a million years expected a Sun Witch to help me, let alone stand beside me against Evanora. "For everything."

"Don't thank me," Brea said, her mouth twisting. "I have never been a friend to the wolves or the Moon Witches." She paused, glancing down at her fingers once more. "But I have many regrets. Perhaps, someday, I will be able to right a few of my old wrongs, or at the very least, free the next generation of such burdens."

"As long as we're alive, we still have a chance to make

things right," I said, thinking of Jordan and Kaden, and how I'd come to forgive both of them for all that they'd done. I'd made plenty of my own mistakes too, and I had regrets of my own, but there was nothing to do but keep moving forward and trying to do better in the future.

"Yes, and thank you for reminding me of that." She came forward and rested her hand on my shoulder for a second, in an unexpected gesture of fondness. "You're the first person I've seen who could actually unite everyone. I wish you luck, Ayla, daughter of the sun and the moon and the stars."

I swallowed harder, the lump in my throat growing. "Thank you again for all of your help. I couldn't have done it without you."

I clutched the journal to my chest as I walked out of her study. Excitement rose in me as I held it tighter, knowing it held secrets about magic I'd never imagined I might know, secrets that could help us win against the Sun Witches. I couldn't wait to look inside.

Jordan and Kaden were waiting for me in the living room when I emerged, and something about their posture made them seem more relaxed around each other. Like they were no longer one second away from punching the other at any moment. Love for the two of them swelled in my chest.

"Let's go for a walk," I said, gesturing for them to follow me outside.

They did, without question, and once we were away from the house I told them everything that I'd learned from Brea, and we began to make plans for what to do next.

"I need to get back to the Leo pack," Jordan said. "I have

a lot of changes I want to make now that the Sun Witches aren't controlling me anymore. I'm sure Bates fucked everything up as well as he could too."

"No doubt," Kaden said.

"I'll try to get the Taurus and Aries packs to join us," Jordan added. "They used to listen to my father, so I'm hoping I can get them to listen to me. Assuming the Sun Witches haven't sunk their claws into them too deeply by now."

"It's possible," I said. "But we have to try."

"We should get back to Toronto," Kaden said, looking at me. "The Ophiuchus should be ready by now to leave for Coronis."

"Are you sure that's a good idea?" I asked, biting my lip. "The Sun Witches know where our pack lands are now. What's to stop them from coming for our people?" *Our people.* The novelty of being an Ophiuchus pack member had yet to wear off. I wasn't sure if it ever would, at this point.

"They will come, no matter where we are. It's time to go home and prepare to face them." His eyes fell on Jordan. "All of the packs need to get ready for the battle that's coming."

"The Leos will be ready," Jordan said.

"I'm coming with you," I said, taking Kaden's hand.

He squeezed my hand with a wry grin. "Obviously."

I turned to Jordan, realizing I would be saying goodbye to him soon. I threw my arms around him. "Be safe. Don't do anything too crazy."

"I'll try, but I am a Leo, after all." He pulled back and touched the moonstone necklace. "I should give this back to you."

"No. Keep it." I rested my hand over it, knowing it would protect him, and feeling unexpectedly pleased that a part of me would be with him still. "Roxandra is still out there. I injured her, but I didn't kill her, unfortunately. She might come for you again."

He nodded and then turned to Kaden. They clasped hands and locked eyes, some understanding passing between them. "Keep her safe."

"Always," Kaden said.

Jordan headed back inside to speak to his mother, and Kaden and I watched him go. I leaned against my mate, feeling his solid presence beside me, as the sun began to set.

"It seems like the two of you are getting along better," I said.

"We had some things to work out," Kaden admitted.

"Oh yeah?"

He took a piece of my hair that was blowing in the breeze and pushed it behind my ear. "I admitted that I'd hated him because he was a Leo and the son of the man who killed my parents. Not to mention, all the horrible things he did to you. But mostly, because I knew you could never truly be mine while Jordan was your mate."

I nodded, trying not to interrupt him. Kaden had been burned before by mate bonds when Eileen—his childhood love—had been mated to the beta of the Sagittarius pack. He'd refused to be with me for a long time out of fear that I would be unable to resist the bond tying me to Jordan. Even after we learned Jordan was my brother, he'd still been afraid, worried that I wouldn't be able to fight the magic.

"But now the mate bond is broken, and everything is different," Kaden said. "And he and I... We have an understanding. We've made peace. I don't think we'll ever be friends, but we're not enemies anymore either."

"That's better than I ever hoped for," I said, before pressing a kiss to his lips. "Now let's go home."

CHAPTER NINETEEN

ONCE WE RETURNED TO TORONTO, I packed my things and said goodbye to the Libras, after giving Ethan a quick run-down of everything that had happened. Larkin opted to come with us to Coronis, though I could see it pained her to leave Toronto, which she'd grown fond of during her time on Earth. Or maybe it was a certain person in Toronto she'd grown fond of.

The drive to the Ophiuchus village in Manitoba took a few days, but everyone in the pack was eager to return. The pack had left Coronis about six months earlier to go into hiding after the Leo attack, when Jordan had taken me prisoner. Then we'd had to move again after some of the Ophiuchus had betrayed us to the Sun Witches, putting the pack in danger once more. We were grateful to the Libras for offering us a safe haven during that time, but the city would never be our home, and we longed for the dense forest filled with the smells of deer and moose, and the sounds of birds chirping and leaves rustling in the breeze.

As we entered the pack lands, I opened my window and breathed in the frosty air. The feeling that I was really home sank into me with a surety that hadn't existed before. I was a true member of the Ophiuchus pack, and no one could take that away from me. Not even Kaden.

"We're home," Kaden said, as he stopped the car outside his house. There was no mistaking the relief in his voice.

The large house loomed before us, surrounded by pure white snow that glittered under the waning moon, untouched by anything except the tracks of our car. I took in the familiar dark wood and cool stone, along with the trees that circled the house like an embrace. I'd learned how to fight in this forest. I'd cried for hours in my bedroom, thinking Wesley was dead. I'd gone through my first heat with Kaden in the living room. So many memories, and so many more that I wanted to make now that we were back.

"It's good to be back," Stella said, as she grabbed her bag and headed for the door.

Kaden opened it and the two of them stepped inside the house, while Larkin hesitated with her bag on the front porch. I hefted my own bag over my shoulder and joined her.

"Thank you again for letting me stay with you," she said, sounding grateful.

"We're happy to have you," I said, giving her arm a squeeze. "You're family."

The inside of the house looked the same as when I'd left

it, and I caught Larkin gazing up at the vaulted ceilings and huge windows that showed off the forest outside. Tomorrow we'd spend some time cleaning and restocking the kitchen, but right now we were all exhausted after hours on the road, and we just needed to crash.

"I'll show you where your room is," Stella said to Larkin. "It might be a bit dusty, but if it makes you feel better, literally everything is dusty."

"Oh, I don't mind," Larkin said, and trailed Stella up the stairs.

I picked up my bag to follow them, wondering what they'd done with my room after the Leo pack had taken me. They'd thought I was a traitor at first. Had they thrown out all my stuff? Not that I'd had much, of course. I still didn't, although the few things I called my own, like my camera and my Moon Witch cloak, I cherished.

When I got to the second-floor landing and headed for my room, Kaden wrapped his hand around my arm.

"No," he said.

Before I could ask what he meant, he picked me up and threw me over his shoulder, then headed for his room. The one I'd once been forbidden from entering.

As he slammed the door shut behind us, I let out a shriek, dropping my bag. "What are you doing?"

"I want you in my bed every night." There was heat in his eyes, and it sparked desire in my own body, instant and unmistakable. He put me down on the bed and stood over me, his masculine presence filling the space between us. "You're my mate, my alpha female. My equal."

"Am I?" I asked, propping myself up on my elbows.

He cocked his head to the side, confused by the hard tone of my voice. "Of course you are."

"Then prove it." I stood up and brushed past him, eyeing the room that was his and his alone, then turned back to face him. Something had been boiling up inside me, something I needed to say, and now that we were mated and home, there was no delaying it any longer. "From the time we met, there has always been an unequal power balance between us. First you were my kidnapper, and then my teacher, and then my alpha. You called me your alpha female, but it wasn't true, not really. You proved that when you removed my pack mark." Kaden inhaled sharply, but I kept talking, refusing to be interrupted. "And even though I like it when you go all alpha male on me in bed, if this relationship is going to work, then you need to show me that you really can treat me like your equal. Starting right here, in this bedroom."

"What do you want me to do?" Kaden asked.

I pushed him down on the bed, using a burst of shifter strength that made his eyes widen. "Nothing. You're going to lie back and let me be in control."

The lust in his eyes deepened, turning them almost black. "I like where this is going so far."

He said that now, but I had a feeling he would have a harder time with this than he thought. I climbed onto the bed and put my hand on his chest. His heart was beating furiously beneath the thin fabric of his t-shirt. "No touching me. If you do, you'll be punished."

"Is that a bad thing?" He reached up to touch me, but I smacked his hand away.

"No touching," I growled.

"Yes, mate." He gave me a cocky grin as he folded his arms under his head.

For a second I simply admired the way his muscular arms and chest pulled at his shirt, feeling my own pulse quicken with desire. My gaze traveled down and I saw the outline of his cock, already hard and straining against the fabric of his jeans.

I removed my jacket, while Kaden's eyes glimmered with something dangerous, something like what I was feeling. The rest of my clothes came off next, and I slid the fabric down slowly, taking my time. He watched every single movement like it was the best show he'd ever seen, barely even blinking. To his credit, he didn't move at all, until I wore nothing but my panties. I hooked my thumbs into them and met his eyes, and that's when he groaned and tried to reach for me.

"Down," I said, pressing my hand to his chest. He was used to being able to take what he wanted, when he wanted it, but that wasn't happening tonight.

When he relented, resting his hands at his side this time, I finally slid my panties off, leaving me naked before him. Then I kneeled on the bed in front of him and slid my hands down my body. Lust poured through me as Kaden's hands dug into the duvet cover like he needed to do something with them or he would explode. He licked his lips as I cupped my breasts and played a bit with my nipples before moving further down. I slid my hands along my stomach and then paused at my hips.

"Ayla," he said, his voice strained. It was obvious that he wanted to touch me, but he was doing his best to hold himself back, even though it was killing him.

I slid my hands between my legs, spreading myself so Kaden could see the gleam of how wet I was. His eyes zeroed in on my pussy and his fists clenched the duvet tighter as I slid one finger inside of myself, letting out a soft sound of pleasure. I watched Kaden's face the entire time I moved my finger in and out, and the look he gave me made me only wetter. He looked like he wanted to devour me.

I picked up speed just a bit, rubbing my thumb over my clit every few strokes. A gasp escaped my lips as the pleasure started building, my hips jerking forward as I chased my own release. I added another finger, the slick sound of it loud in the silence, and let out another moan.

"Fuck, Ayla," he groaned, and then he grabbed my hips, unable to take it any longer.

"No." Moon magic flowed out of me and coalesced into shackles around Kaden's wrists and ankles, tying him down. Kaden fought against it, lips parting in a snarl, but he was no match against my magic.

"What the fuck?" he asked.

I gave him a wicked smile. "I told you that you'd be punished."

He grumbled and thrashed again, but then the fight left him. He watched me through slitted eyes, his breathing heavy, his cock nearly bursting out of his jeans. "Don't stop."

"Be good then." I slid my fingers into myself again. I let my head roll back as I picked up where I'd left off, setting a nice, easy pace. The pleasure hadn't faded when I'd paused to hold Kaden back. No, if anything it had only grown stronger, making him obey me. There was something heady about having this much power over someone as strong as him. What was even better was knowing he was *letting* me. He could use his own moon magic to remove the bonds. He could easily overpower me with his strength. But he did nothing except watch with a strained look on his face.

"How does it feel?" I asked, as I stroked my clit.

"Like torture." He sounded breathless. "This is the hottest thing I've ever seen."

I moved my fingers faster, pleasure sparking at Kaden's words. I fucked myself with my hand, grinding down so that every twitch of my hips brought me closer to orgasm. My pussy fluttered around my fingers, clenching down as I came. A small orgasm, nothing like the ones he gave me, but a little tease of what was to come.

"Fuck." Kaden let out another growl, muscles straining against the magic. "I need you. Let me fuck that beautiful pussy."

There was an edge of desperation in his voice, and I looked down at him as my orgasm faded into a pleasant afterglow. "Not yet."

"Please," he begged. "If nothing else, sit on my face so I can taste you."

I liked it when he was the one begging for a change. "All right. I think you've earned that."

I moved up to straddle his face, then grabbed the headboard as he began licking me with vigor. His arms were still held down by magic, but he didn't need them to eat me out, and he feasted like a man who was starving for every last drop of me. Touching myself had been fun, but nothing I did could ever compare to the pleasure Kaden gave me with his mouth. As he completely devoured me, I rocked back and forth on his face, gripping the headboard so hard I heard it crack. I ground my pussy against his mouth, needing more, needing everything. When he nibbled my clit, a much stronger orgasm rolled through me, and my thighs clenched around his face as he licked me through it.

When I moved back, his beard was soaked with the evidence of my pleasure and he flashed me a cocky grin. "Are you going to keep torturing me? Because I could eat you out all night."

"I have something else in mind now."

I skimmed fingertips down his front, and then grew claws and tore open his shirt. It parted for me easily, and then I smoothed my hands over his muscled chest and stomach, enjoying the feel of his hot, hard skin. My fingers drifted down and snagged the button of his jeans. I unbuttoned his pants slowly, stopping to palm his cock through the fabric of his underwear. Kaden arched his back, fighting against the hold of the magic once more.

I yanked his jeans and boxer briefs down, just enough to give me what I wanted. His cock was so big in my hand, and he sucked in a breath as I gripped him. I brought my lips to the head, then swirled my tongue around him, making him groan, his eyes squeezing shut. Then I took him completely in my mouth, nearly choking on his size, and he jerked against the magic holding him, moaning my name. I gave him a little of the pleasure he'd given me with his mouth, but before he could come, I pulled back, sitting on my heels to admire the need in his eyes.

"Ayla," he groaned. "Torture me however you want. I'm yours to command. Just let me inside you already."

Something softened in me at that, and I decided it was time. I climbed over him and straddled his hips, positioning so his cock was at my entrance. Kaden held himself still, not even breathing, as I sank down on him slowly, inch by beautiful inch. I splayed my hands on his chest as he filled me up, until I was seated completely on his hips. He felt huge inside me, and I ground my hips down, pushing him in as deep as I could.

"Fuck, yes," he said with a rough groan. "Take me as deep as you can. My cock was made for you and you alone."

When I began to move, his jaw clenched with the effort of holding himself back, letting me ride him at a slow and steady pace. A part of me wanted to fuck myself hard on him and lose myself in the heat of it, but not yet. I wanted to make this last.

I raked my nails down his chest as I moved faster, gasping each time I sank down on him. He felt so good as I rode him, and pleasure sparked deep inside of me, growing with every roll of my hips. Kaden's eyes never left my face, but he was breathing faster now, a vein pulsing in his throat. I moved against him exactly the way I needed, the friction on my clit feeling so good I knew I wouldn't last much longer. His cock was driving me quickly toward another orgasm, and I shuddered, gripping onto his shoulders as I brought us both closer to the edge.

"Come with me," I said.

He thrust his hips up and met my pace, and I threw my head back as he pounded into me. We worked together to sate the wild need inside of us, and another orgasm claimed me, the strongest one yet. My pussy clenched down on Kaden's cock, and he exploded inside me. He cried out my name, his head pushing back against the bed, his throat arching toward me. I nipped his neck, tasting the sweat on his skin, as the incredible orgasm continued rolling through us.

I took his hands in my face and kissed him then, releasing the magic at the same time. His arms came up a second later, wrapping around me as he kissed me back harder. But then I pushed him back down.

"I'm every bit the alpha you are," I said. "If you're going to be my mate, you have to treat me like one."

He grinned up at me. "I'll never forget it."

CHAPTER TWENTY

AS MORNING SUNLIGHT slanted through the window, I opened my eyes and stared at the ceiling above me. A heavy weight was draped across my waist, and I was surrounded by the familiar smell of Kaden. I closed my eyes and breathed in deeply, remembering last night. I wasn't sure if it would change anything between us outside of the bedroom, but it was a start.

For the first time in ages, I felt content. Over the last few months, I'd found myself always fighting or running from something, never getting a moment to rest. Until now. Here, with Kaden, in Coronis, I could finally breathe for a bit. It couldn't last, of course. There was too much at stake still, and too much for us to do before we could have peace, but for now I was going to enjoy it.

Kaden's breathing changed from the slow cadence of sleep, and he tightened his hand around my waist. He nuzzled his nose into my hair, inhaling my scent, and let out a contented noise. "I could wake up every day like this," he murmured.

"You can, yes."

"Mmm," he said, his voice still groggy. But then he propped himself up on his elbows, his eyes clear. "I thought about what you said, and you're right. There was a power imbalance in the past, but I want you to truly be my equal now. And I want to make it official."

"What do you mean?" I asked.

He reached his hand up to comb through my hair. "The Ophiuchus typically have a ceremony and a big party for the pack when an alpha finds his mate."

"Like a human wedding?"

Kaden chuckled softly. "Not quite. You don't have to wear a white dress or walk down an aisle. But you would stand beside me, not just as my mate, but as my partner."

"I'd like that."

"Good." His hand came down to trace my neck and my shoulders, his touch tender. "I think it would be good for the pack too. Shifters like their traditions, and the pack needs stability after everything it's been through. A sign that the Ophiuchus are still strong and united."

I grinned and hit him lightly on the chest. "I think you just want to show everyone I'm yours."

"What's wrong with that?" Kaden asked.

"Nothing," I said. "As long as everyone knows that you're mine too."

"That's the whole point of the ceremony." A wicked grin

spread across his lips. "Although we could mark each other again so that no one can miss it."

I laughed and kissed him, weaving my fingers in his hair. Kaden let out a sound of approval, hiking my leg up and pulling me so that we were flush against each other. His cock was already hardening, trapped between us, and the kiss deepened.

"You're insatiable," I said.

"So are you," he said, and I couldn't argue with that. Someone had once told me that a newly formed mate bond always made shifters wild, like they couldn't get enough of each other, and now I knew what they'd meant.

"You had your way last night, but now it's my turn," Kaden growled, pinning me down. "And this time, I'm on top."

I let out a gasp as he thrust his cock into me. I was already wet and ready, and he met no resistance from my body as he slid down to the hilt in one, smooth motion. He set a quick, punishing pace, drawing noises out of me that grew louder as he hit the perfect spot again and again. I grasped onto Kaden, needing something to hold onto as he pounded into me and sent me into a state of catatonic pleasure. He hitched my legs high above his shoulders, taking me deeper, and I cried out his name so loud I swore it shook the walls. He grasped my ankles tight and buried himself deep inside of me, my pussy clenching around him as we both lost ourselves in each other.

He'd taken me hard and fast, a quick tumble in the sheets that satisfied the mating bond, for now at least. We spent some time cleaning up, and then we made our way downstairs.

Stella and Larkin were already in the kitchen, eating cereal at the table. They gave us exasperated looks as we joined them.

"What?" I asked, sensing some tension in the air that hadn't been there before.

"'What,' she asks," Stella muttered, shaking her head.

"Get on with it," Kaden said, as he poured us both some cereal.

Stella rolled her eyes. "Dear brother, need I remind you that the walls in this house are incredibly thin, especially with shifter hearing."

"I didn't even need shifter hearing," Larkin said. "I could hear you just fine without it. You're both so loud."

My face flushed. Both last night and this morning, I hadn't bothered to keep my voice down, and Kaden hadn't either. I'd completely forgotten that the two of them might be able to hear us. In truth, I'd completely forgotten there were other people in the world except for Kaden. "I'm sorry."

Kaden shrugged. From the satisfied smirk on his face, he wasn't sorry at all.

"Are all new mates like that?" Larkin asked, looking intrigued. Probably thinking about some romance novel she'd read.

"So I've heard," Stella said dryly.

Larkin's face turned wistful. "I wish I was a shifter with a mate."

"No, you don't," Stella said. "Then you'd be as insufferable as these two lovesick fools."

Kaden grinned at her. "I can't wait for the day when you find your own mate and become just as insufferable."

Stella huffed and picked up her empty bowl to put it in the dishwasher. "I don't need a mate. I'm just fine as I am, thank you very much."

Okay then. This was getting a bit too awkward for breakfast conversation. "I'm sorry," I said again. "We can try to be quieter."

Kaden snorted, showing how well he thought that would work. "Maybe you two should get your own place."

Stella paused, standing over the dishwasher, her eyes widening. "Really?"

"Why not?" He shrugged. "But only if you want. I'd never ask you to leave."

"No, that's a good idea," she said, nodding slowly. "You two deserve some privacy, and I could use some space."

"You could use Mom's cottage," Kaden said. "Where she used to paint."

Stella's face softened as she considered it. "That might work. It's small, but there should be room for two people. But no one's used it in years, so it'll need to be cleaned out pretty good. What do you think, Larkin?"

She shrugged. "Sounds great."

"We can head over after breakfast," Stella said, her voice growing more excited with each word. "See what needs to be done. Maybe we can recruit help from some of the other pack members too."

"I'll come with you," Kaden said. "I haven't been there in years, but... It's time."

"I'll stay here unless you need me," I said, thinking of the journal I still hadn't had a chance to read, except for a few quick glances in the car. "I need to unpack my things, and go through my old stuff too, if it's still around."

"We kept your room the same after you left," Stella said. "None of us could bear to touch it. All your things are still in there."

"That's good to know."

Kaden leaned close, nuzzling his nose against my cheek. "I hope that when you unpack this time, you do it in my room."

"In *our* room," I corrected.

"Exactly." He rested his hand on my knee under the breakfast table.

"Ugh," Stella said, making barfing sounds. "And this is exactly why we need our own place."

A FEW HOURS LATER, I was unpacked and settled into Kaden's room. It had been pretty sparse before, like all he'd done was sleep in it, so it was surprisingly easy to fit myself into all the empty spaces he'd left behind. Kaden was still over at the cottage, helping Larkin and Stella get it ready. According to his texts, they'd found a couple of spots where the roof was leaking, and he'd enlisted some pack members to get it fixed so the two women could move in immediately.

This house would feel a lot emptier without them in it, and I would miss seeing them all the time, but I was glad that the two of them had become such close friends and would be able to have a place they could make their own. They both deserved it. Stella had always lived under the shadow of her brother, while Larkin had spent her entire life hiding among the Moon Witches in Lunatera. Hopefully, Stella could help Larkin feel more at home with the Ophiuchus pack, so she could stay here and finally grow into her body properly. She might not be a shifter, but I knew the Ophiuchus would accept her as one of them. We were a pack of outcasts, rejects, and misfits, after all.

Once everything was put away, I pulled out the Sun Witch journal and stared at its leather-bound cover. I'd flicked through the pages over the last few days, but I'd wanted to save it for a time when I could devote my entire attention to it. The secrets inside of it called to me, secrets I hoped would make me stronger, or at least give me some insight into how to defeat the Sun Witches and the vampires.

I put on my boots and took the journal outside, through the sliding doors that led out to the back of the house. The sun was out, making the snow glisten, and I'd decided if I was going to read about sun magic, I should probably do it under its light. Besides, it had been far too long since I'd been in this forest.

I breathed in the familiar scents as my boots trudged through the snow, heading for the clearing where I'd once trained with Stella and Kaden. Bright sunlight filtered down into it through the canopy of trees, and I took that as a good sign as I sat on the ground and flipped the journal open to the front page.

The writing inside was neat, but a little cramped, as though the person—Brea, I assumed—wanted to pack as much into the pages as possible. The words were all in ancient Greek, and though I'd studied it with my mother until I was proficient, there were still a few things I didn't recognize. I thought about asking Larkin to look through the journal with me, but decided that felt too much like betraying the trust of my new Sun Witch allies.

I had Sun Witch allies. Huh. What a strange thought.

The first few pages contained very basic spells, similar to the ones Larkin had taught me when I'd begun moon magic training. I read through them carefully, practicing the words out loud, noting how they were both similar and different from what I'd already learned.

Once I'd committed the first spell to memory, I set the book down and hugged my legs. Was I ready to try Sun Witch magic? It had been used against me and my loved ones so many times, and for so long I'd thought of the sun's power as a cause of misery and nothing more. A big piece of my identity was wrapped up in being the opposite of them and everything they stood for. Would I be turning my back on my heritage and my people to use the magic of my enemy?

But then I thought of the way Brea and her people had used sun magic, not to burn or destroy, but to grow and protect. I remembered my mother, using her sun magic to heat up some hot chocolate for me, when I'd needed comfort. And I remembered stories my mother had told me, of how the Sun and Moon Witches had once been united long ago, using their magic in harmony. Magic was a tool, and just like any other, it could be used for good or evil. It all came down to the person using it.

I stepped into a brighter patch of sunlight and tilted my head up, feeling the warmth against my face for a few moments. I imagined that I could feel it soaking into me, awakening the dormant parts of my body that held my sun magic, however slight it might be.

Nothing stirred inside of me, but I refused to be deterred. Brea believed I could do this, so I was going to try. I put my hands together and imagined pulling energy into them. The moon magic leaped to my fingertips, eager to be used, but I gently pushed it back. I reached deeper inside of myself, trying to find something, *anything,* that could give me an indication that there was another kind of magic there too.

I found nothing. Maybe Brea was wrong.

I sighed, frustrated, and read back over the first few pages of the journal, seeing if I had missed anything. It should be similar to learning moon magic, but that had come easy to me, once my magic had been unlocked. Why wasn't this working for me?

I shoved the journal back in my bag, ready to give up and try again tomorrow, when a soft *tap-tap-tap* caught my attention. A little woodpecker with a red spot on its head drummed against a nearby tree, and I watched it with a smile, then studied the way the sunlight dappled the leaves nearby. I'd always felt more connected to the moon, but the sun had its own kind of beauty. As the bird flew to another tree, I understood then that the sun gave life, that nothing in this forest would exist without its gentle light nurturing and providing for us.

I tilted my head toward the sun again and muttered a small prayer to Helios. *Forgive me for any sins I have committed against you or your people. If it is true that I am also your daughter, please bless me with your light.*

I held my hands out, feeling my palms warm under the light of the sun, and inhaled slowly. There was no flash of light or acknowledgment that Helios had heard me, but soon I felt a faint buzzing under my skin. It started in my hands and slowly spread through the rest of my body, filling me with warmth, like I was sitting beside a fire on a cold night.

As it ran through me, I realized *this* was what Sun Witch magic was supposed to feel like—warm and welcoming, like a comforting blanket being wrapped around me. I'd so rarely felt it used in any way other than to harm, and I'd been afraid to touch it, fearing what it would do to me or to others. My subconscious couldn't let the magic break free, not until I had gotten past that mental block.

This time, I didn't try to force the magic. It was already there, underneath my skin. I didn't think it would ever be strong enough to rival my moon magic, but all I needed was enough power to cast the spell that would remove the blessing on the other wolves.

With the sun magic filling me, I thought back to the first

spell in the book. The ancient Greek spilled from my lips as I held my hands out in front of me, envisioning the energy that buzzed under my skin pouring out.

After a moment, a tiny little spark formed between my palms, hovering in the air. I let out an excited whoop, and the energy immediately fizzled out. Oops. But if I could do it once, I could do it again.

With a smile on my lips, I summoned the magic again, trying to make a solid ball of sunlight in front of me. The big balls of heat that the Sun Witches lobbed at us during battle were much bigger and more powerful, but I had to start somewhere.

With patience and a bit of coaxing, I grew the ball into a swirling mass of fiery heat. When I felt like I could barely contain it anymore, I tossed it to the other side of the clearing, toward a big pile of snow. Or at least, I meant to. As soon as the magic left my palms, it fizzled and died.

I let out a noise of frustration. Maybe I'd been a little too hasty, thinking I could learn to do that in one day. Just because I could hold the power didn't mean I knew how to use it yet. Moon magic had taken me months to learn, and that had come much easier to me. Plus I'd had Larkin teaching me, and not just an old journal. Learning this magic would likely take me months, or even years, of practice, and I might never have the strength to do all the spells in this book. But that was okay. All I needed to master was one spell, the spell that would set the rest of the Zodiac Wolves free.

I raised my face to the sun and started again.

CHAPTER TWENTY-ONE

JUST AS I reached for the journal again to find out what other secrets it might hold, my phone rang. The sound startled me and I jerked, dropping the journal in the snow. Swearing under my breath, I grabbed the journal and fished around in my pockets for my phone. After one look at the caller ID, my mood instantly brightened.

"Mira!"

"Hi, Ayla!" she said, sounding just as happy as I felt to talk to her. "It's so good to hear your voice."

"Yours too," I said, tucking the journal back into my pocket. "It feels like forever since we've talked. How are you doing?"

"I'm getting so big," Mira said, sighing. She'd texted me a picture of her baby bump a few days ago, and I'd nearly melted. "I don't know how it's possible that a baby can take up this much space. I feel like I'm going to pop. But other than that, I'm good." She paused. "How about you?"

"I'm doing well. We're finally back in Ophiuchus pack lands, and it's great to be home. Speaking of which, how are you settling into your home with the Pisces? Is everything still going well?"

"Yeah," Mira said, but there was a hint of hesitation in her voice. "The Pisces pack treats me well, especially my mate, Aiden."

"But?" I asked. "You don't sound happy."

"I don't know. I still miss the Cancer pack, even though I want to be part of the Pisces pack completely. Sometimes I wonder if this place will ever feel like home though. How long before I start to feel like I really belong here?"

"Once the baby arrives, I'm sure you'll feel differently," I said, but I couldn't help but wonder if there was a deeper reason that she didn't feel at home with the Pisces. If almost all of the mate bonds were fake, as Roxandra had said, it was likely that Mira's bond with Aiden was fake too. They seemed to adore each other, but what if they were supposed to be with someone else? Now that I was truly mated to Kaden and part of the Ophiuchus pack, I couldn't imagine being anywhere else, and I wanted Mira to feel that sense of contentment too. She would never feel truly at home until she found her true mate. And I had a feeling I knew who that was.

But Mira had told me previously that she didn't want to know the truth about her mate bond. She wanted a family with Aiden, and I would respect her wishes. Mira could make her own decisions, and as her best friend, I would always support her in whatever she did.

"Enough about me," Mira said into the silence. "How are you doing? How are you and Kaden? Have you talked to Wesley lately?"

I sat down on a fallen tree branch and stretched my legs out in the snow. "A lot has happened since I talked to you last." I started telling her a condensed version of events that had happened since I'd last seen her, ending with the fact that Kaden and I were now officially mated, and I was the Ophiuchus pack alpha female.

"Wow," she said when I was finished. "I'd heard about the Convergence from some of the Pisces warriors, but I had no idea about the rest of it. I'm so glad you got the fake bond with Jordan dissolved and that you and Kaden became true mates."

"Thank you," I said, smiling up into the sunlight.

"How does it feel?" she asked. "Now that the Sun Witch blessing is gone, and you're with your true mate?"

I closed my eyes and reached for Kaden, feeling his life pulsing through the bond. He was concentrating, but felt no fear or worry, only a resolve to get something done. "It's incredible. The bond with Jordan always felt wrong, even before I knew he was my brother. Now a weight has been lifted off of my shoulders, and I feel free and wholly myself for the first time ever. My wolf is unchained, and shifting is easier than ever. And the mate bond..." I wasn't sure how much to say, but I wanted to be honest with her. "When the mate bond happened, it was like I'd known all along that Kaden was my destiny, and being with him was like coming home."

Mira was silent for so long on the other end that I thought that she'd maybe hung up.

"Mira?" I asked.

She let out a little shuddering breath that carried even through the phone. "Sorry. I'm fine. I'm really happy for you, and so glad that my child won't ever have the Sun Witch blessing."

"Me too," I said. "I hope we can all be free of this soon."

"I should get going," Mira said. "I'm supposed to have dinner with the Pisces alpha and his family, and it takes me forever to even get off the couch right now. I'm like a beached whale."

I laughed softly, trying to imagine it. "I wish I could come visit you."

"Me too." The smile was back in her voice. "When things calm down, we'll see each other again, I promise."

A lump formed in my throat. I'd never been to the Pisces pack lands, so I couldn't easily teleport there to visit her, and I didn't really have time right now to make the long trip to Alaska. Someday I would visit her though and meet her baby, I swore it.

"Okay," I said. "Let's chat again next week. Otherwise, there's too much to catch up on when we talk."

Mira laughed. "Agreed. Take care of yourself, okay?"

"You, too," I said, trying to put as much love into the words as I could.

We said our goodbyes and I pocketed my phone. I wished I could do more to help her, or at least be there for her during this time, but there was only so much I could do, and I had bigger things to take care of. Like figuring out this sun magic so I could free wolves like Mira, and stop them from being mated to the wrong person.

I was in the middle of practicing a different spell, trying to coax sunlight toward a specific plant to infuse it with growing energy, when Kaden found me.

He pressed a kiss to the top of my head. "How's it going? It looks like you're getting the hang of it."

I blew out a frustrated breath. "It's like pulling teeth. So slow. I wish it wasn't this hard."

"You'll get it. You never give up on anything once you've decided to do it." He grinned at me. "It wasn't that long ago when you started training with me in this very spot. You couldn't even throw a punch back then, and you'd trip over nothing, like a pup learning to walk. I didn't think you'd ever learn to fight."

"I remember," I muttered. "You were such an asshole back then."

"I'm still an asshole, you just grew to love it."

I couldn't argue with that, but I still wanted to wipe that cocky smirk off his face. "I bet I could take you now though."

He arched an eyebrow. "You think you could beat me?"

"With magic? Definitely."

"I wouldn't be so sure."

He charged at me, so fast that he was practically a blur. I shot a burst of moon magic at him, but Kaden deftly swerved out of the way. I teleported away before he could knock me down, and wrapped chains of cold, silver light around him. He glowed brightly, and every single chain broke. He let out a growl and formed his own spear of light, then lobbed it at me. I'd never seen him fight like this before, since he usually preferred his teeth and claws, and it threw me off guard for a moment. I created a shield just in time to make his magic fizzle out, but then he disappeared in front of me, going invisible. My split second of hesitation cost me, and then Kaden was on me.

We tumbled down to the cold ground, and he pinned me beneath him. I squirmed, but Kaden was so much stronger, and he grinned as he grabbed my wrists and held them above my head. I could have kept going, using magic to throw him off me, but I melted into his touch.

"Nice try," Kaden said, and swooped down for a kiss.

"I let you win," I said with a laugh.

Kaden nuzzled his nose into my neck, kissing along the skin there. "You want a rematch?"

"Maybe later," I said, as I felt desire stirring inside of me again. "Right now I want you to fuck me."

"Your wish is my command," he said, as he arched up to pull off his shirt.

He claimed me there, in the clearing where we used to train together, in the forest where I'd first fallen in love with him. I couldn't get enough of him, and I wondered how long that would last. Surely the need would lose its edge at some point. But when?

Once we were both satisfied, we stretched out on the forest floor, feeling the afternoon sun on our skin. The snow in this spot had melted away while I'd been practicing my sun magic, leaving a soft patch of fallen leaves for us to rest upon.

"How are Stella and Larkin settling in?" I asked.

"The house needs more work than I thought it would, and a *lot* of cleaning, but it will be good for them." He toyed with the strands of my hair idly. "It was good to go back and see some of my mom's old paintings and artwork. I've avoided that place for years, but I don't want to run from the past any longer."

"Maybe we can put some of her paintings in the house," I said, letting my fingers trail across his chest.

"I'd like that." He took my hand and pressed a kiss to it. "Stella also volunteered to organize the alpha female celebration for us."

"Thank goodness. She can help me decide what to wear. I'm awful at that kind of stuff."

"I liked that green dress you had on at Christmas. Maybe you can wear that again sometime."

"I tore it while fighting some assholes in the Cancer pack, but I'm sure it can be fixed." I laughed a little. "I guess I never told you about that."

He raised his eyebrows. "No, but I want to hear all about it."

As we walked back toward the house, I told him all about my Christmas with Jordan and Wesley. "That was when I realized I didn't need you to defend me anymore. I can take care of myself."

"You're right, you don't need me. You truly are an alpha

in your own right." He cast me a slanted grin. "But you're stuck with me anyway."

I took his hand and squeezed it. "I'd choose you, even without the mate bond."

"And that makes me the luckiest alpha in the world."

CHAPTER TWENTY-TWO

AFTER A FEW MORE DAYS SPENT SETTLING INTO Coronis, I decided it was time to visit my mother.

I opened my eyes to Lunatera's half-light. Kaden let go of my hand and looked up at the huge moon, before turning around in a circle to take in the beach and my mom's Victorian house up ahead.

"This is it," I said. "Lunatera. Realm of Selene."

Kaden nodded and inhaled deeply. "The magic feels stronger here."

We stepped onto the porch, and Kaden yanked on his shirt collar, adjusting it like it was too tight. He smoothed his hair next. "Do I look okay?"

Was he nervous to meet my mother? How cute. I kissed his cheek. "You look as handsome as ever."

Celeste opened the door, her white hair flowing down her back, her eyes bright under the moonlight. She wore a plain purple dress that had tiny little moons embroidered on it, probably handmade by one of the other witches here.

"Ayla. I'm so happy to see you!" She hugged me tight, but then pulled back long enough to look over my face and tuck my hair behind my ear. "You look good. Oh, I've missed you so much."

"I missed you too," I said.

"And you must be Kaden." She stretched out her arms, clasping Kaden's hands in her pale fingers. "I've heard so much about you."

"Hopefully some of it was good," Kaden said with a grin. "It's nice to meet you."

"Yes, although I have a feeling you're not here just to meet me." She stepped aside and motioned for us to come inside. "Come on in, and we'll talk about it over a cup of hot chocolate. Or tea, if you'd prefer."

Celeste led us into the kitchen, and Kaden admired the strange house that lived out of time with an odd mismatch of older furniture. It wasn't home, but it was comforting to be back here. I relaxed into one of the chairs at the kitchen table, gazing outside at the waves rolling across the sand. Celeste lit the stove with a flicker of sun magic and put a kettle on to boil. She grabbed some mugs out of the cabinets and lined them up on the counter.

"I know Ayla likes her hot chocolate," Celeste said. "What about you, Kaden?"

"That's fine. Thank you."

She smiled as she prepared it for us. "I'm so pleased that you're here. I trust this means that you're together again?"

"We are, yes," I said, and Kaden rested his hand over mine.

"I'm glad to hear it. You should have seen the way Larkin was moping the last time she came here. 'True love is fake,' she kept moaning. I told her that you two would get back together. Sometimes these things take time." She paused as she poured our hot chocolate. "Oh, is that why you're here, to break the mate bond with Jordan? I found something in an old book that might help you."

"Actually, we already broke the fake mate bond," I said, as she handed me my mug. "I'm truly mated to Kaden now, and a member of the Ophiuchus pack again."

Celeste gave Kaden his mug next, before sitting beside me. "I'm so happy to hear that. How did you do it?"

"With the help of some rogue Sun Witches," Kaden said.

"What?" Celeste asked, nearly dropping her mug.

"Hard to believe, I know," I said. "But their leader, Brea, wants to help us fight Evanora."

Celeste's eyes narrowed. "I'm surprised she would do anything to help you. Breanora, as she was called once, was Evanora's second in command, you know. And her best friend."

I took a sip of my hot chocolate. "Not anymore. They've had some kind of falling out, and now she's living in hiding with a few other Sun Witches. Including Jordan's mom."

"Be careful," Celeste said. "It could be another trick."

"I thought that too, but I really think Brea wants to stop Evanora." I told her briefly about what happened to the male

Sun Witches and the curse that resulted, along with everything we'd learned about why they wanted to control Jordan so badly. Then I explained to her how Brea had helped us break the blessing spell, before giving me the Sun Witch journal so I could learn to do it myself.

"You could learn to do the spell too," I said.

Celeste tapped her fingers against her mug, looking a bit troubled. "I'll take a look at the spell, but I'm not sure how much help I will be. It's been a long time since I used sun magic beyond lighting a simple flame or keeping my shower warm. I'm impressed you were able to use it at all."

"Not very well," I admitted. "But I'm getting better."

Celeste nodded, still frowning slightly. "I'll copy the spell down in my grimoire and study it, but I'm not sure what you expect me to do with it. I can't cast it on every Zodiac Wolf, no more than you can."

I stared down into my hot chocolate. "No, casting it one by one would be impossible. We need something like Evanora's staff to amplify the magic. Do the Moon Witches have something like that?"

"We did once, but the Sun Witches destroyed it. I'm sorry."

I sighed. Another dead end. The only option was to get Evanora's staff, and that seemed impossible. I didn't even mention the idea to Celeste, because I knew she would tell me it was too dangerous. But what other choice did we have?

"We'll find a way," Kaden said, meeting my eyes. "But that's not why we're here."

"Right," I said, focusing again. "The Sun Witches were able to get inside Kaden's head and control him. Would you be able to teach him how to shield his mind from their magic, like you taught me?"

Celeste nodded. "I would be happy to."

"Thank you," Kaden said. "I really appreciate that. But I'm not the only one who the Sun Witches have controlled. Would it be possible to get more of those moonstone necklaces for some of the other alphas?"

Celeste shook her head. "I'm sorry, but we already gave Larkin all that we had. We're working to make new ones, but it takes a lot of time and effort to fill them with the energy of the moon."

"We understand, and we're thankful for all your help so far," Kaden said.

"I wish we could do more," Celeste said.

"You could," I said, feeling that flicker of annoyance inside me anytime I thought of the Moon Witches' refusal to help us. "You and some of the other Moon Witches could come to Earth and help us fight the Sun Witches. Like Larkin is doing now."

"Larkin is young, and she needs time on Earth to grow into herself. But the rest of us..." Celeste bowed her head. "We've spent so long hiding that we've forgotten what it's like to fight. We will continue to make the moonstone necklaces, and I will learn this new spell for you, but that is all we can do. I'm sorry."

"I had to ask." I took a long drink of hot chocolate, trying to hide my anger. This had long been a point of contention between us, but I didn't want to spend my time with her quarreling. I knew she was only trying to keep her people safe, and the last thing we needed was more fighting when we should be working together.

"Larkin mentioned there was a vampire here," Kaden said, and I was grateful for the change in topic. "Would it be possible to speak to him?"

Celeste's face looked troubled again. "Larkin told me about the vampire attack on your people. I'm surprised they would do such a thing, but it's been many years since I had any contact with them."

"They're working for the Sun Witches," Kaden said. "We need to know why, and how to stop them."

"I'm sure Killian would be willing to speak with you. I'll ask him to come by."

"Thank you," Kaden said.

We finished our drinks and silence settled between us. Celeste stood and began cleaning up. "How is Jordan? He must be pleased that the mate bond has been broken."

"He's doing well," I said. "He's no longer under Sun Witch control, and he's going to lead the Leo pack in a new direction."

Celeste smiled as she washed up. "I'm glad to hear it. He's a good boy, just a bit troubled."

I leaned back in my chair, trying to relax. "He wants to do better. He *is* doing better. He just needs to figure some things out."

"Don't we all?" Kaden muttered.

"Indeed," Celeste said. "And how is Larkin? She seems

apprehensive when she comes to visit. Is she settling in on Earth?"

"I think so," I said. "She's been a great help to us."

"She's become good friends with my sister, Stella," Kaden said.

"Good." Celeste came back to sit with us again and let her gaze wander over Kaden, taking him in. "You know, I met you both once when you were little. I'm sure you don't remember it."

"Really?" Kaden asked, straightening up a bit. "How?"

"I knew your parents," Celeste said, her voice going soft. "Not very well, but they were kind to me when I was in need." She reached across the table and took his hand. "I'm sorry for your loss. They were taken too soon."

Kaden looked away and cleared his throat, with a bit of a shine to his eyes. No matter how many years passed, the pain of his parents' loss never left him. I couldn't imagine what that was like. My own father had been a horrible person and I hardly missed him at all. And though I would grieve Celeste if I lost her, I'd only known her for a short time as an adult. It wouldn't be the same.

"I hope you can stay for a few days," Celeste said. "It might take some time to teach you to shield your mind."

"We'll stay as long as we need," I said.

"Good." She patted me on the shoulder. "I'll get your room ready. Please feel free to make yourselves at home."

CHAPTER TWENTY-THREE

LATER THAT DAY, Celeste took Kaden down to the beach to start teaching him to shield his mind. He'd looked eager and determined as the two of them trudged through the sand. It would be hard work, but they would make sure he stayed free from Sun Witch control forever.

I stayed inside, claiming the chaise lounge in the living room to read the old book Celeste had uncovered. I still wanted to take a look at the book, even though we'd already broken the mating bond. If there was an easier way to do it, I would gladly learn that spell too.

The paper felt old and brittle under my fingers, and I worried that one swift page turn would break the blessing. The text was written in ancient Greek, of course, and I struggled to get through the thick passages, my eyes blurring together as I tried to make sense of what was in front of me. Though I had gotten pretty good with the language, this book was particularly dense and had many words I didn't recognize. I really needed to spend more time studying the language when I was home. *Add it to my list*, I thought with a sigh. As if I didn't have enough to do. I wished for a moment I'd brought Larkin with us, but I'd wanted it to be just Kaden and me when he met my mother for the first time.

I rubbed my temples and adjusted in my chair. I'd just have to get through this book on my own. It had lots of interesting firsthand accounts from long-dead Moon Witches, and some later secondhand accounts too. They spoke of living with the Ophiuchus pack, and how the other Zodiac Wolves had resented it and then cast the pack out because of it. I already knew all that though, even though it was interesting to read about. But then I found something that made me pause, something that went back even further in time. I read it twice, and then grabbed a piece of paper and a pen.

It took me a few grueling hours to translate the chapter, and I wasn't sure I'd done a very good job when I was done. Maybe I should take this back to Larkin, after all.

Luckily, Kaden and Celeste returned at that moment. I set down my notes and the book, grateful for the distraction.

"How's it going?" I asked, standing up and giving Kaden a kiss on the cheek.

"He's learning very quickly," Celeste said with a kind smile. "He's a natural at this."

Kaden looked exhausted, but his jaw was set in that stubborn way of his. "It's hard, but I'm not going to give up until I have it down. I'm never letting anyone control my mind again."

"You'll get it soon, I'm sure. Now come and look at this." I pulled the book toward me and flipped back a few pages. "I think I found something that could help us." I scanned the text, trying to find the passage. I frowned, running my fingers over the letters. "Here it is. I'm not sure if I'm reading this right, but if I am, it says that when the alphas of all thirteen packs align under a new moon, they can use the magic of the stars."

"I've never heard of anything like that," Kaden said.

Celeste leaned over my shoulder, her eyes skimming the text. "Yes, that's correct. It says here that this is how the Zodiac Wolves broke free of slavery from the witches all those years ago. This is what I thought might help you break free of the mate bond."

My heart raced in excitement at this new idea. "So if we got all the thirteen packs to align at the new moon, whatever that means, we might be able to remove the blessing spell on all of them."

Kaden snorted. "Getting all the packs to unite would be a miracle. We'd have more luck getting Evanora's staff."

He was probably right, but I wasn't going to dismiss this chance. I skimmed the passage again. "Why a new moon?"

Celeste sank down into a chair across from me. "Probably because it's when the sun and moon are the weakest, and the stars are the brightest."

"Of course." I thought of Kaden showing me the Ophiuchus constellation while standing on his roof. The constellations... It seemed so obvious now, I wonder how I'd never realized it before. "The stars are where we get our Zodiac powers from!"

"Obviously," Kaden said. "What have they been teaching you in those packs?"

"A lot of Sun Witch nonsense," I muttered. "Otherwise we would have known about this sooner."

"This knowledge has been buried for a long time," Celeste said. "The witches of old wanted to make sure the Zodiac Wolves never did something like that again. I didn't know about it either until I found this book, and I only looked at it because I was searching for a solution to the mating bond problem."

"This is why they keep the packs fighting with each other," I said, as everything clicked into place. Roxandra had told us they did it to keep us weak and easy to control, but I realized her words went even deeper than I realized. The Sun Witches wanted to make sure the alphas never performed this ritual ever again, and the best way to do that was to make sure they all hated each other.

I sat up straighter, my head spinning. "So you're telling me we can use our star magic, the magic we've always had, to break free of the blessing spell? All it takes is us working together?"

Kaden scowled. "You say that like it's so easy."

"Maybe it is. You saw how the Scorpio pack became our allies after we gave them proof that the Sun Witches were controlling everything. Jordan is working on the other packs too. We just need to get the other alphas to listen to us."

"Fine. We'll call another meeting of the alphas when we get back, but I wouldn't get your hopes up."

I nodded, looking down at my translated notes. The other alphas needed to know about this. It might be our best chance of freeing everyone.

A knock sounded on the door, interrupting our discussion. Celeste's face lit up. "That must be Killian. He agreed to come talk to you today about the vampire problem. I'll let him in."

"Are you sure this is a good idea?" Kaden asked me, as Celeste went to the front door.

"Yes, as long as you refrain from attacking him." I shut the book and pushed my notes aside.

Kaden shot me a look. "I can control myself."

"We'll see."

"Please, come sit with us," Celeste said, motioning for Killian to join us in the living room. "Ayla and her mate, Kaden, would like to ask you a few questions. I'll get us some refreshments."

"Hello again," I said, though my wolf immediately reacted to his presence with an inner growl. It didn't matter that I knew he was a friend, or that he'd never done anything to harm me. Something in my blood thought him my enemy, filling me with the instinctual need to pounce on him and rip his throat out. I coughed behind my hand to compose myself.

"Ayla, it's a pleasure as always to see you," Killian said, sweeping into the room with an unnatural grace. He was shockingly beautiful, and it was hard not to stare at the perfect lines of his face, or the way his black hair fell across it. Even though I wanted to kill him, I also wanted to look at him for hours, like a priceless painting in a museum. It made no sense, but that was the nature of vampires and wolves.

Beside me, Kaden had his hands clenched into fists, and every muscle in his body was tense. He'd never had a positive experience with a vampire, so it was probably even harder for him to stay calm in the face of the instinctive urge to take down his foe. I could tell he was ready to pounce at a moment's notice, and if he didn't get himself under control, we were about to lose the one vampire ally we had.

"It's okay," I murmured at him. "Just sit down."

Kaden sat, though he never took his eyes off the vampire, and his body didn't lose any of the tension in it.

"Kaden of the Ophiuchus pack. I'm pleased to meet your acquaintance." Killian was either very good at acting, or he didn't notice the obvious tension in the air. The former, I guessed, because he stayed on the other side of the coffee table and didn't try to get any closer.

"Likewise," Kaden said, but it sounded more like a growl.

I put my hand on his knee and dug my fingers in a bit. Kaden finally stopped glaring at the vampire and looked over at me. *Play nice,* I thought, trying to send the message through the mate bond, along with a sense of calm.

Kaden's jaw was clenched as he looked back over at Killian, but his voice was a bit less murderous. "Thank you for coming to talk to us."

Progress, I thought, and sent an apologetic smile toward Killian. "It's good to see you again. I hope you've been well."

"It's the same as always here, which I suppose is a yes." He flashed me a smile, showing the tips of his fangs, and Kaden stiffened once again next to me. "I heard you have a vampire problem."

I nodded. "The Sun Witches have gotten the vampires to work with them. We're trying to figure out everything we can about them, and how they can go out during the day."

"And how best to defeat them," Kaden added, through gritted teeth.

I dug my elbow into his side, but didn't correct him. He was technically right, but he was being very rude about it. He flashed me an annoyed look, but didn't say anything else.

"Yes, Larkin came to speak to me too," the vampire said. "I'll tell you the same thing I told her. They shouldn't be able to go out in the sun. Vampires still suffer from the Sun Curse, as I'm sure you know. It makes it so we can't step outside during the day." Killian held his own hand up toward the pale light from Lunatera's moon. "I don't have that problem, of course, since it's always night here, but I'm the exception."

"Is there any way they would be able to go out during the day?" I asked.

"Perhaps. Was it very cloudy, or late in the afternoon where there wasn't any direct sunlight?"

"No," Kaden said. "They went out in broad daylight."

"There is another way." Killian paused. "If the Sun Witches let the vampires drink their blood, that would allow them to walk in the sunlight, but only for so long. It wouldn't be permanent, so they'd have to keep going back to them for more."

"That sounds about right," Kaden muttered. "The Sun Witches like to make everyone dependent on them."

The vampire smiled sadly, as if remembering something from his past. "Indeed. If I had to guess, the Sun Witches probably offered to remove the curse eventually in exchange for their servitude, and the vampires accepted, from the sounds of it."

"And knowing Evanora, they were never going to keep that deal," I said.

"Probably not," Killian agreed.

Celeste returned with some tea and passed it around, and everyone calmed down a little. Killian took a seat and sipped his tea, thanking Celeste for her hospitality, while Kaden watched with narrow eyes.

"So you can drink things other than blood," he said. "What else?"

"Oh yes, we eat and drink like anyone else," Killian said. "We just have an...extra dietary need."

Kaden leaned forward, resting his arms on his knees, ignoring his tea completely. "Tell me about your powers."

I rolled my eyes. He really was going to spend the whole time on the verge of starting a fight. He was mine, and I loved him, but sometimes I just wanted to throttle him too. I looked over at Celeste, who just shrugged, as if to say, *what can we do?*

Killian stirred his tea, like we were having a normal

conversation. "Speed, strength, and immortality, of course. Rapid healing. We're very hard to kill, as you might have noticed."

"No shit," Kaden growled. "What else?"

"Fangs, naturally. Oh, and we can grow these." He lifted a hand, modeling it from side to side as his nails extended into razor-sharp points.

Kaden gripped the edge of the couch like he was holding himself back. "Anything else?"

"We have some other tricks too... Different bloodlines have different powers, similar to your packs, actually." He said nothing more, only offering a mysterious smile that rankled Kaden more.

"We're nothing alike," he snapped.

I got the sense that Killian was enjoying winding him up because his smile only got wider. "Ah, if only you knew, my young friend. Perhaps someday I'll share the full history of the wolves and vampires, but that would be a longer story than I have time for today, I'm afraid."

"Just tell me how to kill them," Kaden said.

"You already know how. Decapitation. Stabbing through the heart. Fire." He waved his hand, his nails already back to normal. "There are other ways, but those are the most common."

"What about the other stuff?" Kaden asked. "Holy water, crosses, garlic...?"

Killian let out a laugh that was so lovely my ears ached to hear it again. "All nonsense, just like silver and werewolves."

I frowned as I mulled over his words. Most of what he'd told us we'd already known, or at least guessed. No wonder Larkin had told me she hadn't learned anything useful from him when she'd come to see him. I'd wanted to talk to him on my own, just to be sure, but now it seemed like a waste of time.

"Is there any way we can get them to turn on the Sun Witches?" I asked Killian.

Killian shook his head. "It's unlikely, unless you can find a way to break the Sun Witch curse. If nothing else, we vampires always remain true to our word. If the others have made an oath to serve the Sun Witches, it would be hard to break."

I sighed and looked over at Kaden, who appeared just as frustrated. We'd hoped that this trip would yield more answers, and yet here we were, with even more questions.

"Is there anything else you need?" Killian asked, as he set down his empty tea cup. "I'd be happy to answer more questions, if you have any."

"I don't think so," I said, trying to keep the frustration out of my voice. "Thank you, Killian."

"It's been a pleasure. Next time you come to Lunatera, I hope you'll join me for a meal." At this last word, Killian's eyes flickered to Kaden, and there was a brief gleam of humor in them before he slipped back behind his perfect, gentlemanly mask.

Kaden's muscles tensed again at the joke, obviously not finding it very funny, and he only relaxed once Killian had left the room with Celeste. The vampire, meanwhile, looked perfectly at ease despite the glare Kaden had leveled at him.

"A *meal*?" Kaden asked, as soon as he was gone. "Is he serious?"

I ignored that and said, "I was hoping we'd learn more from him."

Kaden blew out a long breath. "At least now we know for sure what we're up against."

"In more ways than one." I picked up the book again, flipping to the chapter I'd been studying. This was our only solid lead and I would chase it as far as I could. If we could get all the packs to work together for long enough to break the curse, this could all be over. I just prayed Kaden was wrong about needing a miracle to bring the alphas together.

CHAPTER TWENTY-FOUR

KADEN WAS A FAST LEARNER, and even Celeste was impressed by how quickly he was able to shield his mind. Once he had it down, we said our goodbyes and returned to Coronis, feeling disappointed. It had been nice to spend some time with my mom, and we'd gained some new knowledge about how to possibly break the blessing spell. We'd also had our suspicions about the vampires confirmed, and learned a little bit more there as well. But that was it.

Would it be enough? I wasn't sure. The Zodiac Wolves hadn't been united for as long as anyone could remember, and the book didn't tell us what exactly to do during the new moon. Even if we convinced the alphas to work together, who knew if it would do anything?

The spell that Brea had created though, that was something that I knew worked, and so I kept practicing sun magic whenever I could. Of course, using it on a grand scale still required Evanora's staff, which seemed impossible to get.

But two plans were better than one, and I liked having as many options as possible.

We called a meeting of the other alphas as soon as we got back, though it was tricky finding a time when everyone could meet. Ethan and Jordan had helped us contact them all, and then all we could do was hope for the best.

"Do you think they're going to come?" I asked, as the clock ticked closer and closer to the start time. So far, no one had joined our Zoom meeting, but I was hoping that we'd get a good turnout. I already knew that Ethan, Jordan, and Wesley were planning to come, as well as Amos, the Pisces alpha. But what about the others?

"They better," Kaden growled, as he adjusted his laptop so it got both of us on the screen a little more. We were sitting at the kitchen island since it had the best lighting, but we'd already discussed turning one of the other rooms into an office that we could share. Possibly Stella's room, since it was the biggest.

With only a few minutes to go, the alphas began to arrive. To my surprise, more and more showed up, and our screen filled with squares. I let out a long breath, watching the other alphas appear. Even the Taurus and Aries alphas showed up. I could hardly believe it. I stared at the screen as I counted the numbers. A few of the packs still had their cameras off, but they were all here. Every single one of them.

Even Kaden looked impressed. "Maybe it won't take a miracle."

I let out a short laugh, still shocked by what was happening. We might not be united yet, but something had struck a chord in each of them, and they were ready to listen. It was progress, at least. Maybe we *could* get everyone on the same page. I hoped so, at least.

When it was time, Kaden unmuted us and started talking. "Thank you for joining us today. I won't beat around the bush. You all saw what happened at the Convergence, when every pack lost valuable lives because of the Sun Witches' control. You all watched the interrogation of Roxandra, when she told us the truth about everything they'd done to us. You all heard about the vampire attack in the heart of Libra pack territory, when Roxandra was freed. You all know what's at stake now, and that we will never be free until the Sun Witches are stopped."

Theo, the Sagittarius alpha, unmuted himself. "We saw, yes," he said, sounding a bit tired. "But what do you propose we do? Do you have a plan, Kaden?"

Everyone looked to Kaden as their leader still, but he bowed his head. "I can no longer lead you. Not after what we learned they did to me. Luckily, there is someone else who does have a plan, who will be a better person to lead you in the upcoming battle." He turned toward me. "Ayla."

"What?" I asked, nearly falling off the kitchen stool. We hadn't talked about this in advance, and I wasn't sure I was the right person for the job. Kaden had much more experience, and he was protected from Sun Witch mental attacks now. Why would he pass this to me?

"You're the best person for this," Kaden said, sounding sure.

"I agree," Wesley said.

"Me too," Jordan added.

Ethan unmuted himself. "I back Kaden up on this. If he says it's best, I trust his judgment."

Amos, the Pisces alpha, and Theo agreed to follow me too. But I saw shock on other faces, and the Aries alpha was shaking his head. He was probably in his mid-forties and had a shock of ginger hair cut into a buzz cut, along with a strong jaw.

"Why should we listen to a half-witch mutt?" he asked. "Is she really even a true Zodiac Wolf?"

Kaden growled low in his chest, but to my surprise, Wesley was the first to verbally defend me. "You're one to talk," he said, glaring through the screen. "Why should you have any more say than Ayla just because you're a full-blooded wolf? Why should we even give you a vote, when you helped decimate the Cancer pack? You've been allied with the Sun Witches this entire time. How do we even know if we can trust you?"

The Aries alpha snapped his teeth at Wesley, his voice rising in anger. "We only did those things because the Leo pack was working with the Sun Witches, and we were allied with them. If you want to blame someone, blame Jordan and his dad for getting us into this mess with the Sun Witches."

"I agree," the Taurus leader said, unmuting himself. He was a bit older than the Aries alpha, with a full head of gray hair and a matching shaggy beard. "We were just doing what we were ordered to do. Can you blame us for that?"

"Yes," Wesley said. "I can."

The Taurus alpha looked ready to say something else, but the Aquarius alpha cut him off. He was about the same age as the other two men but had no hair at all. "They're right. Jordan and the Leos should be held accountable for all of this. They took over my pack and held my daughter hostage, forcing me to work with them. Why should we listen to anything Jordan has to say now?"

"Because I'm the Leo alpha now," Jordan said loudly, drowning out both of them. "For too long the Leos have been led by people under the control of the Sun Witches. My father. His beta. Even me, at one point. But that's not happening anymore. They can't control me ever again. I've had my mate bond removed, the blessing spell has been broken, and I'm a free wolf now—and I'm taking the Leos in a new direction."

Wilson, the cranky old Capricorn alpha, unmuted himself and let out a derisive snort. "I don't believe it. There's no way we can trust the Leos or their allies. What if they turn on us again? Then what?" He zeroed in on me. "Do you have a plan for when it all falls apart, girl?"

"Let's not be too hasty," Ethan said. "We need to hear everyone out, and try to come to a peaceful resolution."

"Shut up," the Aries alpha snapped. "We all know you're on their side no matter what."

Ethan looked affronted, but didn't say anything else. Many of the other alphas unmuted themselves and all started talking at once, trying to get a word in, but no one could be heard. It quickly devolved into shouting and a complete cacophony.

I groaned and turned to Kaden. "This isn't what I had in mind for this meeting. I thought we'd make it through the first ten minutes, at least. I don't know how to handle this."

"Can I just kill them all now?" Kaden asked, his lips twisting up into a wry smile.

"No. We need to get them to listen to each other rather than pointing fingers. I have to fix this... Somehow."

I sat and listened to them bicker for a few moments. If only I could make them all shut up for a minute. I remembered our time with the Libra pack, when Ethan had muted them all at once so he could get a word in edgewise. I searched for the mute button, and blessed silence settled in. They kept shouting for a few moments, but slowly each alpha realized that it was useless, that no one could hear them except themselves. They sat back one at a time, though some of them glared at me and made gestures for me to unmute them.

"This is what the Sun Witches want," I said slowly, staring into the camera. "We heard it from Roxandra's own mouth. They want us to fight amongst ourselves so we can never unite and take them down. They'd let us rip each other apart just to protect themselves. We have to be better than this. How are we supposed to defeat the Sun Witches when we can't even get along for ten minutes?"

I paused, letting the words sink in. Kaden rested a hand on my knee, out of sight of the camera, and gave me a nod to continue. He trusted me to lead them, as his equal in every way, and it gave me the strength to go on.

"The only way we'll ever be free is to remember who the

real enemy is, and to unite against them. And if you let me explain, I have a plan to do it." When the other alphas seemed to be listening, I continued. "As you saw in the interrogation, Roxandra said the blessing spell that keeps our wolves locked away, among other things, can be removed. It took a lot of time for us to figure it out, but we did it. Jordan and I are no longer mated, and we're completely free of any Sun Witch magic now."

The Virgo alpha, an older woman with kind eyes, raised her hand. I unmuted everyone, and she asked, "How?"

I took a deep breath. They weren't going to like this. "The powers of a Sun Witch and a Moon Witch can be combined to break the spell."

"A *Sun Witch?*" Amos asked. The rest of the alphas looked equally unsure about the prospect.

"There might be a way around that," I said quickly, before I lost them. "I'm trying to learn how to do the spell on my own. The real problem is that it can't be cast on a large group, not without something to amplify the magic. Something like the staff Evanora used at the Convergence. If I can get that, I can use it to cast the spell on a large number of shifters at once."

"How can we get the staff away from Evanora when she has the ability to take control of us?" Dasan, the Scorpio alpha, asked.

Ethan spoke up. "We were able to get a few moonstone necklaces from the Moon Witches." He pulled one out of his shirt. The rest of the alphas looked at it with varying degrees of disbelief and apathy. "Not enough for all the alphas, but it's a start."

"There might be another way," I said, before the alphas started arguing again. "I've been studying an old book that the Moon Witches had, and it talks about star magic, the magic we all have as Zodiac Wolves. If all thirteen packs align during the new moon, we can use this star magic to possibly remove the Sun Witch magic."

"What does that mean exactly?" the female Gemini twin asked, looking at her brother. They were both gorgeous with golden blond hair and curious eyes, but they sometimes had a hard time agreeing on things.

"Yes, how do we align and use star magic?" her brother chimed in.

"I'm still figuring that out," I admitted. "But it's our best bet, and the only way we can do this without getting hold of Evanora's staff."

"This is how the Zodiac Wolves originally broke free from the slavery of the witches long ago," Kaden said from my side. "If we did it once, we can do it again."

"If there's any chance of breaking the spells on us, we have to try it," Theo said. "Until then, we're at risk of being controlled by the Sun Witches at any time, made to turn against the people we love. Look what they did to us at the Convergence. Look what they did to Jordan and Kaden. I don't ever want them in my head again."

Thank you, I thought. *Finally, someone gets it.* Some of the other alphas nodded, looking like they were seriously considering it for the first time.

"All of us should plan to meet during the night of the new moon to try it," Kaden said. "With your best warriors, of course."

Ethan looked thoughtful. "Yes, I think that's our best course of action right now."

"I agree," Jordan said, nodding. "Even if we can't make the star magic work, Ayla can break the blessing spells on the alphas one at a time. That will give us a huge advantage when we face the Sun Witches again."

"What happens if the Sun Witches attack us when we meet again?" Amos asked.

"Then we'll try to get the staff from them," I said. "We need to prepare for every possibility."

"If the Sun Witches come, we'll be ready for them," Wesley said.

"But what happens when the blessing spell is removed?" the Aquarius alpha asked. "Roxandra said our mate bonds were wrapped up in it. What will happen to them?"

I swallowed hard, knowing this next part would be difficult for some people to hear. "Yes, when we remove the Sun Witch blessing spell, you will probably lose your mating bonds too."

"I don't want my mate bond removed," the Capricorn alpha said. "I've been with my mate for thirty years. We have children and grandchildren together!"

The Aries alpha snorted. "Your female will always stand beside you. You're both stubborn as hell."

"Is there another way?" the Virgo alpha asked.

"Unfortunately, no," I said as gently as I could. I was

only now realizing how big a problem this might be. For wolves like Mira, they could decide not to have their blessing spell removed. But the alphas? They had no choice but to go through with this, or risk being controlled by the Sun Witches forever. "You might want to bring unmated warriors with you, so they're not affected."

Many of the alphas, the ones who had mates, looked stricken by this complication. I knew this was where we might lose them. It was a lot to ask of them, even if their mate bonds were fake, especially for the people who had been together so long. But they also had to realize by now that their mate bonds were likely created by the Sun Witches as a way to manipulate them and to breed them like dogs with the shifters they chose, either to emphasize a trait, or to create an alliance here and a rivalry there. It had to end.

"We have to do this for our people," Theo said slowly, as if he was coming to the realization himself. "I don't want to lose my mate either, but I trust that we will always be together, no matter what happens."

The Aquarius alpha nodded solemnly. "It will be a great sacrifice, but it will be worth it if we can all be free of the Sun Witches forever. It has to end here, with us."

Most of the alphas were nodding, but a few didn't look so agreeable, and I wasn't sure they would all go along with this plan. I cleared my throat. "The next new moon is about a month away, on February twentieth. That should give us some time to prepare. We just need somewhere to meet."

"We can meet in the Gemini pack lands," the male Gemini alpha said.

"No," the Aries alpha said, with a low huff. "I'm not doing this unless it's on neutral territory."

"The neutral territory we used before is controlled by the Sun Witches," Ethan pointed out.

A few alphas suggested some places but were quickly shot down. I wasn't sure what more we could do at this point. We were all together, but no one seemed willing to *work* together.

Finally, the Virgo alpha spoke up. "My extended family has some land in Texas. They're human, so the land is not connected to any of the packs, and it's far away from anyone's territory."

I raised my eyebrows at that. How did the Virgo alpha have humans in her extended family?

The other alphas discussed it a bit and seemed to agree that since the Virgos had always been neutral in the Cancer-Leo war, this was the best choice. Once it was decided, they left the call one by one, and then I sighed and dropped my head into my hands. Getting the other alphas to work together might be the hardest fight of all.

CHAPTER TWENTY-FIVE

AS THE DAYS PASSED, there was enough to do in Coronis that it was easy to forget my fears and doubts for the time being. I spent many long hours practicing my magic and poring over the two old books, trying to tease out all of their secrets. Every day, my sun magic grew stronger, but I wasn't sure I would ever be good enough to cast the unblessing spell, as I'd come to call it. I also had to settle into my new role as alpha female—starting with the pack celebration to honor me on the night of the full moon.

I peered out of my tent, admiring the village center. The snow had been cleared away, and in the center of the grass stood an archway decorated with twinkling lights, twirling vines, and dark blue flowers. Two walkways lined with the same flowers led up to the archway, one from my tent, and one from the other tent across the grass. More lights hung from the trees, and soft music played as Ophiuchus pack members gathered around, waiting for the ceremony to start at sunset.

I dropped the tent curtain, then smoothed the soft fabric of my gown, wondering if it was too much. I touched my hair next, checking if it had fallen out of place.

"You look pale," Stella said. "Are you feeling okay?"

I nodded and gave Stella an unconvincing smile. She and Larkin had helped me get ready earlier, and they'd done my hair up into an elaborate style that left my neck untouched to show off the beautiful blue-violet tanzanite necklace I wore. The December birthstone, Stella had told me, which made it precious to the Ophiuchus. This neck-lace had been her mother's, and Kaden had insisted that I should wear it tonight.

"Just nervous," I admitted. It seemed silly when I'd faced so many horrible and terrifying things in my life, but I couldn't help it. *What if they don't accept me? What if I'm not good enough to be their alpha female?*

"It'll be okay." She took a piece of my hair and tucked it back in place. "Everyone in the pack loves you."

"Do they? Just a few months ago, not everyone wanted me here. Tanner even challenged Kaden for the position of alpha because of me." I still remembered how many people had supported him, and many more who had been on the fence, unwilling to choose a side.

"That battle was a long time coming. You were just the catalyst. Besides, a lot has changed since then. You've won everyone over, and we all know you truly belong here with us." She squeezed my arms and grinned at me. "I'm excited for you to officially become my sister."

I blinked rapidly, my throat closing on a sudden wave of emotion. "Me too."

"I'm sorry to say this, since you're both having a moment," Larkin said, as she peered inside the tent. "But it's time to start."

I nodded and stood up straighter. "I'm ready."

Larkin moved close and slid a delicate silver tiara into my hair, which was decorated with the phases of the moon. "No, now you're ready."

I held up a small hand mirror to admire myself. A crown fit for a Moon Witch and a necklace made for an Ophiuchus. It was perfect. "Thank you so much for all your help."

"It's what family does," Stella said softly, and then motioned me toward the edge of the curtain. "Now go, before Kaden comes over and bites me for letting you take so long."

I moved to the curtain and inhaled deeply, steadying myself. I'd faced enemy wolves, Sun Witches, and vampires. I could face the Ophiuchus pack too.

I stepped out of the tent and the shifters closest to me fell silent. As more pack members realized I was there, the silence spread, except for a few gasps that could be heard. I couldn't blame them for being shocked. I looked like a completely different person tonight, wearing a silvery gown that appeared to be spun from starlight. The bodice hugged my breasts but dipped low between them, showing off the

Ophiuchus mark above my heart, while the skirt draped gracefully to the ground.

From across the grass, Kaden emerged from his own tent, wearing a black tuxedo that fit him perfectly, with a bow tie the same color as my necklace. He looked so handsome in that moment that my heart did a somersault in my chest. Sometimes I still couldn't believe that he was mine.

Kaden met my gaze from across the lawn, his eyes raking me up and down, and my body flushed with heat. Seeing the appreciation in his gaze gave me a confidence boost, and I used that to start walking forward.

The flower-lined walkways led us to the arch, and to each other. As we met under the twinkling lights and blue flowers, we stared into each other's eyes for a few heartbeats, and I could see everything I felt reflected back to me. I sensed his emotions too, pulsing through the mate bond. Love, desire, happiness, and a sense of rightness and contentment.

Kaden reached his hand out, and I took it, my pulse racing. He twined our fingers together, pulling me closer, and my anxiety melted away. My heart was overflowing with the love I had for Kaden, and it felt so right to be here, doing this in front of everyone.

Kaden stared into my eyes, but he raised his voice so everyone in the pack could hear him. "From the moment I met Ayla, I knew she was my mate. I didn't want to admit it at first, but I couldn't deny it either. Though our enemies tried everything they could to keep us apart, our destiny was to be together, and we fought for it with every breath we took. Not even death could keep us apart, and I know we will get through everything we face next, as long as we're together. I present her now to the pack, as not just my alpha female, but as my equal in all things."

Tears filled my eyes and I tried to blink them away. I didn't want to cry in front of everyone, but I hadn't expected Kaden to give a speech like this. His words meant more to me than I could ever express, but I knew he could feel it through the bond between us, which seemed stronger than ever tonight.

He looked over at me, and I knew it was my turn. I'd had an entire speech prepared, which I'd practiced over and over to myself, but all the words disappeared in the jumble of nerves and love I felt toward Kaden and the entire pack.

The Ophiuchus pack—my pack—waited patiently, and I gazed out at them. Their eyes were trained on me, but I didn't see a single hostile face. Some were neutral, but almost everyone was smiling, proud and happy for their alpha and his mate. Stella was right. I'd won them over.

I swallowed, bolstered by the sudden burst of confidence, and then raised my voice so it would be heard by everyone. "Kaden took me in when I had no pack, no home, and no family. He trained me, protected me, and made me one of your pack. He taught me that love was possible, even when it was hard, and I know that the trials we've been through have only made us stronger because we got through them together. I'm honored to be his mate and your alpha female, and I swear to always serve the Ophiuchus. I will do everything in my power to make sure that our lands are kept safe, and that we have the peace we deserve."

Love from Kaden flared through the bond, along with pride. He pulled me closer and pressed his lips to mine, kissing me in front of everyone. All around us, the pack started to howl, tilting their heads up toward the night sky as they celebrated their two alphas. The sound washed over me, sinking deep into my soul, and I knew they were truly accepting me as Kaden's partner.

The howls died down and the ceremony ended with Kaden leading me away from the arch and into the dark forest. It was part of the ceremony, he'd explained, a throwback to the old days when the alpha would take his female into the woods and ravish her. As soon as we were out of sight, the pack began to cheer, and Kaden pressed me against a tree and kissed me harder.

"They're happy," Kaden said, as he nuzzled my neck.

"So am I," I said. "I'm glad they accepted me."

"I would have challenged anyone who didn't." His mouth brushed across my skin. "And you know I would have won."

I laughed and shook my head. "I have no doubt."

His hands trailed down my gown, gathering the fabric to lift it up. "Now, can I fuck you against a tree in this dress, or should I remove it first?"

"Later," I said, pushing him away with a smile. "We can't miss our own party."

"Fine," he grumbled. "I could use some food. I'll need fuel for everything I have planned for you tonight."

"Is that a threat or a promise?"

"I'll let you decide that." He pinched my ass through the dress with a wicked grin, before leading me out of the forest.

A few howls welcomed us as we joined the party. Food had been brought out and set on tables, along with all kinds of drinks and alcohol. Loud music played from speakers, and people were already starting to dance. A few pups raced through the grass, playing and nipping at each other, and I smiled as I watched them go. Kaden was pulled away by Clayton, Jack, and Dane, while I headed for the food table, where I spotted my friends.

Harper gave me a congratulatory slap on the back. "Welcome to the pack," she said, grinning. "Again."

I gave her a hug. "Thank you."

Stella was practically vibrating at Harper's side. "Can I give you another hug? Our first one as sisters?"

I rolled my eyes. "You've been my sister for months now. But yes, go ahead."

Stella let out a squeal and proceeded to try to squeeze the life out of me. I laughed and patted her back, and then Larkin wanted to hug me too, and soon all of us were one big mess of laughter and tears.

"Come on, let's dance," Stella said, dragging me away from the food, which I'd never even gotten a chance to try.

Time passed quickly, and the full moon shined brighter as we danced to some music, while pack members stopped by to give me personal congratulations. I'd never been filled with so much joy.

As the party wound down, I finally got to sit down and

eat a proper meal, though I wasn't sure Kaden ever got a chance to rest. Every single person in the pack wanted to talk to him, even if they were still a little shyer with me.

Then the music changed to a slower song, and Kaden grabbed my hand and pulled me into his arms. "Dance with me."

"I don't know how," I protested.

"Me neither. We'll figure it out together." He touched the necklace above my breasts as we swayed in each other's arms. "Have I told you how fucking stunning you look yet?"

"I don't think so," I said. "You'd better say it again to make up for that mistake."

"Ayla, you're so beautiful, I can't believe you're real. But if this is a dream, I never want to wake up from it."

The sincerity in his words made me speechless for a moment. "You're not so bad yourself."

"Oh, 'not bad'?" Kaden asked, but I could hear the teasing note in his voice. "That's the best you've got?"

"What do you want me to say, that you look so good in that tuxedo that I'm dying for you to bend me over one of these tables and fuck me in front of everyone?"

Kaden let out a soft growl, his hands gripping onto my hips tighter. "Don't tempt me."

"That's why I didn't say it."

"Mmm, but now it's out there, and it's all I can think about. That was cruel."

I slid a hand down his chest. "When we get back, you can punish me."

"We can take turns," he said with a small grin.

I was about to reply, when every hair on my body stood on end, and warning bells sounded in my head. I jerked away from Kaden, looking around. "Something's wrong."

"It's the wards." His face turned hard, and he yanked off his jacket, preparing to fight. "They've been broken."

"No," I whispered, filled with dread. Not tonight. Why did they have to attack tonight?

"Prepare for an attack," Kaden shouted, and the music cut off sharply.

People cried out all around us as the news quickly spread. Parents scooped up their children and sprinted toward their houses, and the fighters gathered around me and Kaden.

"Sun Witches?" Jack asked, looking on edge. Before Kaden could answer, someone sounded the alarm bell. The rest of the shifters who couldn't fight hurried to get to safety. I had an awful sense of déjà vu. The last time this happened was when the Leos had attacked, months ago.

"Not just Sun Witches," Larkin said, her eyes closed. She'd done something to the wards, I remembered. A new spell, that allowed her to sense more than just witches. "A large group of vampires. They're coming. Fast."

Kaden and our warriors shifted, and I yanked off my dress and set it aside, not wanting it to get ruined, before I joined them on four paws as a wolf. Larkin flew up above us, creating a shield to protect us from any Sun Witch attacks they might throw at us. It was so quiet without the music playing, without the laughter and the merriment that had existed just a few minutes ago. Why did the Sun Witches have to ruin every good thing in my life?

We waited, tense and unsure, as the forest rustled around us. There was almost no warning, just the slightest noise in the bushes to my left, and then the vampires arrived. They swarmed us, but Kaden had been training our warriors over the last few days with new techniques specifically designed to defeat vampires, and we sprung into action.

Our wolves fought with their teeth and claws, tearing through the ranks of the vampires with brutal efficiency. The vampires attacked with equal ferocity, moving quickly and gracefully, striking at the werewolves with their sharp fangs and nails. The Sun Witches stood to the side, working together to break Larkin's shield with a burst of heat.

I summoned my moon magic to blast them, but two of the vampires circled around me, moving so fast it was hard to tell them apart. I jumped back from an attack that took some fur off my back, then let loose a stream of magic from my mouth. The vampires stumbled back, momentarily stunned, but I knew it wouldn't stop them for long.

But Kaden was there by my side, and he leaped on the closest vampire and took it down with a spray of blood. With his powerful jaw, he rendered flesh and bone with ease, driven by an animalistic rage to kill the vampires invading his land. I felt it too, that primal urge to tear apart the vampires, and this time I didn't hold myself back.

Yet no matter how many vampires we took down, more surrounded me, their nails reaching out to grab me. The Sun

Witches aimed magic at me too, but Larkin managed to keep them at bay.

You're their target, Kaden said, his blue eyes meeting mine for a second, before he leaped on another vampire that got too close to me.

A bolt of sun magic stuck me then, so hot it felt like fire burning my fur, and it knocked me down. A vampire was on top of me instantly, and all I saw was a flash of fangs coming for me. I roared and grew spikes of ice from my fur, impaling the vampire on them, then threw him off me. Another vampire grabbed me by the tail and yanked me toward him, while another burst of heat slammed into me.

With a fierce roar, Kaden threw himself in front of me, and the vampire's claws sliced into him instead of me. The shock of seeing the vampire hurt my mate pushed me into my own frenzy, and I tore the fucker's head off with my teeth. I didn't even know what I was doing until the red haze cleared, and I spat the blood from my mouth and saw the head rolling away. I went for the Sun Witch next, but she disappeared in a poof of smoke, abandoning the vampires to their final deaths.

While the other shifters took down the remaining vampires, I rushed to my mate. We both shifted back, and blood seeped from deep gashes in his side where the vampire had clawed him.

"Ouch," he said dryly.

I kneeled beside him and examined his wounds. "You idiot. You could have been killed."

He shrugged, although his face clenched with pain as he did so. "I'd gladly die again to keep you safe."

"Don't you dare." I leaned down and licked a path along his wounds. The Ophiuchus healing saliva kicked in immediately, stitching the skin back together before my eyes. It wouldn't be a complete fix, but it would help him heal faster.

When it was done, I sat back and gazed sadly at our home, once again ravaged by war. The smell of blood and death filled the air, and the bodies of fallen vampires littered the ground, mixed in among trampled blue flowers. Tables of food were overturned, and the archway had been shredded to pieces. One of the string lights had been torn from a nearby tree and was flickering on and off.

Our wolves let out a chorus of triumphant howls, their fierce battle cries echoing through the forest. It was a relief to see that none of them had fallen, but it still didn't feel like a victory.

CHAPTER TWENTY-SIX

WHEN HORRIBLE THINGS happened in life, sometimes there was nothing to do but take a deep breath and keep going, no matter how hard it seemed. I knew that better than anyone.

I thought about that as I took another bite of my sandwich, while Stella and Larkin argued about the plot of a book they'd just finished reading.

"Is it really enemies to lovers though if they always secretly want each other?" Larkin asked.

"Definitely," Stella said. "You can hate someone and still want to fuck him."

"I suppose so," Larkin replied, her voice thoughtful. "The sex does seem to be hotter when they finally do it, anyway."

Harper shot me an amused glance from across the table. "Maybe I need to start reading these books."

I laughed out loud. When Stella had invited me to lunch, I'd almost turned her down, but she'd demanded I take a break and join my friends. It had been a few days since the celebration-turned-battle, and though we'd all recovered from the attack, it had only pressed upon me that it was more important than ever to figure out how to break the blessing spell. The new moon would be here soon, and the other alphas were relying on me for a solution.

I'd been working nonstop, either practicing my sun magic or reading the section of Celeste's book over and over again until all the words blurred together into nonsense. I'd even given the book to Larkin for a second opinion, but she couldn't uncover anything more than I'd already found.

This morning I'd set a bush on fire accidentally with my magic and nearly had a complete meltdown over it. That's when Stella had dragged me out of the forest, telling me that getting upset about it wasn't going to change anything, and that I needed to take a break so I wouldn't spend the weeks leading up to the new moon working myself to sickness. I'd fought her at first, saying that I didn't have time to take breaks, but she'd been firm. Now I was glad that she'd been so insistent. For the first time since the attack, I found myself smiling and relaxing.

We were at Stella and Larkin's new house, sitting in the little nook that had just enough space for all of us to eat lunch. They'd quickly turned the cottage into a cozy home, and though it still needed a lot of work, the place had plenty of charm. Sure, the kitchen and bathroom looked like something from the eighties, but the cottage had two bedrooms and a living room with windows that looked out onto a little stream and a large, ancient tree filled with birds even at this time of year. But the part that Stella loved most was the random splashes of paint in the house, proof that her mother had once worked in here, creating some of the beautiful art that now hung in my house. My favorite was a painting of two wolves walking through the snow with two little pups at their side. It took my breath away every time I saw it, filling me with both sadness and hope. I wanted that future with Kaden, more than anything. But we would never be safe until the Sun Witches were defeated. The attack on our lands had proved that much.

"You're quiet, Ayla," Larkin said, breaking me free from my thoughts. "Is everything okay?"

"Sorry," I said. "I'm fine. Just frustrated. My sun magic has come along, but I'm still not good enough to do the unblessing spell. Our only other option is to get the alphas to align, but we still have no clue what the book means by that, or what exactly it will do if we do succeed."

"I'm sorry I wasn't able to get anything else out of the book," Larkin said, sounding a bit more subdued than she had a few moments ago.

"It's not your fault." I mentally slapped myself. She'd been so happy talking about her romance novels, and here I was, bringing her down because of my own inability to figure this out.

"There has to be an easy answer," Stella said. "It can't be too complicated, or they would have explained it in greater detail in the book. It must have been obvious to them, right? And if the alphas did it years ago, they should be able to do it now."

I sighed. "If only we could go back and ask one of those wolves what they did, this would be a whole lot easier."

"Maybe you can." Harper set her sandwich down. "You know that Dane can look into the past using a pool of moonlight, right? It's his Moon Touched gift. Maybe he can help you."

I'd heard about Dane's gift, though I'd never seen him use it in person before. "But this happened a long time ago. Centuries, even. Can he see that far back?"

"I'm not sure. I don't think he's ever tried." Harper shrugged and took another bite of her sandwich. "Might as well give it a shot. I'm sure he'd be willing to help you."

"I'll take any help I can get at this point." My shoulders relaxed a little. I wasn't going to get my hopes up too high, but at least I had something else to try. I flashed the girls a warm smile. "Now tell me more about this book you were reading. Why are they enemies?"

"He's an evil fae king, and she's the assassin sent to kill him, but when she tries, they end up in bed instead," Larkin said, getting excited once more.

"Naturally," Harper said. "Damn, I just hate when that happens to me."

"Same," I agreed. "Although I've always been a sucker for a bad boy."

"Especially one with a tragic backstory," Stella added, pressing a hand to her heart dramatically.

"Is that what you're into?" I nudged her with my elbow. "I think I know a few of those."

She flushed bright red. "Not in real life. I just want a nice guy with no drama."

"Like Ethan?" Harper asked, not noticing how Larkin's eyes widened before she quickly looked away. "Did you two get it on after the Christmas party? I heard him invite you to his room."

"No." Stella ducked her head. "Nothing happened between us."

Harper grinned, oblivious to the tension. "Too bad. I've always wanted to know if he has more tattoos under those suits of his." She finished her sandwich and leaned back. "I need some of these books to read. It has been way too long since I've gotten laid."

"I think Ayla's the only one having any luck there," Stella said dryly, and I tried to look as innocent as possible.

"No shit. I think everyone in the pack has heard them by now." Harper waggled her eyebrows. "But you don't need a mate to have some fun."

I rolled my eyes, but I couldn't stop smiling. It was fun to joke around with them, almost like everything was normal, although I couldn't help but notice the wistful look on Larkin's young face. Being stuck in a child's body had prevented her from ever having a relationship, even though she wanted one more than anything. Romance novels were her only way to experience that sort of thing, for now, anyway. As long as she stayed on Earth she'd eventually grow into her body properly, and then I had no doubt that plenty of men would be interested in her. The problem was that a certain Libra alpha would likely find a mate before then, especially if I was able to remove the blessing spell on him. But Larkin had to know that already, so there was no point bringing it up. Someday she would find the right match, I was sure of it.

Harper took a long sip of water. "This has been fun, but I should head back out. Kaden's ordered us to double down on our training in preparation for the new moon, and he'll growl at me if I'm late."

"How is training going?" I asked, as she put on her jacket.

"Good. Now that we've had more experience fighting vampires, we have a better idea of what to expect. But some of our wolves are still too slow."

"It's tough to match a vampire's speed," I said.

"True. The real problem is that some kind of frenzy takes us over when we're near them, and it becomes hard to remember our training. Kaden's hoping if he drills it into us over and over, it'll be like muscle memory."

"I had no idea it was so bad," Larkin said. "Do you all feel that way when they're near?"

Stella nodded. "There's some instinctive urge to kill them deep inside of us. No one seems to know why."

"It must be an evolutionary thing." I shrugged. "After all, I even feel it around Killian and I know he's not going to harm me."

"Wolves were enslaved by the witches to fight vampires, long ago," Larkin mused, her gaze far away. "It must have something to do with that."

"Probably." Harper waved as she headed for the door. "Thanks for lunch. Let's do it again soon."

While Stella and Larkin jumped into a discussion about the next book they wanted to read, I finished off my sandwich, thankful I'd taken the time to join my friends today. The only thing that would make it better would be if Mira was here too. She'd always gotten along well with the other girls, and I missed spending time with her. Hopefully, someday we'd all be able to get together again, though it would be harder once Mira had her baby. I made a mental note to call her later and check how she was doing.

We carried on a bit after lunch, but eventually I took my leave of them after helping with the dishes. Then I headed home to grab a bottle of water before venturing back into the forest and was surprised to find Kaden in the kitchen, instead of out training with Harper and the others.

He turned around with a phone to his ear. He wasn't smiling, and he looked especially grim, even for him. I paused in the doorway, waiting to hear what he said, fearing the worst.

"Understood. Yes." There was a long pause. "Thank you for calling me. Let me know if you hear anything else." Then he hung up, and set his phone on the counter with a frown.

"What is it?" I asked, as I walked up to him.

He reached for me and pulled me close, like he was relieved to see that I was safe. "That was Ethan. The Capricorn alpha is dead."

"Wilson?" I went cold, looking up at Kaden in horror. "What? How?"

"Vampires." Kaden's arms tightened around me. "Ethan doesn't know many details yet, but it sounds like a small group of them sneaked into the Capricorn pack lands late at night and assassinated the alpha. No one even knew it had happened until they were already gone."

"No," I whispered, leaning against Kaden. I couldn't believe we'd spoken to him only days before, and now he was gone. Sure, he'd always been cranky and sometimes harsh, but he'd been tough too, and a good leader, in his own way. "Wilson has been the Capricorn alpha my entire life. I thought he'd outlive all of us, to be completely honest."

"I'll never forget that he was one of the first alphas to ally with the Ophiuchus pack," Kaden said.

"Could that be why he was targeted?" I asked, straightening up. "He was one of our first and strongest allies, even if he often disagreed with us. Everyone respected him too."

Kaden nodded slowly. "If the Sun Witches want to make sure we don't unite, it would make sense to take him out, especially since their attack on us failed."

"But that means they might go after our other allies next." Fear shivered down my spine. Ethan, Jordan, and Wesley were all in danger. "We have to warn them."

Kaden sighed. "I'll call another Zoom meeting."

CHAPTER TWENTY-SEVEN

KADEN WALKED PROTECTIVELY beside me as we made our way into the forest that I knew like the back of my hand. Even though I was nervous about what we were about to do, it was a relief to get out of the house and breathe in the brisk night air. Especially after the day we'd had.

Earlier it had been a nonstop game of trying to get all the alphas on a Zoom call so we could get everyone's opinions on the latest attacks. Everyone was in a panic, demanding answers, and wondering if they were next. Our hasty agreement to all work together seemed even more strained than it had the first time around. The Capricorn alpha had held a lot of respect among all of the packs, and the other alphas were all shaken after seeing a pillar of the Zodiac Wolves fall so easily to vampires. Some questioned whether Wilson had done something specifically to anger the Sun Witches or the vampires. Others blamed me, since the vampires came after me first, but no one had any answers or solutions. The only thing we'd been able to agree on was that we needed to be careful and stay on the defensive in case of another attack. The best we could hope for was to figure out how to free the other alphas before the Sun Witches struck again. Hopefully tonight we'd get some of those answers we so desperately needed.

The forest was quiet tonight, and I suspected most of the animals were burrowing in whatever warm place they'd found. Overhead, the moon cast soft light through the trees, but a few clouds kept moving over it, muting its light.

"Will there be enough moonlight for Dane's magic to work?" I asked.

Kaden glanced up. "I think so. It helps that the full moon was only a few days ago."

"Does he need anything else for the spell? I brought the book, just in case."

"No, just tell him what you want to see, and he will try to show you." Kaden shrugged. "I don't know how he does it, and he's not exactly the most talkative guy."

No kidding. I'd never heard Dane say a word. He seemed to communicate with Harper somehow, maybe through some telepathic twin thing like the Gemini had, but otherwise he didn't speak. "Do you know why Dane never speaks?"

Kaden was silent for a moment as we walked around a fallen tree. "There are some humans who know about our kind and wish to hunt us. Very few, luckily, and even fewer who do it well. When Dane was five years old, he and his parents ran into two of these hunters in the forest. He watched his parents get killed in front of him, and there was nothing he could do except run. He never spoke again after that."

"How awful." I shuddered and rubbed my arms, though the chill was inside me. "Was Harper there too?"

"No, she stayed behind with her grandmother that day for some reason or another."

"What happened to the hunters?" I'd heard of human hunters before while living in the Cancer pack, of course. It was something my dad worried about since our lands were near Vancouver, but to my knowledge, no hunters ever bothered us during my lifetime. I'd started to think they weren't really a threat, but it sobered me to know that sometimes they were.

"My father led a hunt against the humans and stopped them from hurting anyone else," Kaden said. "But it was too late for Dane's parents."

We entered a small clearing with a pond in the center of it, and the trees overhead seemed to frame it, allowing a pool of moonlight to land perfectly on the smooth, flat water. It had been unusually warm today, maybe a sign that Helios was watching my progress, and I counted it lucky because the pond wasn't frozen over tonight.

Dane stood beside it, hands in his pockets as he gazed into the dark forest, his head slightly cocked as if listening to something. He turned toward us as we approached and bowed his head in respect.

I gave him a warm smile. "Thanks for meeting with us."

Harper emerged from the trees in the direction Dane

had been looking, her caramel-colored hair tied back in a tight ponytail. "Sorry, I thought I heard something, but it was just a mink. Can't be too careful these days."

"Indeed," Kaden said.

"How does this work?" I asked.

"You simply tell Dane whatever info you have, and he'll do his best." Harper exchanged a glance with her brother, their green eyes meeting in some kind of silent understanding. "Dane isn't sure it will work. He's never reached back further than his own lifetime. But he wants to try anyway."

"We appreciate any help you can give us," Kaden said.

I nodded and took out the book, opening it to the correct page. "I'm trying to figure out how the Zodiac Wolves broke free of slavery from the witches all those years ago. I have a book that describes a certain ritual where the alphas of all thirteen packs aligned under a new moon and were able to remove any magic on them. It sounds like the same ritual might work for us now, except I have no idea what exactly we're supposed to do or how it works. If I could just see the ritual they were performing, we might be able to replicate it."

Dane nodded, looking thoughtful. Harper glanced at him again before saying, "I think that will be enough information, but Dane is sorry in advance if it doesn't work."

"No need to worry," I said, though I was breathless at the thought of possibly getting answers tonight.

"It might help if he can hold the book," Harper said with a shrug.

"Of course."

Dane took the book carefully and knelt by the glass-smooth water that shone bright with the light of the moon. The rest of us gathered around the pond as he closed his eyes and drew the book in close to his chest. I could feel the magic in the air around him, like I could when Kaden used his power to become invisible, and I edged closer.

Dane sat for a few minutes with the book in his hand. The slight breeze rustling the empty branches froze, and the forest seemed to hold its breath as the magic gathered. When Dane opened his eyes, they glowed like the moon reflecting off the water.

I let out a breath, captivated. "Is it working?"

"I think so," Harper whispered.

I glanced back at Kaden, raising an eyebrow. He shook his head and jerked his chin back toward the water.

Dane dipped his hand into the water, scattering the moonlight across it. A pulse of moon energy went through him and into the water, making the pool glow even brighter for a few seconds before fading.

Something flickered in the depths of the pond, but then it was gone in a flash, so fast that it could have been a fish. Dane frowned and tried again, sending another pulse of moon magic into the water. It flashed again, before fading away. I reached for Kaden's hand and clenched it tight, suddenly terrified this would fail, and we'd be no closer to answers than we were before.

Dane looked up at Harper and shook his head, while my heart sank even more. Harper chewed on her lip, casting a glance at me, and then went to kneel beside Dane.

"Let me try to help," she said, taking his hand. "Like Larkin did with Ayla. I don't have a Moon Touched gift of my own but..."

Dane glanced at her and then nodded, his face determined. He did the magic again, and this time Harper's eyes glowed too. That flickering came back in the pond and lingered there, but it was still too blurry to really see anything. I glanced up at the moon and muttered a quick prayer to Selene, asking her to help her children.

With the next pulse of moon energy, the ripples spread across the pond and then went still. An image appeared on the water, so clear it was almost like watching a movie. A dark forest reflected back at us, but the trees were different, and there was no moon in the sky. Men began to emerge from between the trees, along with one woman. They each had a different pack mark on their chest, and they were naked as if they'd just shifted from their wolf forms. They gathered in the forest one by one, their faces somber, and a few of them spoke to each other, but there was no sound with the image. I looked briefly over at Dane and Harper, whose eyes were open and reflecting the moon's power once more. They seemed far away, as if they were back in the past with these people, rather than here in the clearing with us.

In the vision, other shifters emerged from the trees, creating a small crowd of people watching and waiting, but they were on the outskirts of the vision and a bit hazy. Once everyone was there, the alphas formed a circle, switching up their positions as they did so. It took me a few seconds to realize they were lining up in order of their astrological signs, starting with Aries and ending with Pisces. Once in place, they shifted into their wolf forms, all of them large and gorgeous, as alphas usually were, and took a few steps forward, tightening the circle. They stood shoulder to shoulder with their noses almost touching, their tails facing out toward the forest.

Then the Aries alpha lifted his head and started to howl. I couldn't hear it, but it sent chills down my spine all the same. Next to him, the Taurus alpha did the same, and then down the line they went. Each alpha added their howl to the mix, and about halfway through they all began glowing. Slowly at first, and the glow was different from that of sun and moon magic. This was like tiny little flecks of glitter in the air that kept getting bigger and brighter. By the time Pisces began to howl, the alphas were sparkling brightly like fireworks. This, I realized, was the magic of the stars.

Awe filled me as starlight began cascading from their pelts like water, sloughing off the sun and moon magic that held them captive. Each shifter seemed to spark a bit brighter as they continued howling up at the dark sky, their fur so bright and brilliant that I nearly shielded my eyes against it. I saw the moment the sun and moon magic gave way completely, setting them free all at once, leaving only the power of the stars behind. Then the magic spread out like a burst of starlight across the other gathered shifters before it faded away.

The alphas stopped howling as the power soaked back into their bodies. Only their eyes still glowed, sparkling with the power of star magic, and it tugged at something inside of my chest. I blinked back tears, moved by the sight of seeing them empowered and free from the enslavement they'd been subjected to.

The image slowly faded to black, the magic disappearing until it was once again just normal water. I hadn't realized I'd been leaning over the pond so far until my reflection looked up at me. I sat back, processing what I'd just seen. Something so simple, yet so powerful.

Dane and Harper relaxed their shoulders, their eyes no longer glowing. Both of them were breathing hard, their faces flushed. I knew how much magic could take out of someone, and sympathy for them went through me.

"Thank you," I said to them both, as Dane handed me the book.

"Was that helpful?" Harper asked.

"I think so." Excitement bubbled up in me as I thought about what we'd seen and what it meant for our future. "From what we saw, it all seems pretty simple."

Kaden shook his head. "Simple doesn't always mean easy."

"We should call the alphas tomorrow and let them know what we found." I ignored his surly tone, clinging to the tiny bit of hope inside me. "This might actually be doable. Surely they can form a circle and howl together, right?"

Kaden snorted. "You have a lot more faith in the other alphas than I do."

CHAPTER TWENTY-EIGHT

I LOOKED out at the ocean, letting the breeze hit my face. The horizon was far away, the midday sun sparkling off of the water in a mesmerizing pattern. It was nice to be back by the ocean, as it always was. The sound of the waves made me feel at peace, and I could finally think of them without thinking of my father.

Wesley also stared at the horizon, a small frown on his face. "Are you sure this is going to work?"

"No," I said truthfully. "That's why I need to practice it on you. You won't rip my throat out for not being able to do it."

"Well, those are pretty low standards," Wesley said dryly. "But I better get the brother of the year award for this."

"Careful," I said, grinning at him. "Those are fighting words if you let Jordan hear them."

Wesley snorted. "I'd like to see him even try to compete with me. Have I ever tried to kill you?"

"Yes, you did. During the winter Convergence."

He scoffed. "That doesn't count. I was under the control of the Sun Witches."

"Jordan could probably say the same for many of his crimes." I waved the Sun Witch journal at him. "Now stop distracting me so I can do this spell already."

He rolled his eyes but clamped his mouth shut. I opened the book and went over the spell for the hundredth time, making sure I knew it all by heart. I had no idea if this was going to work, but I had to try. The horror of my own brother attacking me was something I never wanted to relive, and we had to assume that the Sun Witches would try to stop us on the new moon. Removing the blessing spell from him now would keep him safe, and if it worked, I could do it on Ethan and possibly some of the other alphas too. Between that and the moonstone necklaces we'd gathered, we'd be able to keep the alphas out of Sun Witch control long enough for them to do the alignment spell.

Back home in Coronis, we'd been preparing for the new moon meeting of the alphas as it drew steadily closer. After learning what exactly alignment meant, Kaden and I got the alphas on Zoom again and explained what we'd seen. Some of the alphas seemed skeptical that it would work, others refused to trust anything in a vision, but they all said they would be there at the new moon, and that was enough. It had to be.

But as the days passed and we drew closer to the new

moon, I started to wonder if they would keep their word, especially as more alphas were attacked by vampires in other assassination attempts. Ethan was the first, but he'd been well prepared for such an attack, and he managed to fight them off. Scorpio and Sagittarius were next, but their alphas both survived with only minimal damage done to them. Our theory that the vampires were attacking the Ophiuchus allies seemed correct, and I worried for Wesley constantly. I suspected the only reason he hadn't been attacked too was because his pack was already in hiding on a remote island, and the vampires had no idea where he was.

I worried for Jordan too, but for a different reason. The Sun Witches didn't want him dead, but they did want him. But every time we talked, he assured me he was fine, and that he hadn't seen any sign of Roxandra or any other Sun Witch in his village. For now, they were leaving him alone.

Unfortunately, the Virgo alpha wasn't so lucky. The Virgos were healers, not warriors, and the vampires took her down with ease before disappearing into the night without a trace. It was another huge blow to our alliance, since the Virgos had always remained neutral in every pack war. Even at the Convergence, they'd made a point to heal the packs we'd considered enemies at the time. No pack would ever turn against them, and we relied on them for their kindness and wisdom. Not to mention, we'd been planning to meet at the Virgo alpha's land for the meeting. She had no daughters either, so we had no idea who would take over as alpha, or if we would still have a place to meet.

Everything had been thrown into chaos by one alpha's

death, which was exactly what the Sun Witches wanted. We'd had another Zoom call after the Virgo alpha had died and somehow it was even worse than the ones before. Everyone was in a complete panic, not listening to each other and resorting to shouting once again. The Pisces alpha accused the Aries alpha of telling the Sun Witches their plan, believing that was why the alphas were being attacked. The Aries alpha got so upset about the accusation that he'd ended the call and refused to rejoin. Others suggested we cancel the new moon meeting, but Kaden had slammed his hands down on the kitchen counter and said there was no way they were turning back now.

"This means we're on the right track," he'd insisted. "The Sun Witches wouldn't be trying this hard to stop us otherwise."

I'd suggested that the alphas go into hiding with some of their most trusted warriors until the new moon, if they could. Then I promised I would break the blessing spell from every alpha who showed up at the new moon, even if the alignment spell wasn't possible. But I wasn't sure very many of them cared, at this point. The fear of dying overshadowed everything else. I only hoped they'd see reason in the end.

Now, with only a few days until the new moon, I feared half of the alphas might not show up after all. Which is why I needed to make sure this spell worked, more than ever. If the alphas wouldn't align, this was our only hope.

"Are we going to do this?" Wesley asked.

I realized my eyes had glazed over as I'd been staring at

the book. "Sorry, I got lost in my thoughts. There's a lot going on right now."

"No kidding."

I went over the spell one last time and then closed the book and put it aside. It was now or never, and I had to trust that I could do this.

I reached for sun magic first, gathering it in one outstretched palm, and then called up my moon magic into the other hand, as sweat beaded on my forehead. I'd foolishly thought that learning to use sun magic would be the most challenging part of the spell. What I hadn't counted on was how difficult it would be to control both types of magic at once. They were opposite energies in every way and it was difficult to get them to play nice with each other. At first, they hadn't wanted to come out at the same time at all. I'd had to spend almost an entire week trying to get them to stop separating like oil and water every time I tried to use them together, but eventually I'd gotten it to work. I had a feeling it would never be easy though.

I moved my hands in the motions I could do in my sleep, and began chanting in ancient Greek. Wesley stood with his hands at his sides and waited patiently. The magic began to form around him...and then it slipped away. I swore under my breath.

"You got this," he said. "Keep trying."

"Thanks," I said, hoping that he was right. I closed my eyes and took a few deep, calming breaths before starting again. I had a feeling that my anxiety about being able to do it was most of the problem. I'd practiced the magic so many times by myself, and I'd finally gotten it to flow together, to work the way I thought it was supposed to. It worked when I was alone, so why couldn't I get it to work now for Wesley?

I'm scared of hurting him.

Maybe that was the problem. Subconsciously I remembered the pain I'd felt during Brea's attempts, and I didn't want to harm someone I cared so much about.

You won't hurt him, I told myself, and reached deep inside to find the dual wells of magic. I tried again, but this attempt didn't work either. I let out a frustrated shout that was carried away by the sea breeze.

Wesley put a hand on my shoulder. "It's okay. It's just me."

As usual, he knew exactly what was wrong. I hung my head. "I know. But after you, it's all of the other alphas. What if I can't even do it for you?"

"Ayla, I have complete faith in you. Now remove this damn blessing spell so I won't ever be forced to attack you again."

I nodded, his words filling me with determination. There was nothing I wouldn't do for the people I cared about. Wesley trusted me, and he was counting on me to help him. No one else could do this for him. It all came down to me.

I summoned the two types of magic again, and this time they flowed through me a little easier. Sunlight and moonlight wove a pattern across Wesley's skin, like a sweater being wrapped around him. He glowed all over as the dual magic settled into his body, and when his face grew taut, I knew it was working. I kept chanting and doing the hand gestures and footsteps, dancing around him slowly as I continued the spell. Then there was a burst of light and Wesley sucked in a breath, and I sensed the blessing spell breaking like a *snap*. Wesley stumbled a little, and I caught his arms to steady him.

"How do you feel?" I asked.

Wesley rolled his shoulders. "I don't know. Lighter maybe? Are you sure it worked?"

I shoved his arm lightly. "What happened to that complete faith?"

Wesley held his hands up. "I just thought it would feel more...dramatic."

"You didn't have a fake mate bond to break, so I guess the magic is more subtle. Try shifting and see if it feels any easier."

He began removing his clothes and I turned away to give him a modicum of privacy. As I did, my phone buzzed in my pocket. I pulled it out and saw Mira's name on the screen. I quickly answered. "Hey, Mira."

Mira sobbed into my ear, babbling something incoherent, and the smile fell off of my face instantly.

"What is it?" I asked, as fear spiked through me. "Is it the baby?"

"No, no. I'm okay. The baby is okay. But Amos..." A little sob escaped her. "He's dead."

"Oh, no." I closed my eyes as the sadness hit me hard. Amos had been a kind but strong leader, who'd always done what he thought was best for his people. Even though I'd asked him for help after my family was killed and he'd turned me down, he'd later come to regret that decision and had apologized to me. Since then, he'd been one of my strongest supporters, and had never balked on his alliance with the Ophiuchus pack. He'd been one of the first to acknowledge Kaden and the Ophiuchus, and without him, we wouldn't have been able to get the other packs to listen to us at all. And now he was gone.

"What happened?" I managed to ask.

"We wanted him to go into hiding, but he wouldn't do it." Mira sniffed. "The vampires came for him sometime in the early morning. We had guards posted, but they weren't enough."

I found myself nodding, even though she couldn't see it, of course. Like the Virgos, the Pisces were not warriors, but instead artists, fishermen, musicians, and so forth. They wouldn't have stood a chance against the vampires, which is why I'd hoped Amos would go into hiding.

"I'm so sorry," I said, unable to find any other words to express my grief. "He was a great man."

"Yes, he was." She let out another sob. "He was always so kind to me."

"Will his son become the new alpha?"

"No, he was injured badly during the attack trying to save Amos. He's recovering but he's declined the position of alpha. At least for now." She sniffed. "Aiden has been made alpha instead."

"Your mate?" I asked, sucking in a breath. I remembered that Aiden was Amos's nephew.

"I'm scared, Ayla. What if they come for him next?"

"He should be safe. They haven't attacked any pack twice, and the new moon is only a few days away. But he might want to go into hiding somewhere to be safe." I paused, opening and closing my mouth, trying to find a delicate way to ask the next question and failing. "Do you think you will be able to convince him to come to the meeting?"

Mira let out a shaky little noise. "Yes, he'll be there. The Pisces pack will uphold Amos's promise."

I closed my eyes, clutching the phone tightly. "Good."

"Tell Mira she can come to the Cancer pack if she's worried," Wesley said, from behind me. He must have heard the entire conversation, thanks to his shifter hearing. "We'll protect her."

"Is that Wesley?" Mira asked with a soft sigh. "Tell him I can't leave my pack, but I appreciate the offer."

I was certain Wesley could hear her, especially from the way he grunted in response. I spoke to Mira instead. "Stay strong. Just focus on keeping healthy and safe, okay? For your mate and for your baby."

"I'll try," Mira said. "But Ayla... I'm worried."

My hand trembled a little as I held the phone. "Me too."

CHAPTER TWENTY-NINE

KADEN WAS in the kitchen when I returned home, wearing an apron and wielding a chopping knife. I'd completely forgotten that tonight we were having dinner with our closest friends, since it was our last chance to be together before we began traveling to Texas. The journey would require a long plane flight plus a long car ride, so we had to leave a few days in advance to make sure we were there on time.

The sight of Kaden cooking usually made me smile, but I couldn't muster one as I took off my shoes and headed toward him. He turned and put down the knife, studying my face.

"What is it?" he asked. "Did it not work?"

It took me a second to realize what he was asking about. "It worked. Wesley is free."

"Then why do you look so miserable?"

"Mira called me. The Pisces alpha is dead."

"Damn." Kaden closed his eyes, his face twisting with grief. "Not Amos too."

He took me in his arms and held me close, and I clung to him as sorrow passed through us both. No words needed to be spoken. We both knew what a huge loss this was, both for us personally, and for the Zodiac Wolves as a group.

I pressed my face to Kaden's shoulder and let the tears flow. I cried not just for Amos, but for the other alphas who had died, all because we wanted to be free. I cried because the task ahead of us seemed even more impossible than ever, and time was running out. I cried because I knew the Sun Witches would never stop until we defeated them.

Kaden held me through it all, slowly rubbing my back. He must have sensed that I needed a good cry. For weeks, I'd been holding everything inside, trying to be strong for everyone else, but now it was like a dam had burst and the emotions all came pouring out. With Kaden, I was safe to feel them all, knowing he understood what I was going through.

When the tears stopped flowing and I regained control of myself, Kaden asked, "Is Mira okay?"

I wiped my eyes and nodded. "Physically, she's fine. But her mate is now the Pisces alpha, and she's worried for him."

"Understandable."

I gripped Kaden's shirt and looked up at him. "Are we making a huge mistake?"

"What do you mean?"

"What if we're wrong about bringing all of the alphas together? They're risking their lives for this, but what if the

ritual doesn't work?" I bit my lip as my thoughts kept spiral-
ing. "If they even show up. At this point, I wouldn't be
surprised if half of them stayed in hiding, and who could
blame them?"

Kaden stroked my hair. "The alphas will come. They're
scared, but they will come."

"How do you know?" I asked, feeling despondent.

"Because the thought of their children growing up as
Sun Witch slaves is more terrifying than anything else."

I shuddered at that. Now that Kaden and I were
mated, there was a very real possibility of us having children someday. I silently resolved that they would never
live in fear of the Sun Witches, and that I would do what I
could for the other packs too. Even if only a few of the
alphas showed up at the new moon, I would remove their
blessing spells one by one so they would be free. But that
would just be the beginning. If I had to travel to every
single pack over the next few years to free the other
wolves, I would do it. And if the Sun Witches tried to stop
me? Well, I had plenty of friends and family who had my
back.

I took a deep breath. "You're right. Whatever happens,
we'll deal with it. And we won't stop until all the Zodiac
Wolves are free. Even if we have to stop the Sun Witches by
ourselves."

Kaden pressed a kiss to the top of my head. "We're a
force of nature, with a love that burns like the stars. Who
could ever stand against us?"

I smiled up at him, my spirits bolstered by his support

and confidence, but our moment was interrupted when Stella breezed into the kitchen like she still lived with us.

"Get a room, you two," she said with a grin.

"Did you forget that you don't live here anymore?" Kaden asked, his arms still around me.

"Hey, you invited me over." She carried a covered casserole dish and set it down on the counter. "I even made your favorite potatoes."

"I guess you can stay," Kaden said.

Larkin arrived a few seconds later, with a lemon cake she'd baked. She looked at us and flushed. "Are we too early?"

"No, you're right on time," I said, pulling back from Kaden with a smile.

We'd decided to do a potluck tonight so everyone could share their favorites with the group. Kaden was making a classic roast beef as our main course, which smelled amazing, and while he checked it, I finished chopping the carrots and cucumber for the salad.

The others showed up a few minutes later. First Harper and Dane, with a huge bowl of pasta salad, then Clayton and Grant, with a tray full of butter tarts. I greeted each of them with a hug and a smile, my mood instantly brightening now that they were here.

Jack was the last to arrive, his arms full of beer and wine. "I can't cook, so I thought I'd make up for it by bringing booze. Lots of booze."

"Our hero," Harper said, taking some of the wine off his hands, while Dane helped with the beer.

Kaden pulled out the roast beef and sliced it, while Jack passed around beers, and Stella opened a bottle of wine. We arranged the food on the kitchen island, and everyone grabbed plates and served themselves, sampling a bit of everything. Our friends all seemed to be in good spirits, laughing and joking with each other as they sat at the dining table.

Their voices died down when Kaden stood tall and commanding at the head of the table. His gaze swept over his friends and family, his eyes shining with pride as he raised his glass of red wine.

"My brothers and sisters," he began, his voice strong and steady. "The new moon quickly approaches, and many of us will be leaving for the meeting of the alphas, while the others stay to defend our village in case of an attack."

This had been something we'd worked out with the alphas during our last Zoom call. All of the alphas would attend the meeting with ten of their strongest warriors, but the alpha's mates and the pack betas would stay behind. Not just for their protection, but to defend their pack lands in case of an attack while the alphas were away. I was the one exception to the rule.

"The Sun Witches will try to stop us," Kaden continued. "They want to make sure the other Zodiac Wolves never experience the freedom we've always had in the Ophiuchus pack. If they win, they will enslave the packs again, including ours. This is why we must fight." He met the eyes of every person at the table as he spoke. "Now I ask you all to raise your glasses and join me in a toast, to our pack, home of misfits, outcasts, and rebels, and to the family we have built here. Together, we are unstoppable, and I know we will emerge victorious."

"To victory," I said, raising my glass,

Everyone raised their glasses and echoed my sentiment, the excitement and camaraderie palpable in the room. I couldn't help but feel a sense of pride and belonging as I looked around the table at my pack members, my family, and my mate.

"And to hopefully finding mates once this is all over," Jack said with a grin. "Once all those other shifters are free, the rest of us might finally have a chance."

Harper laughed. "Yes, if we were going to be mated to anyone in this pack it would have happened by now. We need some fresh blood."

"Are you both so eager to be mated?" Grant asked, raising an eyebrow.

"Maybe not right away, but someday," Jack said with a shrug. "It's what a lot of the shifters are fighting for though."

I hadn't realized that was such a huge concern among the Ophiuchus, but it made sense. It was why Kaden wanted to join with the Zodiac Wolves in the first place, and why he'd been willing to do it through force if necessary. The pack did indeed need some new blood, and our people needed to find their mates to do that. Once the other wolves were free, they would have that chance.

"I just wish I could go with you," Stella said, deflating a little. Kaden had convinced her to stay behind to help protect Coronis in case the vampires or Sun Witches attacked. "I'm itching to kill a few vampires."

"We don't even know if the vampires will show up at the meeting," Clayton said. "For all we know, they might use it as a diversion to attack here again."

"I guess," she said with a sigh.

"Don't worry, I'll kill some for you," Harper said.

Jack downed the rest of his beer with a grin. "We've started a bet to see who can kill the most vampires. Right now, Dane is in the lead."

Dane looked proud at that, flashing a handsome grin, while Harper rolled her eyes.

"Just be careful without me there to watch your backs," Stella said.

"We've been training for months," Jack said. "We're not going to let those bloodsuckers get the best of us."

"Or the Sun Witches," Larkin said. "If they show up, we'll be ready for them."

As the night went on and the party began to wind down, I couldn't help but feel a sense of sadness that it was coming to an end. No matter what happened, things would change after tonight, for better or for worse. But then I thought about how far I'd come, from a scared Cancer outcast on the run from my mate, to the Ophiuchus alpha female with sun and moon magic in my veins. I had a mate I loved and respected, who treated me as his equal, and a pack that had become like family to me. The Sun Witches didn't stand a chance.

"Ayla, you're very quiet," Clayton said. "Is everything okay?"

I smiled at him. He'd been one of the first people in the pack to offer me kindness. "Yes, I was just feeling thankful for all of you. You've always been such good friends to me, even before I was in the pack."

Harper nudged me in the side, but her smile was gentle. "Don't get all emotional on us now."

"I can't help it. You all accepted me and helped me when no one else would. You've truly become not just my pack, but my family."

"You were always meant to be one of us," Stella said. "We all knew it from the moment we met you. Even if it took Kaden a while to admit it."

Kaden let out a grunt, and everyone at the table laughed. I suddenly had an idea, and I got up and grabbed my camera off a table near the front door.

"Let's head out to the deck and get a photo," I said, once I'd returned. "This might be the last time we're all together. I want to remember this moment."

"Don't be so dramatic," said Harper, as she tugged on her ponytail. "We'll come back victorious and will do this again."

"Yeah, and next time we'll have even more to celebrate," added Jack.

"I hope so," I said, feeling a lump form in my throat.

Everyone shuffled outside onto the deck behind the house and gathered together, while I worked on my camera, fiddling with the settings until I got the timer ready. I set the camera up on one of the outdoor tables, making sure everyone was in view. My friends grinned as they huddled together, making silly faces and laughing as I snapped a photo to test it.

"Here we go!" I pressed the button and quickly ran to get into the picture. Kaden held out an arm for me and I snuggled into his side and smiled as big as I could. Everyone else leaned in and grinned at the camera until it flashed.

I hurried over to look at the picture, making sure no one was blinking or making a weird face. To my relief, everyone was looking at the camera and smiling, their faces cheerful and their eyes bright. It was perfect.

I showed it to everyone, feeling the warmth in my heart expanding. We went back inside and poured some more wine, before tucking into the dessert. Everything might change after tonight, but for now, I was surrounded by my pack and the warmth of my home, and I knew that no matter what happened, we were all in this together.

CHAPTER THIRTY

KADEN SURVEYED the land in front of us with a steely gaze, and I couldn't help but feel a sense of unease as I did the same. The vast expanse of flat, dry ground stretched out before us, the only relief from the monotony being the occasional shrub or patch of tall, brown grass. It was much warmer in Texas than in Canada this time of year, and the sun cast a harsh light over everything and made the air feel thick and heavy. There was a sense of emptiness and isolation here, as if we were the only living creatures for miles. It was the perfect place for a battle, but it also made me feel small and insignificant. I couldn't help but wonder if this was where we would make our last stand.

A large farmhouse stood in the distance, with some horses grazing in a corral outside of it. They must have belonged to the Virgo alpha's human relations. We'd decided to stay as far away from the family as possible to avoid bringing them any trouble.

In the other direction, a small lake glistened, and some of the other packs had already set up a few tents nearby. It reminded me of my first Convergence, although on a much smaller scale, and I was relieved to see the symbols of the Libra and Cancer packs, among others. But there were still many packs missing.

Don't panic, I told myself. *It's only midday. The others will come.*

Our warriors began to gather around us, their faces focused and determined. They were all in their human form, but their eyes had taken on a fierce gleam, betraying their inner wolves. Every single one of them was ready to defend Kaden with their lives so he could perform the ritual, even though it wouldn't have any effect on them. They were already free, but they knew we would never have peace until the other wolves were free too.

"Jack, get a command tent set up and begin patrols," Kaden said, back in full alpha mode. He glanced at me, waiting for me to add my input. He really was trying to treat me like his equal.

"Harper, stay with Larkin while she sets up wards around the area. Kaden and I will greet the other alphas." I paused and glanced at Kaden. "Do you have anything else to add?"

"No, that all sounds good," he said with a small smile. "We'll meet back at the tent when we're done."

The other warriors nodded and the group split up as people went in different directions. Kaden and I headed toward the lake, where the other packs waited. Ethan and

Wesley were already walking toward our vans as we approached, and I was happy to see them, even though I'd visited them both recently. The day after I removed Wesley's blessing spell, I'd gone to Toronto to remove Ethan's too. Now they were both free, unable to be taken over by the Sun Witches and used like puppets ever again. They might even find their mates too, once all of this was over.

They both gave me a quick hug and shook Kaden's hand. "About time you two showed up," Wesley said with a grin.

"Kaden got us lost," I said, nudging Kaden with a grin of my own. He just grumbled in response.

"About half of the packs have arrived," Ethan said. "Capricorn, Sagittarius, Virgo, and Scorpio are here already. Plus our packs, of course."

"I'm sure the Leo and Pisces packs will be here soon, but the others..." I swallowed. They all said they would be here, but the assassinations had changed everything, and I wouldn't believe they were all coming until they stood before me.

"What do we do if they don't show up?" Wesley asked. "You said the spell needed all of the alphas to align."

"We'll try to do it with as many as we have," I said. "Maybe it will work."

"If the Sun Witches come, we'll try for plan B—getting the staff from Evanora," Kaden added. "Then Ayla can use it to remove the blessing from large groups of shifters at once."

Wesley cocked his head. "And if the Sun Witches don't come?"

"They will," Jordan said, as he walked up behind me.

Relief washed through me as I took him in. He looked tired, but also surer of himself, like having full control of his mind and pack again was doing wonders for his self confidence and mental stability.

"I'm so glad you made it," I said, hugging him as he came up to me. He shook hands with Kaden and Wesley, and gave Ethan a polite nod.

"The rest of the Leo pack is getting into position, and I brought a few of the rogue Sun Witches as well." He jerked his chin over his shoulder, and I saw four Sun Witches emerge from a van. Brea spotted me and raised her hand in a tentative wave. I waved back, pleased to see her again. She was here, willing to fight with us, and that was more than I'd ever thought possible. It gave me hope that the other packs would face their fears and join us too.

"We'll be ready for whatever happens," Jordan said.

"That's all we can do," Ethan said with a nod.

One of Jordan's warriors called him over, and he excused himself and went to speak with him. Ethan promised to meet with us later and headed back to the Libra tent. We were about to check on the Ophiuchus tent to see if it was ready, when Wesley gestured toward the Virgo tent.

"Come with me. There's someone I want you to meet."

The Virgos had found possibly the only patch of green grass in the entire area, and that's where they'd set up their tent. A young woman wearing a flannel shirt and jeans was speaking with two older women, who nodded at her before heading toward the lake.

"Hey, Wesley," she said, as we walked up to her. She flashed a friendly smile as she pulled her chestnut brown hair back into a quick ponytail. She was beautiful in a down-to-earth way, but there was something unusual about her too, but I couldn't put my finger on what exactly it was.

Wesley grinned at the woman. "Madison, this is my sister, Ayla, and her mate, Kaden, the alphas of the Ophi-uchus pack."

Her moss-green eyes widened. "Oh! I've heard all about you. It's so nice to meet you." She stuck out her hand. "I'm Madison."

As I shook her hand, I realized what was off about her. She was half human. Like I'd always believed myself to be.

"Madison is the new Virgo alpha," Wesley explained. "She's also the best healer in the pack. She's the one who saved my life after the Scorpios nearly killed me at the summer Convergence."

Madison slapped Wesley's arm playfully. "Don't hype me up so much. We're all good healers. I just happened to be the one who found you first."

"This is her family's land," Wesley continued. "She was kind enough to let us use it tonight."

She nodded, a flicker of sadness crossing her eyes. "I never expected to be alpha, but I hope to fill my aunt's shoes as best I can. Starting by honoring her promise to provide you the land for the ritual tonight."

I found myself both surprised and impressed that this

half-human had somehow become alpha. The Virgos must not have considered her an outcast, which made sense. They'd always been the most sensible and sympathetic pack, and the only one ruled by a woman alone. If any pack would be accepting of someone with mixed blood, it would be them.

"I'm sorry about your aunt," I said. "We were all devastated when we heard."

"Her wisdom and kindness will be greatly missed," Kaden added.

"Thanks. It's been quite a shock." She drew herself up straighter. "But I'll stand with you tonight, and the Virgos will help however we can."

Kaden and I visited the Sagittarius pack next to meet with their alpha, Theo. Now that three of the oldest alphas had fallen to vampires, he was one of the most senior alphas, and I guessed him to be in his fifties. His pack was preparing their bows as we approached since they usually fought in human form first. He gave us a warm smile as we approached and a friendly hug.

"It's so good to see you again," he said. "Especially in these dark times."

"Yes, we were relieved to hear that the vampires failed in their attempt on your life," Kaden said. The two of them had known each other for many years—the Sagittarius were once the only allies of the Ophiuchus pack, though they'd kept that fact a secret from the rest of the Zodiac Wolves.

Theo snorted. "They were no match for our arrows or our claws."

"How is Mae?" I asked, remembering his kind, funny alpha female.

"She is well, thank you." A crease formed on his forehead. "I must admit, I'm nervous about what will happen to us if we succeed with this ritual. I don't want to lose my mate bond with her. She is my everything."

"Have faith," Kaden said, resting his hand on his friend's shoulder. "She is your true mate, I know it."

Theo nodded, his face taut. "I pray to Selene that you are right. But even if you're not, I would still do the ritual. The only worse thing than losing my mate bond is being forced to turn against her through Sun Witch control. I could not live with myself if I hurt her in any way."

"That will never happen," I said. "Even if we fail tonight, I will remove the blessing spell from you myself. I swear it."

"Thank you, Ayla."

"Kaden..." a soft female voice said behind us.

Kaden stiffened at the sound. We both turned to see a beautiful woman with long black hair standing at the entrance of the tent. Eileen—Kaden's first love. She'd been an Ophiuchus once, until the mate bond had activated with a Sagittarius, breaking Kaden's heart at the same time. But then her mate had died in one of our fights against the Sun Witches. I hadn't seen her since.

"You are truly mated," she said, glancing between the two of us. There was no hostility in her eyes, only a lingering sadness that I didn't think had anything to do with us. "Congratulations. I'm happy for you."

"Thank you, Eileen," Kaden said. "What are you doing here?"

"I've come to avenge my mate." A little tremor of emotion ran through her. "And to protect my alpha." She glanced between Theo and Kaden. "Both of my alphas."

The sadness in her eyes touched something inside of me. Now that I'd been mated to Kaden, I understood the depth of her pain, to some degree. To watch your mate be killed in front of you, to lose that connection with him in an instant... It would be unbearable.

"You honor your mate," I said. "His death will not be in vain."

She nodded and gripped her bow tighter, before walking out of the tent. I let out a long breath, wondering if I would see her alive again.

As the sun dipped lower on the horizon, more packs arrived. First the Geminis, led by the golden-haired twins, followed by the Taurus pack, and then the Pisces.

As the Pisces got out of their vans, I left the Ophiuchus tent to talk to Aiden. When he'd been mated to Mira, I remembered thinking how lucky she was. Aiden was handsome and muscular, with hair the color of sand, though he looked a lot more tired than I remembered. Then again, everyone seemed more tired lately.

He smiled at me in greeting, though he looked a bit nervous. "Ayla. It's good to see you again."

"Same to you. I'm sorry to hear about Amos's death. He was a good man, and I will miss him a lot. But I'm glad that you decided to uphold his word."

"Of course," Aiden said, with a wry smile. "I'm pretty sure Mira would have killed me if I let you down."

"You can set up next to the lake if you'd like," I said, motioning over to the banks. "It might be a good place for your people, in case of an attack." The Pisces pack could breathe underwater, like all water signs, but they could also swim faster than anyone in the water. On land, they were not fighters, but get them in the water, and they were unstoppable.

"Good idea." He waved over one of his men and said a few quiet words to him. The Pisces nodded and headed off to unload the van.

"How's Mira?" I asked.

"Very pregnant," Aiden said with a soft smile. "But healthy. Worried, of course. She misses you."

"I miss her too. I want to come visit, once this is all over."

"She'd like that." He ran a hand through his hair. "I just hope we make it through this."

"We will," I said, trying to sound confident.

"You know, I was never supposed to be alpha, but no one else wanted to come here. Honestly, I don't think I'm cut out for it."

"The fact that you're here proves you have the strength and courage to be alpha." My voice softened and I gave his arm a squeeze. "I know Mira is proud of you."

He sighed. "What will happen if you succeed in removing the blessing? Will I still be mated to her?"

"I don't know," I said, wishing I could lie to him.

Aiden let out a shaky breath but then shook his head. "I

believe we'll still be mates. I love Mira and I want to be with her. We'll raise our child together as a family, no matter what happens after tonight."

"Mira feels the same," I assured him. "She loves you and wants to be with you. No matter what."

His face brightened at that, and I was glad I'd been able to take away some of his worries. "Thank you, Ayla."

He went to help his packmates get ready, while I returned to the Ophiuchus tent. The sun was nearing the horizon, and there was still no sign of the Aries pack. It was a miracle that the other eleven packs had shown up, but we couldn't do this with only twelve. We needed all thirteen. But I was starting to lose hope that they would come.

As I stepped into the tent, Kaden immediately came up to me with a plate of food. "Here. Eat this. You need your strength."

"Thank you," I said, taking it from him. It had a sandwich and some chips, but I was too nervous to really taste any of them. I ate all the same, because Kaden was right. I needed as much energy as I could muster in case I needed to use my magic tonight.

The other Ophiuchus were using this time to eat too, although I heard Jack tease Larkin about the fact that she'd brought a book to read. "What?" she asked, shoving him away playfully. "We knew we'd be doing a lot of waiting around."

"Jack's just jealous he didn't think of the idea himself," Harper said.

Kaden snorted. "Jack, read a book? Are we talking about the same guy?"

"Hey, I read Harry Potter as a kid," Jack said with a laugh.

"That doesn't count," Harper said. "Everyone's read that."

"What's Harry Potter?" Larkin asked, which just made everyone laugh harder. She grinned, pleased to be part of their joking around, and warmth filled me as I glanced around the tent at my friends.

But when Ethan poked his head inside our tent to tell us the sun had set, the warmth instantly evaporated as I remembered why we were here.

"It's time."

CHAPTER THIRTY-ONE

THE OTHERS FILED out of the tent to get into position, but Kaden and I stayed behind, sharing a long look. Anticipation made my heart beat faster, and even though I'd been waiting for this night to come, now that it was here, I didn't feel ready.

Kaden pulled me close and I buried my face in his chest and wrapped my arms around him, listening to the steady beat of his heart. He pulled back and cupped my head in his hands, so many emotions swirling in his eyes, before he leaned in and kissed me. I closed my eyes and melted into him once more, trying to engrave this moment on my memory forever.

"You're not allowed to die again," I said, trying for stern. It came out shakier than it should have.

"Don't worry. Once was enough." The smile dropped from his face, and he stroked my cheek with his thumb. "You be careful too. I can't lose you again."

"You won't," I whispered. "I love you."

"I love you too," Kaden replied and squeezed my hand once more before letting it go.

He stripped out of his clothes and folded them neatly in a pile. I left my clothes on, but grabbed my Moon Witch robes, thick purple and embroidered with moons, and pulled them around myself. Kaden would be performing the ritual in the circle with the other alphas, but me? I was there in case everything went wrong.

We exited the tent side by side. The sun had completely set by now, leaving the night pitch black. Since there was no moon, only the light of the stars and our shifter senses let us see the dry land around us. We walked to the lake, to a space without any tents where the other alphas were gathering. They were all naked and moved silently to stand together in a group, while the warriors spread out around us. Our Sun Witch allies waited on one side, wearing pale yellow robes, while Larkin stood on the opposite side, wearing her own purple robe. She eyed the other witches with distaste and suspicion.

The alphas all looked toward me as I approached. I counted their numbers and my heart sank. There was still no sign of the Aries alpha, and I didn't think this would work without him. But we would still try.

Kaden nodded at me, but as I stood before them, my heart pounded in my chest. I had never been one for public speaking, but I knew that this moment was crucial. The fate of all of the Zodiac Wolves was riding on this moment.

"Thank you all for coming," I said, making eye contact

with each alpha one by one. "I know it wasn't an easy decision, but you've proved you are truly alphas with your
bravery and selflessness."

Many of them bowed their heads in response, their eyes
flashing with determination. Others looked wary, shifting
from one foot to the other, or gazing out into the darkness as
if worried about an attack. But they all stayed.

"Tonight we'll do whatever it takes to free the Zodiac
Wolves from the invisible shackles the Sun Witches have
chained us with for generations," I continued, keeping my
head high. "There is a very strong chance that they will try
to stop us, but we have trained and prepared for this
moment for weeks. They may think they have the upper
hand now that they've gotten the vampires to do their dirty
work, but they do not know the power of our packs. If our
enemies do come, we will fight for our families, for our children, and for the generations to come. We will fight for our
freedom with every last breath, so they will never be able to
control us again. We are strong, we are united, and we will
stop the Sun Witches for good. And we will win."

The alphas howled in response, their voices rising to the
stars in a fierce and united cry. The warriors around us took
up the howl too, and I felt the energy and determination of
the other shifters fill the air.

As the howls died down, Larkin moved among them,
handing out moonstone necklaces to each alpha who
didn't have one already, to protect them from being
controlled in case Evanora arrived with her staff. Larkin
had visited my mother again the other day, and the Moon

Witches had managed to provide us with a few more of the gems. Combined with the ones we'd already received, it was just enough to protect all of the alphas. Unfortunately, the Moon Witches still refused to do anything more to help us.

Larkin gave me the extra necklace, which was meant for the Aries alpha. I sighed and put it around my neck, prepared to hand it over in case he showed up after all.

Once the alphas wore their moonstones, I asked, "Are you all ready and willing to align?"

Jordan stepped forward first. "The Leo pack is ready."

Wesley spoke out next. "Same for the Cancer pack."

I smiled at both of them, grateful that they were both here and on the same side. Ethan joined in next, and one by one, the other alphas stepped forward. A few of them hesitated, but none of them backed out.

Kaden was the last alpha to speak. His eyes met mine with love and determination. "The Ophiuchus pack is ready and willing."

I nodded. "Now form a circle in the order of your astrological signs and we will begin."

The alphas began to move, but there was an awkward pause as the Taurus alpha looked at the space where the Aries alpha should be. He covered his reaction easily enough, but I could tell that everyone was on edge from the missing alpha. They shuffled about, forming the correct order, and I checked it to make sure no one was out of place.

Once they were all standing in a circle in the right order, I nodded. Each alpha shifted at the same time into their wolves, and the sight of so many large, gorgeous wolves of all different colors was so beautiful it took my breath away.

The shifters moved forward until they were standing almost nose-to-nose. This was when the Aries alpha would start the ritual, and again, the alphas hesitated. Taurus started to howl first, followed by the Gemini twins. They were pressed close to each other, their tails twined together, as they acted as one alpha for the ritual. My brothers went next, one after the other, followed by Madison and then Ethan. Around the circle they all went, adding their lovely, keening howls to the night, their noses pointed toward the stars.

I held my breath and waited for them to start glowing, but nothing happened. There was no change in the air, or any sign of the magic working. Damnit. We needed the Aries alpha. A bolt of blind rage went through me. Every single other alpha had come through, putting aside their differences and facing their fears to be here. Why couldn't the Aries alpha do the same?

The alphas realized it wasn't working and their howls cut off, leaving the night silent once more. Everyone turned to me for a solution, and I swallowed hard.

I opened my mouth to address them, but then I paused as I felt a flicker of magic in the distance, like a small *pop*. Every one of my hairs stood on end as I realized it was the wards being broken.

"They're here!" I called out.

Before any of us could move, a huge beam of sunlight shot through the clearing and knocked into the alphas, sending them all flying backward. At the same moment, dozens of Sun Witches in orange robes appeared out of nowhere in a burst of smoke, forming a circle around our people. Unnaturally beautiful vampires in black clothes slinked through the night beside them, along with a group of shifters, much to my surprise. The gray and brown wolves snarled, their eyes feral and their teeth snapping. I caught sight of a pack mark on one of their flanks and my blood ran cold.

The Aries had turned on us.

Our enemies charged, and in an instant, the battle was upon us. The alphas recovered quickly while their warriors jumped into action, preparing to defend their leaders with their lives. Shifters threw themselves at vampires with animalistic rage, while Larkin, Brea, and her people tried to stop the Sun Witches. I threw up shields around my allies to protect them from bursts of blazing hot sunlight while searching for a glimpse of Evanora and her staff or Roxandra in her red robe. At least one of them had to be here, but I couldn't see them in the swarm of bodies.

Sagittarius warriors fired arrows from the sidelines with deadly accuracy, while Capricorn wolves used their goat leap to tackle their enemies in a flash of claws and fangs. A Scorpio wolf near me stung a Sun Witch with his tail, poisoning her instantly. The Sun Witch screamed, but before she could retaliate, a Pisces shifter dragged her into the water. Her screams were cut short on a gurgle as she went under.

Meanwhile, the Geminis worked in pairs to take out the

nearest vampires, their twin mind link turning them into brutal, efficient killers. The twins nearest me moved as if they were one person, working in tandem to pull a vampire down and kill him with precise strokes of their claws. A few of the vampires managed to get past them but were met by the Aquarius wolves, who activated their power of foresight to temporarily dodge every blow.

But none of us had counted on the Aries wolves being our enemies too. I knew just how deadly their ram charge could be, but as the Aries pack surged forward at an impossible speed, the Taurus formed up in a line, using their bull stance to protect as many of us from the attack as they could. The Libras moved alongside them, using their powers to nullify the Aries' magic, slowing them down instantly.

I hissed out a breath as a vampire caught my arm, tearing at it. I quickly shot it back with a burst of moon magic, straight into the open mouth of a Leo. A Cancer shifter dodged in and helped the Leo tear it apart, and the sight of the two of them working together made me momentarily breathless.

"Are you okay?" Madison asked, startling me. She motioned to my arm. I nodded, barely noticing the blood dripping from the tear in my robe, but she reached out a hand and quickly healed me before going on to the next shifter who needed her.

"Thank you," I said, but she was kneeling beside a fallen wolf and had already forgotten me.

I felt Kaden wince through our bond as he was injured, not badly enough to take him down but enough to sting. I spun around, searching for him, but couldn't find him in the midst of the battle. I did spot Wesley attacking some vampires, using his crab armor to remain impervious to their attacks, while Jordan fought beside him, using his roar to send other vampires fleeing.

As they did, the crowd opened up just enough for me to catch sight of Kaden. His black wolf glowed with silvery moon magic as he used it as a shield against a Sun Witch fireball. Then he went invisible for a few seconds, before appearing behind the witch and sinking his deadly Ophiuchus poison into her. She went down screaming.

Kaden's wolf eyes looked toward me and panic shot through the bond. I had only a second to feel his warning before a huge reddish-brown Aries wolf came hurtling toward me. I froze as my memory flashed back to when I'd been hit by an Aries ram charge before, but then I managed to teleport away at the last second. The wolf tore a chunk of my robe as he went, though I'd narrowly avoided any actual damage this time.

The Aries wolf spun around and growled at me, blood dripping from his teeth. He was huge, and I sensed massive power coming from him—the alpha, it had to be. Rage at his betrayal boiled up inside me until I saw his eyes. Wild, glassy, almost soulless. I'd seen this before when Wesley had attacked me at the winter Convergence.

He was being controlled by the Sun Witches.

CHAPTER THIRTY-TWO

IF THE ARIES alpha was under Sun Witch control, it stood to reason that the other Aries were too. Which meant Evanora was here somewhere with her staff.

I had to get it.

That thought snapped me out of the fog of battle, and I shot chains of moon magic at the Aries alpha before he could charge me again. I wrapped them around him, holding him in place, and pulled him closer to me. He fought like a feral creature, rising up on his hind legs, claws slashing everywhere, spit flying from his mouth. He was so strong I wasn't sure I could hold him, until Kaden arrived, tackling the reddish-brown wolf and bringing him to the ground. The two alphas scuffled in a frenzy of sharp teeth, but Kaden managed to scrape a poison fang along the Aries's flank, which was just enough to daze him.

I scrambled for the extra moonstone necklace and lifted it over my head. Kaden held the alpha down and I wrapped more silvery chains around the snout that tried to bite me. They would only hold for a few seconds, that was how strong the Aries alpha was, but it was just enough time for me to slip the moonstone necklace over his head.

The moment it settled around his neck, his eyes cleared. He blinked, shaking his huge head, and let out a soft whine. Kaden growled at him, still holding him down, but when the Aries alpha submitted, my mate let him go.

The reddish-brown wolf shifted back to a muscular male with a ginger buzz cut. He dropped to his knees in front of me. "Thank you."

"Where is Evanora?" I asked.

"Back there," he said, pointing to a spot by some of the tents. She must have been using the tents to conceal herself.

"Good. Now use your alpha command to tell your wolves to fight the vampires and Sun Witches instead of the other shifters."

He shifted back to relay the command, just as a Capricorn wolf fell from the sky and landed on top of Kaden. The two wolves rolled and fought, while I noticed other shifters turning on their allies too, attacking with a blind, mindless rage. Evanora was controlling them too now.

Kaden took the Capricorn wolf down with a quick bite, putting him to sleep, but I was already moving toward the tents. I had to take Evanora out. It was the only option.

"Larkin!" I called, hoping she'd hear me over the sounds of battle. She flew down from somewhere above me and hovered in the air. "Evanora's controlling our wolves. Can you shield as many as you can until the alphas break them free?"

"I'll try," she said, but she looked doubtful as she gazed across the battlefield. "There are so many though."

"I know," I said, with a pang of despair, knowing that each second we delayed could lead to more shifter deaths. "I'm going to find Evanora and get her staff."

I teleported away, to the tents that the Aries alpha had indicated, but didn't see Evanora anywhere. I spun around, searching for any glimpse of her pale hair or her staff, but all I saw were shifters fighting vampires, witches, and other shifters. Larkin was shielding as many shifters as she could, but it wasn't enough, and the Sun Witches had caught on to what she was doing and were attacking her too. A Scorpio wolf with glassy eyes attacked me, and I teleported away like a coward, unwilling to fight him. A wave of hopelessness washed through me. If I couldn't stop Evanora, we stood no chance of winning.

A cool, bright light suddenly appeared out of nowhere. The night air filled with the power of the moon, and I gasped as a woman with pure white hair and a silver crown stepped out of the light. My mother! A dozen other women in purple robes followed her, along with one beautiful, black-haired vampire. I cried out in relief at the sight of them. The Moon Witches had come to help us. They'd actually come!

I couldn't believe it, but I pulled myself together and teleported to Celeste. "You're here."

She embraced me quickly. "I managed to convince a few

witches that we would regret it forever if we did nothing. Now, what can we do to help?"

"Evanora and her staff are controlling the shifters and making them attack each other. If you can shield them, I can work on stopping her."

"I'll make sure that no harm comes to you," Killian said to Celeste, as he pulled a sword from a sheath.

"Go," Celeste told me. "We'll handle this."

"Thank you." I gave them both a look filled with love, before turning back to find Evanora. I felt the Moon Witches use their magic, wrapping it around the wolves, and felt lighter knowing we had their power on our side.

If I could feel their magic, surely I could feel a large amount of sun magic coming from one person too. I closed my eyes and steadied myself, reaching out into the night with my senses—and there, in the middle of a small group of vampires, stood Evanora and her staff.

"Jack!" I called out. I'd need some help getting past that group quickly. If I took too long, Evanora would vanish again.

Jack's black nose nudged against my leg only a few seconds later, and I reached down to touch his furry head. I spotted Harper and Dane, also in their wolf forms, just behind him.

Relief washed through me, seeing them all alive and unharmed. "I need your help," I said. "All of you."

Jack and Harper let out little yips to show they understood, and I teleported us as close to the vampires as I could. The three wolves instantly launched into a coordinated attack, while I came face to face with Roxandra, who blocked my path to her mother.

She wore red robes and had a horrible scar running down one side of her face from when we'd last fought, thanks to my claws. She'd always been so beautiful, but now her face matched how hideous she was inside. Her eyes glowed with angry magic as she faced me, blocking me from reaching her mother.

"I'm going to flay you alive," she snarled, as sunfire gathered in her hands.

"Nice scar," I said to her, as I grew my claws. "How about I put a matching one on the other side?"

"No," Jordan said, behind me, in human form. "She's mine."

"Jordan—" she started, but was cut off when his giant golden-red wolf lunged for her. She screamed as he took her down.

I saw a flash of magic as they fought, but I was already moving past them toward my target. Evanora was resplendent in a golden robe and a crown with a sunburst on it that matched the staff she held, and her beautiful, timeless face was cold and cruel. She was surrounded by four vampires wearing all black. I gestured at them, and my three Ophiuchus wolves charged, drawing the vampires away. Leaving Evanora alone to face me.

A smile spread across her lips as I approached, but there was nothing kind about it. "Thank you for gathering all my enemies together in one place. Now I can destroy them all at once."

She blasted me with sunfire, but I used my moon magic to throw up a shield. Her sun magic was so strong though that I gritted my teeth as I felt it breaking through my shield. I remembered a spell in Brea's journal, one I hadn't been able to practice yet with anyone else, and chanted the words I'd memorized. Evanora's sun magic became mine, and I threw it back at her. She made a gesture with her hand and it vanished, though her eyes widened in surprise.

"You've learned some new tricks."

"I have, *auntie*," I said, as I called forth a bolt made of both sun and moon magic.

She sniffed. "No matter. You're still no match for me."

I tossed my bolt of magic but she threw up her own magical shield to block it, before leveling her staff at me. Red hot sun magic poured out of it and I let out a cry as it slammed into my shield and tore it apart. The blast of heat made me stumble back, and I fell straight into the path of one of her vampire guards. He slashed at my robes, tearing them with his razor-sharp nails, and I fell to the ground to avoid his attack. Evanora blasted me at the same time and I managed to roll out of the way, but then the vampire was back, and pain sliced along my side as he grabbed me. I found myself pinned between the vampire and Evanora, both of them preparing to kill me. I tried to teleport, but nothing happened. Evanora was blocking me somehow. I gathered my magic but feared it wouldn't be enough.

But then a gray wolf came barreling out of nowhere, charging Evanora with a snarl, just as two caramel-colored wolves leaped on the vampire. Harper and Dane took the vampire down, while Jack took the blast of sunfire meant for me. It hit him in the chest just as he reached Evanora, and I let out a wordless cry. He took her down with a roar, but then his body went limp on top of her, his fur blackened and smoking.

"No!" I screamed as I rushed toward them.

Evanora shoved Jack's body off her but struggled to get up. Jack had taken a huge bite out of her shoulder, and she was bleeding profusely from it.

I ignored her and ran to Jack, hoping to heal him, but he was already gone. "No, no, no," I mumbled, running my hands over his fur, crying for the friend who'd given his life protecting me.

"I'll kill every one of your shifter friends to get to you," Evanora said. She pressed a glowing hand to her injury, trying to stop the bleeding with her magic. She cauterized the wound, her face twisting with pain.

Rage and despair like I had never known filled me, and I wanted to use every last drop of moon and sun magic inside of me to tear her apart. I was about to do it when I saw the staff lying on the ground a short distance from her. She must have dropped it when Jack attacked her.

I won't let you die in vain, I thought, as I lunged for the staff. I wrapped my fingers around it and Evanora let out a sound of protest. With the staff's power, I could free all the wolves here of their blessing spells.

But Evanora grabbed the staff at the same time, gripping it tightly. We both sent our magic through it, glaring at each other, our faces only inches apart, neither of us willing to back down. Sun and moon magic swirled through us and into the staff, making it glow so bright it blinded me, but I didn't stop. I bared my teeth, readying my claws, willing to take the staff any way I could, when I heard a loud *crack* and was blasted back in a burst of light.

When my vision cleared, I was lying on my back in the dirt. I pushed myself to my feet, my head swimming, but the staff was gone. All that remained were a few burnt shards of metal and melted crystal scattered on the ground.

"No," I cried, stumbling forward. I picked up a piece of what had once been part of the sun at the top of the staff, but I couldn't even see the other parts of it. The staff was gone, and with it went any chance I had of freeing the Zodiac Wolves by myself.

Our only hope was for the alphas to align.

CHAPTER THIRTY-THREE

DESPAIR NEARLY DRAGGED me down again as I looked at the broken shards of the staff and the fallen gray wolf near me, but then there was a spark of hope. I watched as one of the Sagittarius shifters shook her head, blinking at the Scorpio shifter she had pinned down on the ground, and then let him up. Just behind them, a Cancer wolf had a Virgo woman cornered, but let out a whine and backed away slowly. All around the battlefield, shifters came back to their senses as the control spell dissipated now that the staff was broken.

I turned back, but Evanora was gone. I swore under my breath, while Harper and Dane began howling mournfully as they found Jack's body. They'd completely ripped apart Evanora's vampire guard, and their snouts and paws were covered in blood as they nudged the gray wolf. Larkin landed at their side, her feet gracefully hitting the ground, and she let out a sob and pressed her hands to her mouth.

"He's gone," I said, my voice breaking with the words. "But we can honor his memory by finishing our task. Harper, tell Kaden to get the other alphas back in a circle. Larkin, get the other witches to form a shield around the alphas to protect them while they align."

"What will you do?" Larkin asked.

My hands clenched into fists. "I'm going to take out Evanora for good."

Harper bowed her furry head, and the two wolves darted off to relay the message and get the other shifters in place. Larkin nodded too, giving me a brief hug, before flying off again to get the two groups of witches to help her.

With that done, I tore off my shredded robes and tossed them aside. I'd fought Evanora as a witch, using both my moon and sun magic, but now it was time to fight her as a wolf. My white paws hit the ground and my tail swished behind me as I shifted in the blink of an eye. I raised my nose to the sky, inhaling sharply, breathing in the scents of the battle. So many smells, all of them horrible, and so strong they almost overwhelmed me. But there—Evanora's faint smell, like a mix of coal and lemon. I lumbered after it, intent on taking down my prey, knowing nothing would stop me this time.

I darted around shifters, past vampires, and through groups of witches, until I found Evanora, standing with a group of Sun Witches behind the Cancer tent, of all ironies. I crept around the tent and heard them speaking.

"I ordered you to create a sunfall in the sky," Evanora snapped. "Why do you hesitate?"

"That will kill everyone," one of the orange-robed women protested, her voice nervous. "Including our allies."

"I don't care! Just do it!"

"Yes, Evanora," the woman said, and a few others muttered similar words.

I had no idea what a sunfall was, but it couldn't be good. I prepared my attack, when sharp claws dug into my back and dragged me back. These fucking vampires! I snarled and twisted, snapping my teeth, but the vampire was too damn fast and strong. He had a sun pinned to his shoulder, and I realized I'd spotted him earlier, tearing through our shifter allies like they were tissue. He had to be their leader.

"Get your hands off my mate," Kaden growled. He prowled over in human form, naked muscles shining with blood, and tossed the vampire off me like a doll. He shot me a look that was a mix of fury and protective love. "I've got your back. Take her down."

I raised my snout in thanks and spun around, though I moved a little slower with my new injuries. Blood dripped off my white fur as I charged toward Evanora.

She was chanting softly in ancient Greek with five other Sun Witches. Sun magic began spreading overhead, blanketing us all in bright, warm light, like a huge sun radiating deadly heat down on us. This had to be the sunfall magic they'd been discussing, and I feared what kind of damage it would do if they released it. I pictured Jack's burnt, blackened body and shuddered, imagining that same thing happening to everyone here.

I wasn't strong enough to fight against that. Not on my

own, at least. But I wasn't alone. I was surrounded by my allies. Shifters of every single pack. Brea and the rebel Sun Witches. Celeste and the Moon Witches. They had all the magic I needed.

As I faced Evanora, I drew the energy from everyone around me. Sun, moon, and star magic all in one place, and all there for my use. I breathed in the power, letting it fill me, and then I tilted my head back, howling.

It wasn't to warn the other shifters, or a battle cry, or even a song for the fallen. I was calling to the stars, asking them to listen to me, to recognize me as the alpha that I was. Their magic stirred, far away and faint, but I felt it. *Please*, I prayed. *Evanora has thrown the balance off between the sun, moon, and stars, and now it needs to be restored.*

I called out to Selene, the goddess of the moon, and begged for her help. I called out to Helios, god of the sun, and pleaded for his assistance. I was the daughter of the sun, moon, and stars, and I needed them all right now.

And they all listened.

My body was suffused with massive power and I became pure energy. I shone like the sun. I glowed like the moon. I glittered like the stars. Celestial magic turned me into a luminous being, and then went *beyond* my body, unable to be contained within my small wolf frame.

I turned the magic toward Evanora and let out a massive roar. Fire flew from my mouth. Ice formed on my paws. Electricity raced through my fur.

She threw up a shield, barely able to protect herself and

her witches. "Impossible," she stammered. "How can you have this kind of power?"

"You have displeased the gods," I told her. "It's over, Evanora."

"No!" she yelled. "Release the sunfall!"

The Sun Witches chanted faster and louder, and the bright sunburst overhead radiated heat—and began falling down toward my friends, my allies, and even my enemies. They were all frozen, watching up in horror as their death approached, but I refused to let this be the end. I sent my magic out, forming a huge, shining shield over everyone, protecting them all with my magic. The sunfall plummeted against it in a burst of light that turned the night into day, but then it dissipated. My shield absorbed it all, only strengthening my power with the addition of their sun magic.

Evanora screamed and shot magic at me, and the witches beside her did the same. It hit my body and did nothing. If anything, it made me stronger. I opened my mouth and released my energy toward her in a luminous torrent, and she burst into a thousand little pieces of light. *That was for Jack, and for every other life you've stolen.*

The Sun Witches beside her met the same fate. I spun around to see if anyone else wished to challenge me, but Kaden had already taken down the vampire who'd attacked me. Everyone else was fleeing or already dead. But I still had so much power, and so much grief and anger, and I had to use it on someone. I found another group of vampires and opened my mouth to destroy them, but then I felt Kaden's hand on my back.

"That's enough, little wolf."

His voice and his calm presence beside me brought me back to myself. I was Ayla, his little wolf, his mate. With a long breath, I slowly released the magic, letting it back out into the sky, sending it to the heavens once more. It flowed up into the night, and then everything went dark again, with only the distant stars lighting the black sky.

My body gave out under me. I felt hollow, weak, lost. All that power, now gone. But Kaden had his hands on my face, rubbing my snout, stroking my ears. Through our bond I felt his love, his pride, and his relief. I licked his face, letting him know I was all right, and then I shifted back. He held me, naked, in his arms as I shivered and clung to him, overwhelmed by everything that had happened. I wept for all we had lost, and all we had won, and all we still had to do.

I looked up at him through tear-filled eyes. "You need to align with the other alphas or this will all be for nothing."

He gave me a soft kiss and then rose to his feet. His voice rose across the battlefield. "Alphas, circle up!"

He shifted and moved into place, while the other alpha wolves gathered together. I feared we might have lost one of them, but they were all still alive, though most were injured, and some were worse off than others. I watched the Aquarius alpha limp over, finally closing the circle with all thirteen packs represented.

As the Aries alpha raised his head, a mournful howl echoed through the air, sending shivers down my spine. The

Taurus alpha added his voice next, and one by one, the other alphas followed suit, creating a haunting melody that pierced the night. The stars listened, and the alphas began to shine, just like in the vision Dane had shown me.

Their howls reached new heights as they sparkled brighter and brighter, their fur so radiant that I had to squint. Star magic radiated out from each alpha, washing away all traces of the Sun Witch spells on them, and then it rippled outwards, enveloping the other shifters around us in a burst of power. It washed over everyone in the area, including me, before it disappeared.

When it was done, many of the other wolves around us let out soft howls into the night, some triumphant, some sorrowful. The alphas shifted back and looked at one another with surprise and awe, as if they were still in disbelief. Kaden's eyes met mine, and he gave me a little nod.

It was over. We were free.

CHAPTER THIRTY-FOUR

I SANK TO THE GROUND, finally giving in to my injuries, and to the exhaustion and grief that were just as strong as the relief. The last remaining vampires and Sun Witches fled quickly, disappearing in a poof of smoke, probably back to Solundra. There were few of them left, but we'd lost many people too. I saw dead shifters all across the battlefield, along with fallen witches from both sides. So many lost in one night, yet so much gained too.

Sometime later, perhaps a minute, perhaps an hour, Kaden gathered me in his arms. He smoothed his hands over my hair and wiped the tears off my cheeks. "Are you all right?"

"I think so," I said, my voice shaking. "Are you?"

He shrugged. "I'll heal."

I knew what he meant. We were all injured, inside and out, but we would get better over time. But there were others who wouldn't.

"Jack..." My throat tightened and another tear slid down my cheek.

"I know." Kaden's entire body sighed. "I saw."

"I'm sorry. I couldn't—"

"Stop. You have nothing to feel guilty about. Jack was one of my closest friends, but he was also my most trusted warrior, and he died protecting his alpha female. There is nothing braver than that. I can't believe he's gone, and I will miss him terribly, but we will honor his memory among the Ophiuchus forever."

I sniffed and nodded. "I will never forget his sacrifice."

"When we get back, we will howl for him, and for everyone else we lost tonight."

Something in his voice made me worried. I sat up and looked at him. "Who else was lost?"

Kaden's face was grim. "Every pack lost too many."

"My brothers?" I whispered, terrified of the answer.

"They're fine, but..." Kaden stood and offered me his hand. "I think you should come with me."

Getting up was hard. I hurt all over, and I was bleeding from at least three places, although I was healing fast. Faster than usual, even. Holding so much power inside of me must have helped with that.

Kaden led me through the dark battlefield toward the spot where the alphas had aligned, careful not to disturb any of the dead or the Virgo shifters healing those they could. Many of the alphas had already wandered off to tend to their pack mates, and we came upon Wesley speaking with one of the Cancer warriors. He'd found some clothes and had a bit of dried blood on his forehead, but otherwise seemed to be unharmed.

I limped over to him and hugged him tightly. "I'm so glad you're okay."

Wesley hugged me back. "I'm glad you are too. You were pretty amazing out there."

"I'm still not sure exactly what I did. But you alphas are the true heroes. You freed everyone here."

"Only because you two told us how and got everyone to work together." Wesley gazed across the land. "It's hard to believe we really did it."

"Yes, and this is only the beginning," Kaden said. "Many more wolves need to be freed. But now we know we can do it."

We found Jordan next, being healed by one of the Virgo females nearby. He winced as she moved her hands over a big gash in his chest, but his face brightened when he saw us approach.

"Are you okay?" I asked, kneeling beside him.

"This? Just a scratch." He smirked. "You're not rid of me yet, sorry."

"Good." I squeezed his arm. "And Roxandra?"

He shook his head, his face twisting in a grimace. "I wounded her badly, but she got away."

"Damn." I was hoping we'd seen the last of her. As long as she was alive she would still be a threat, especially to Jordan and his younger brother.

Jordan rolled his shoulders. "If she comes back, I'll tear her apart."

"All you have to do is call, and the Ophiuchus will be there to help," Kaden said, offering Jordan his hand. They shook, and some of the despair inside me melted away.

We moved on, and my worry grew as Kaden led me toward something he wanted me to see, in the clearing where the alphas had aligned.

"Who didn't make it?" I asked around the lump in my throat.

"We lost the Taurus alpha early in the battle," Kaden said. "But one of his warriors stepped up and declared himself alpha. I'm grateful for his quick thinking, or it wouldn't have worked. But Aiden..."

I gasped as I saw Aiden's body on the ground, surrounded by the other Pisces wolves who had survived. They kneeled beside him, heads down, mourning the death of another of their alphas.

I stumbled forward and fell to my knees. "No," I said, taking Aiden's hand. His chest had deep, fatal gashes all over it from the vampires, and one side of him was completely charred from Sun Witch fire. The sight of it made me sick, and tears streamed down my face.

Kaden stood behind me, his hand on my shoulder. "Despite his many wounds, Aiden held on long enough to do the ritual. As soon as it was over, he returned to the stars. He was a true alpha of his pack, even if only for a short time."

The Pisces shifters nodded solemnly at Kaden's words. I wept openly for Aiden, and even though I hadn't known him well, I still felt his loss deeply. The Pisces pack had long been our allies, and they had suffered so much at the hands

of the Sun Witches. But more than that, Aiden was Mira's
mate and the father of her child, which was due to be born
any day now. Mira would be devastated to learn that her
mate had fallen. The two of them had been willing to fight
to be together, even without a mate bond, and Aiden had
truly loved Mira until the very end. I wept for the life they
might have had together. But Mira was strong, and she'd
known what she was sending him into. She'd let him go,
knowing he was risking their mate bond and his life to free
his people. She would mourn him, but hopefully she would
also see his sacrifice for the gift that it was.

With heavy hearts, Kaden and I continued our journey
across the battlefield. I felt like I had to see every one of the
dead, to know the price of what we had earned today. We
did what we could to help the living too. We healed those
we could and called the Virgos to help with those we
couldn't. We brought water to the thirsty and carried the
injured back to their pack's tents. But then we stumbled
upon a body that made Kaden stop in his tracks.

The beautiful woman who was once Kaden's first love
looked peaceful as she gazed up at the stars, even with her
throat torn open. Eileen clutched her bow in one hand with
the other hand over her heart. Kaden's face was pale as he
looked down at her. I knew he didn't love her anymore, not
like he once did, but he'd known her since they were children and he would still mourn her loss. I took his hand,
weaving our fingers together, quietly sharing my strength.

"She's with her mate now," I said softly.

Kaden nodded, his hand tightening around mine. He

bent down and closed Eileen's eyes, then lifted her and brought her to the Sagittarius tent so she could be with her packmates. I watched him go and then went to help Madison, who was healing an injured Aries shifter.

"We lost too much," Madison said, looking up at me with haunted eyes. "No one should have to suffer this much. Was it even worth it?"

"It was," Ethan said, moving beside us. He looked exhausted and sad, but his eyes were bright and hopeful too. "The wolves who survived the battle are free now, and their children will grow up without ever knowing what it was like to be under Sun Witch control. Evanora is dead and her staff is gone, so we will never fall under her spell again. But most importantly, we know the ritual works, and we can do it again and again, as many times as needed, until every wolf tastes freedom."

"Assuming we can keep the alphas from turning against each other again," I said.

"You can." Ethan cracked a smile at me. "They'll listen to you. Especially after what they saw you do tonight."

"It was incredible," Madison said. "I've never felt such power before."

I ducked my head. "I just did the best I could, same as all of you. None of us could have won this battle alone."

"True, but none of us would be here if not for you," Ethan said. "You're the reason the alphas aligned, and the reason the Zodiac Wolves will be free someday."

His praise made me blush and a little more of the darkness inside me faded away. I hoped Ethan was right, and that this marked a new beginning for the Zodiac Wolves.

Larkin waved me over from where she stood beside my mother. Their robes were black in a few places and torn in others, but for the most part, they looked all right, much to my relief.

"I'm so glad you're okay," Larkin said, as she squeezed me tight.

My mother hugged me next. "I'm so proud of you," Celeste said, pulling back to gaze at me. "Truly, you are a blessed child."

"Thank you for coming to help us," I said.

"It was time for us to stop hiding in the shadows. We had to fight for our freedom too." She glanced between me and Larkin. "The two of you taught me that to really live we cannot stay in a timeless realm. We must return here to Earth."

"Do you think you will?" I asked.

"I hope so, eventually. I doubt everyone will go, but perhaps enough of us would be willing to start a new life somewhere."

"The Moon Witches will always be welcome with the Ophiuchus," I said.

"It would be nice to have some other witches around," Larkin added with a smile.

"Speaking of other witches..." I muttered, as Brea walked up to us.

Larkin and Celeste both stiffened at the Sun Witch's

approach, but none of the ladies attacked each other, so I took that as a good sign.

"Peace, sisters," Brea said, holding up her hands. "I come to you as a friend, not as an enemy."

Celeste's eyes narrowed. "You have never once been a friend to the Moon Witches."

"No, but I hope to change that." She offered a small smile to Celeste, as her eyes traveled over her. "It has been many years, Celeste. You look well."

"What is it you want, Breanora?" Celeste asked.

"I want peace and safety for my people, just as you do, and I want the favor of Helios once more." She turned her timeless gaze on me with a kind smile. "You seem to have it. I take that as a sign that I'm on the right path."

"I think you are," I said. "With Evanora gone, Helios might look kindly on you once again."

"I hope so." She stood a little taller and announced, "I'm going to declare myself the new High Priestess of the Sun Witches."

I arched an eyebrow. "Roxandra might have a problem with that."

Brea jutted out her chin. "She can fight me for the position if she wants it. But I think I'll be able to convince the other Sun Witches to follow me now that Evanora is gone. Everyone was too scared of her to oppose her, but I hope to lead them in a different way." She looked at Celeste once more. "I'd like to start by forming an alliance with the Moon Witches and the Zodiac Wolves."

Celeste crossed her arms. "We'll think on it."

"Mom..." I said gently.

"What?" She threw up her hands. "You cannot expect us to forget hundreds of years of genocide because this woman supposedly had a change of heart."

"No, you're right," Brea said, her face thoughtful. "I realize an alliance will take some time to work out, between all of us. I can't expect any of you to trust us yet, though I promise we will no longer hunt neither witch nor wolf. I plan to gain control of the Sun Witches first and guide them onto a new path, one of peace and harmony. Once that is done, I hope we can speak about this again. That is all I ask. For a chance to talk."

"We would like that," Larkin said, though my mother still looked uncertain.

"And the vampires?" Killian's melodic voice asked, as he joined our group. His clothes had smears of blood across them, but otherwise he looked as beautiful as he always did. "I don't know what sort of deal they had with the Sun Witches, but I have a feeling we won't see the last of them."

"I'm not sure either," Brea admitted.

Kaden joined us then too, and he rested his hand on my lower back. "If the vampires want to fight us again, we'll be ready for them."

I leaned against him, welcoming his steady presence. I knew I could face whatever happened next as long as Kaden was by my side.

A sudden chorus of excited yips had us all turning to look at the commotion. By the lake, a gray Cancer wolf and a reddish Scorpio wolf were rolling around, nipping and nuzzling each other, their tails wagging. Other members from their packs rushed forward, in both wolf and human forms, some of them concerned, others confused, and others laughing.

"What's happening?" Larkin asked.

A huge smile spread across my face because I knew immediately what was happening and how they were feeling. I knew, because I'd felt it myself once. I still felt it now, as I took Kaden's hand. That joy. That sense of coming home. That feeling of being complete.

"The ritual worked," I said. "They've found their true mates."

CHAPTER THIRTY-FIVE

AS THE AFTERNOON SUN DESCENDED, my excitement grew with every passing moment. The last two weeks had been a roller coaster of emotions as we settled back into a normal life after the new moon battle that had freed us all. We were back in Coronis, and though we had mourned the warriors we had lost, including Jack, the pack was slowly healing and preparing for the future. I suspected the other packs were doing the same. Starting with tonight— the full moon.

Every full moon made shifters a little wild, perhaps from a lingering trace of the Moon Curse still in our blood, or perhaps because each one made a different pack go into heat —and this full moon belonged to the Ophiuchus.

This time, I wasn't packless, and I had my real mate. I could hardly believe it. I'd be going into true heat tonight, with the possibility of getting pregnant. The thought sent shivers down my spine.

But first, we would hunt.

As a wolf, I stood on the edge of the forest and inhaled the crisp, fresh air. The Ophiuchus pack had already begun their hunt, and the scent of their pursuit was easy to pick up. I raced through the trees, my paws pounding against the ground as I followed the trail of the other shifters. The thrill of the chase coursed through me, my heart pounded with excitement as I caught sight of Kaden's large and majestic wolf through the brush. His black fur shone under the setting sun as I approached, and he greeted me with a short bark, then rubbed up against my side.

About time you showed up, he said with a wolfy grin.

I nipped his neck playfully. *I thought you might need a head start.*

He huffed at that. *Don't forget who taught you to hunt, little wolf.*

Why don't you show us how it's done then? Stella asked, her black wolf watching us with amusement.

I'd be happy to, Kaden replied. *But let's get on with it already. I've got some things to do tonight.*

More like someone to do tonight, Harper said, her caramel wolf rolling on the ground with laughter. Beside her, Dane looked up at the heavens, like he was exasperated with all of us. Clayton and Grant both snickered nearby.

Kaden raised his nose to the air and then took off running. I dashed alongside him, and together we became a fierce duo as we tracked a deer. We worked in perfect harmony, with me keeping the deer in sight while Kaden moved in for the kill, and the rest of the pack creeping behind us, ready to pounce. The deer stood no chance against our combined strength and agility, and we brought it down with ease.

With the kill made, Kaden and I howled to the sky in triumph. The rest of the pack joined in, their voices filling the forest with a wild and beautiful chorus. I felt like I was truly a part of something special, a member of the pack and their true alpha female. I was finally home, and nothing could ever tear me away from this place.

The sun was setting and the moon was rising. Soon, the pack would be heading back to the cookout in the center of the village, but for now, we were all here, together, taking part in this ancient and sacred tradition. My heart swelled with pride and joy as I ran through the forest, surrounded by my packmates, with my true mate by my side.

Afterward, the village feasted and celebrated, but when the moon rose, people began to pair off with their mates to settle into a long night of going into heat and hopefully getting pregnant. Those that were unmated stayed at the party, though many of them left together to enjoy themselves on this beautiful night.

I expected Stella to pair off with someone, like she'd done at other full moons, but instead, I saw her heading back to the cottage with Larkin. Even though many of the unmated males would gladly spend the night with her, she'd turned everyone down. I wondered if it was out of solidarity with her friend, or if there was another reason she'd turned them all down. Perhaps someone she wanted, though she would never admit it to herself...

I heard a growl behind me, and it put all thoughts of Stella aside. My heart sped up as I turned to face him. Of course I knew who it was. I could feel his desire through our mate bond.

"Kaden," I said, breathlessly, as the heat started to take hold of me, the lust crawling under my skin, the need pulsing between my thighs.

He strode toward me with hunger in his gaze, and I let out a squeal as he hoisted me up and threw me over his shoulder. He carried me back to the house, just like he did during that first full moon, which seemed so long ago now. I laughed and kicked, but I wasn't really putting any effort into my fight. No, I very much wanted him to win this battle.

Desire thrummed between us as he opened the door and carried me into our house. I squirmed in his grasp, needing to touch him. "Let me down."

"Not yet." He slapped my ass, and I let out another squeal. "I feel it too, but I'm not going to be rushed tonight. Last time I held myself back because you weren't my mate. Not yet anyway. Not fully. But now you're all mine, and I'm not going to hold anything back."

"Those are big words from someone who isn't fucking me," I said breathlessly.

"Patience." He didn't let me go, even as I tried to rub myself off against him, unable to help myself. He threw me down on the couch we'd first done this on, and then stood over me. His eyes were heavy with lust as he reached out to put his thumb on my bottom lip, moving it back and forth until I parted my mouth for him. He slid his finger inside and I sucked it gently, looking up at him with a seductive gaze and hoping he got the hint.

"I love seeing you like this." He removed his finger and took my chin in his hands, tilting my head up. "Flush with your rising heat, and so needy for my cock."

"You're such a tease," I said, panting.

A smile lifted his lips, and he pushed me back onto the cushion. "If you think that's teasing, you haven't seen anything yet."

His eyes flashed with primal lust as his claws came out. He slid them down my dress, slicing it open like it was made of tissue paper. Then he hooked one claw into my panties, and they ripped easily too. Any other night I might have complained about my ruined clothes, but not now, not during heat. Besides, it turned me on seeing him let his animal side loose like that.

He ran those claws along my naked flesh, and the hint of pain only made it hotter. I knew Kaden would never hurt me, and I threw my head back as those sharp claws ran along my breasts, making them tingle. Then they traveled lower, down my stomach and my hips, while I grew wetter with every touch.

Those claws spread my legs wide, and then Kaden's face was between my thighs, his tongue tasting me. "Fuck, you're so wet," he growled, low and deep, and I felt his hot breath against my pussy. "You taste so good."

I cried out as he circled my clit with the tip of his tongue and then dipped lower, swirling around my pussy before sliding inside. Then his mouth was fully on me, licking and sucking like he couldn't get enough. I wonder if I tasted different during heat, or if it was just the wild need in both of us that had him devouring me like a starved animal.

I squeezed my eyes shut and arched my back while he fucked me with his tongue, feeling my climax building quickly. My body writhed beneath him, wanting more, wanting everything he had to give me. I gripped my fists in his hair, holding him there as I worked my hips in time with his tongue, feeling the uncontrollable need take over my body. It wasn't enough though. I needed his cock. We both knew from last time I went into heat that nothing else would do.

I bucked my hips, trying to force his mouth away, to bring him back up to me, but he just held me down, grinding against my clit, making me cry out again. "Please," I begged, panting. "I need your cock, Kaden."

But Kaden wouldn't listen and he wouldn't stop. He kept eating me out, his tongue driving me crazy as the pleasure built, my orgasm crashing over me. I shuddered, biting down hard on my lip as he tried to wring every last drop of my climax out of me. It was torture, wonderful torture, because all it did was make the desire for him even stronger. Like a little taste of what I needed, but not nearly enough. The heat demanded more.

He rose up and looked at me with a satisfied smile, his mouth wet with the taste of me. "Delicious."

I propped myself up on my elbows. "Enough teasing.

You can go down on me for hours on any other night, but tonight, I really need you inside of me."

"Do you?" He licked his lips as his hungry eyes gazed along my naked body. He lifted one hand and ran it down my thigh, and when he reached my pussy, he spread my lips apart, exposing my swollen clit. I whimpered, and he pushed two fingers inside me, stretching me open. "Are you sure you're ready for this?"

I tilted my head back and moaned loudly. "Yes. Hurry."

He slid his fingers in and out of me slowly. My head fell back, desire pulling my spine taut and lifting my hips to try to get more friction. He growled low in his throat, and then his fingers withdrew. I whimpered a little.

"Do you want me to fuck you, or not?" he asked, as he tore off his shirt and tossed it aside. I devoured the sight of his naked chest, all those rippling muscles and hard abs, and nodded eagerly. Then he popped open the button on his jeans and pulled out his cock, staring down at me with an amused look on his face.

"Finally." I grasped his cock and jerked it slowly, loving how big and thick it felt in my hand. He was fully hard, and I could smell the arousal on him. I leaned forward and ran my tongue along it, unable to help myself.

He groaned, a deep sound of satisfaction, and then he shoved me down onto the cushions, pushing my legs apart so he could slide between them. He kissed me hard, letting out a sound that was half curse and half promise as his cock pressed at my entrance. The ache between my thighs grew, wanting nothing more than to feel him inside me, as full and hard as possible.

But then his strong hands gripped my body and turned me over, bringing me up on my hands and knees. The animal in my blood practically screamed *yes* as he got in position behind me.

"Take me, claim me, rut me, do whatever you want, just do it now," I begged. "I'm yours."

"Mine," he growled.

He lined himself up and pushed his cock into me in one, smooth motion. I groaned, shifting my hips and trying to take him deeper. He felt so good, so big and hard, filling me up completely. He really was made to be my mate.

His hands ran along my ass, squeezing and kneading it, as he pulled out and slammed back into me. He thrust hard and I dug my nails into the cushions, moaning out loud. I couldn't stop myself from rocking back against him as I cried out his name.

He made a satisfied sound, and began fucking into me earnestly, so primal and wild that my eyes rolled back into my head. He grabbed my hips and started pounding me, hard and fast, matching my movements perfectly. I screamed my pleasure into the cushions as his cock hit that perfect angle inside of me, driving me closer and closer to orgasm.

We were like wild animals, the heat taking over and driving us to act on our instincts alone. His claws were out again, raking along my skin. Mine came out too, tearing into the cushions. Kaden was absolutely feral as he thrust into me, and I loved every second of it. I threw my head back and gasped out loud, riding out the waves of ecstasy surging through my body.

Kaden arched over my back and growled as his sharp teeth sank into my neck. I cried out, my senses overwhelmed by the bite, the pain mixing with the pleasure as he made me come again. His hands tightened on my waist, pulling himself as deep as he could. He came as I did, biting my neck and marking me as his mate once again.

I let out a scream and shuddered around him as he kept coming and coming, like he couldn't stop. His cock swelled, stretching me wider, more than I'd ever been stretched before, as he kept pumping into me.

"Oh my god," I cried out, as my orgasm kept going on and on with this strange new sensation. "What's happening?"

Kaden groaned and rocked himself against me, sending waves of intense pleasure through me again. "It's called knotting. The base of my cock is expanding to hold me inside of you so that nothing leaks out. It's to increase the chances of pregnancy."

"It feels so good," I said, grinding back against him, chasing that pleasure. It was like this was what I'd needed for this heat, without even knowing it.

He gripped my hair, running his tongue along the bite on my neck. "I'm going to stay locked inside of you until every last drop of my seed is deep in your core."

I moaned and nodded, pushing my hips back into him. He snarled, and then he slammed into me again, setting off another wave of pleasure that seemed to go on forever.

Finally, he lowered us onto the couch, wrapping his arms around me, his cock still locked inside me from behind.

"Why hasn't it happened before?" I asked, as I snuggled back against him.

Kaden nuzzled my neck. "It happens during heat between two true mates. Especially with alphas."

"I had no idea."

"It was probably rare among the Zodiac Wolves," Kaden said. "But that should change now. More people will find their true mates, and more wolves will be born as a result."

I hummed, content with the feel of him so big and hard inside of me still. "I could get used to this."

He idly played with my hair, twirling it around his finger. "Me too. Especially if it puts a baby in you faster."

I twisted around to look at him with a laugh. "I didn't realize you were such a caveman, wanting to knock me up so soon."

"I didn't realize it either until now." He leaned forward and pressed a kiss to my lips. "Ayla, we've defeated the Sun Witches, freed the Zodiac Wolves, and secured a future for the Ophiuchus pack. Now all I want is a family with you."

"I want that too," I said, my heart soaring as Kaden held me tighter.

Sometime later, Kaden's cock returned to normal size, and I found that I missed the feeling of him locked inside me already. I whined, pushing my hips back, the heat calling to me again. I needed him to fuck me again, and to feel his cock knotting me again.

Kaden pulled out long enough to turn me toward him,

drawing me close to his body. He kissed me as my legs wrapped around him, his cock hard between my thighs.

"I think I'm ready to try for that baby again now," he said, as he slid back home.

I had a feeling that we'd be going all night, but I was ready for it, and for everything that came next with Kaden.

CHAPTER THIRTY-SIX

I GAZED upon the sprawling meadow that served as the venue for the Convergence, taking in the vibrant display of pack tents dotted across the landscape. The summer solstice was upon us, and the air was alive with energy and excitement as shifters from all thirteen packs bustled about, exchanging greetings and catching up with old friends. The sounds of yipping and howling, along with the smells of fresh grass and cooking fires, all combined to create an atmosphere of hope and joy.

This Convergence was a fresh start for the Zodiac Wolves, and I felt incredibly grateful to be a part of it. The old tensions and conflicts that had previously defined our packs were a thing of the past, and we were all coming together as one, united and truly free for the first time in centuries. It was a time to celebrate, and I basked in the warmth of the sun and the love of my fellow shifters.

I took in the sight of some younger shifters playing in the

grass, experiencing their wolves for the first time now that they were no longer bound by Sun Witch magic. I remembered how I'd been so desperate to get my wolf, and I couldn't believe it had been a year since the last summer Convergence when all of this began. My last two Convergences hadn't gone well at all, but I could feel in my heart and soul that this one would be different.

There had been some big changes, after all. The first was that all of the wolves here were free of any Sun Witch magic. The alphas had performed the new moon ritual again last night, giving thanks to the stars that it had coincided so closely with the summer solstice. Hundreds of shifters had come to this Convergence with the purpose of getting the blessing spell removed, and many hoped to meet their true mates tonight. Many other shifters had purposefully stayed at home, keeping the blessing spell so as to not lose their mate bonds. The alphas had decided it would be up to everyone to make that choice for themselves.

I raised my camera, which hung on my neck from the strap Kaden got me at Christmas, and snapped a shot of the pups playing. The sun was setting, casting a beautiful hue over the tents, so I zoomed out a bit and got a landscape photo too. I'd made it my mission to document everything. The first Convergence of the new, freed Zodiac Wolves. This time with zero witches present. Not even Larkin.

She'd been invited, of course, but we'd all decided it would be better if she stayed behind. It would have been nice to have her company, but this marked an important time: the first Convergence with only shifters. Although a part of me secretly wondered if the main reason Larkin had decided not to come was because she didn't want to see if Ethan got his mate today.

Larkin was still living with Stella at the moment, and she'd even convinced a few of the other Moon Witches to stay with the Ophiuchus for a while. She'd taken it upon herself to help them adjust to life back on Earth and slowly reintegrate them into society again. We were happy to have them visit for as long as they wanted, since they'd played such a crucial role in the final battle, and Larkin hoped they might set up a permanent residence somewhere. My mother agreed, though she was staying in Lunatera for the moment. Eventually, the goal was to bring the Moon Witches back to Earth for good, but that would take time. Many of them were still convinced the Sun Witches were a threat, which was true in some ways. Roxandra was still out there, though most of the Sun Witches had decided to follow Brea and had accepted her as their new High Priestess. The vampires had vanished, and we weren't sure where they were or what they were planning, but as long as they didn't bother us, they weren't our problem. If they did come for us again, we would be ready.

I snapped another photo and spotted Mira heading toward me, holding her baby girl, who cooed happily when she saw me. She had a shock of dark hair, big brown eyes, and the chubbiest little cheeks.

"Hey, you two," I said, giving Mira a quick hug. "I'm so glad you're here. How's my little friend?"

Mira propped Adriana up on her hip. "She's good. Finally sleeping a little better. Aren't you, my sweet girl?"

"She's getting so big." I held out my finger and the baby grabbed onto it. "And how are you?"

"I'm doing as well as can be expected," Mira said, with a sad smile. She'd lost weight, and there was a sorrow in her eyes that had never been there before. After her mate had died, Mira had been distraught and didn't know what to do. She had no family with the Pisces and didn't feel like she belonged, but she didn't want to return to the Cancer pack either. All of her family there was gone too. I'd brought her to the Ophiuchus pack and she'd had her baby there, protected and surrounded by her friends. We'd taken care of her, helping as much as we could with her grief and the trials of being a new mother. We'd offered to let her stay as long as she wanted, but eventually she'd decided to return to the Pisces pack so Adriana could grow up there.

"I'm surprised you decided to come," I said.

Mira shrugged. "I felt like I had to come, to get some closure on everything. I owe it to Aiden to be here for him and honor his sacrifice."

"I understand," I said quietly. Tonight the packs would hold a big ceremony to mark this new Convergence, and as part of that, we would honor everyone who had fallen during the new moon battle, celebrating them as brave warriors who had given their lives to free us, with a special moment for Aiden. I could see why Mira wouldn't want to miss it.

Adriana started making fussy noises, and Mira bounced

her on her hip. I reached my arms out for her. "Can I hold her for a moment?"

"Of course," Mira said, and passed her to me.

I took Adriana in my arms and cuddled her close, and she calmed immediately. "I've missed you, little Pisces girl. I'm going to come visit you again real soon, okay?"

"You're so good with her," Mira said. "It's good practice for when your own baby comes."

I ran a hand over my stomach, smiling softly. I wasn't showing very much yet, but I knew it would only be a few months before I started getting as round as Mira had been not long ago. Kaden had gotten his wish that night and had put his baby inside of me, after all.

"I'm so glad that our children won't ever have the Sun Witch blessing on them," I said.

Mira sighed, a mix of relief and sorrow. "Me too."

"Ayla?" someone asked, and I turned as Wesley stepped out of a nearby tent. "Have you seen Mi—"

He trailed off as his eyes landed on Mira beside me. They stared at each other for a long, heated moment. Wesley's brows pinched together in a pained expression. "Mira," he finally said.

"Hey, Wesley." Mira drew in a sharp breath and took her baby from me. "It was good to see you, Ayla, but I should get back to the Pisces pack. I want to talk to the new alpha for a few minutes before the ceremony starts. We'll talk again later, okay?"

She rushed away before Wesley could get another word out, and he looked like he was about to follow her, like he wanted to say something but was holding himself back.

I put a hand on his arm. "She just lost her mate. She needs time."

"I know." He let out a breath and then shook my arm off. As he straightened his back, he looked like the Cancer alpha suddenly, not just my brother. "Everyone is gathering. Shall we head over?"

"Don't wait for me. I want to take a couple more photos first."

Wesley grinned. "I'm glad to see you attached to a camera once again. Just like old times."

"Except better."

"Better," he agreed. He gave me a warm smile before heading toward the spot where everyone was gathering.

I took a few moments to snap some more photos of all the shifters from various packs mingling together with some of the beautiful forest as the background. This Convergence was being held at a spot in Canada that the Sagittarius used during their travels and considered part of their broad pack lands. Over many Zoom calls with the alphas, we'd decided we could no longer use any of the previous Convergence spots since they belonged to the Sun Witches. Instead, each pack would host a Convergence, much like a different city hosted every Olympics. We would rotate between all thirteen packs over the years, giving everyone a chance to have it in their own pack lands. The Sagittarius had volunteered to host the first one, and the Capricorns would be hosting the winter Convergence later this year. We would continue in the order of each Zodiac sign to be fair to everyone, with the Ophiuchus last. That would give our people plenty of time to adjust to the idea of being part of the Zodiac Wolves.

That was the other big change at this Convergence—the Ophiuchus finally had an official spot alongside the other packs. Kaden and the others had proved without a doubt that we belonged as part of the Zodiac Wolves, and no one would dare question our right to be at the Convergence anymore. We were no longer the boogeymen of the Zodiac Wolves, but equals. Heroes, even.

I was taking one last photo when I caught movement out of the corner of my eye. My gaze was drawn to Stella, who stormed out of the forest with a scowl on her face.

Jordan emerged from the same spot a moment later, looking frazzled as he tried to catch up with her. "Stella, wait!" he called out.

She walked right past me, her annoyance palpable, and snapped, "Tell your brother to stay away from me." She disappeared into her tent and I heard her roughly closing the flap behind her.

I raised my eyebrows at Jordan. "What was that about?"

Jordan jerked a hand through his hair as he stared at her tent. "Nothing."

"It didn't look like nothing."

He let out a frustrated huff. "Well, if you figure it out, let me know."

With that, he turned on his heel and walked away. I was tempted to go after him, or to ask Stella what had happened between them, but decided it wasn't my problem. Not tonight, anyway. If they needed me, I would always be there for either of them, but it seemed like they had some things to work out on their own.

The sun had set, so I left the tents to head toward the circle where everyone was gathering. Unlike at the previous Convergences, there were no divided pack lines at this ceremony. Shifters from packs that had once been enemies were now freely conversing with each other, mixing and mingling together, sitting wherever they pleased. I knew that it wouldn't always be so easy, but I hoped that without the Sun Witch magic driving us to hate each other, we'd be able to stay on better terms.

I spotted Ethan among the alphas and waved a hand at him. He'd become like a brother to me over the last few months, and I would never forget all he had done, not just for me but for all of the Ophiuchus. Beside him stood Madison, who offered me a tentative smile. A new friend I was excited to get to know better, and the first half-human alpha. I hoped it was the start of a change among the Zodiac Wolves, a chance for us to become more tolerant of those among us who were a little different.

Wesley and Jordan walked over to them, greeting Ethan and Madison warmly as they all took their positions for the ceremony. Four young, bright alphas ready to lead the Zodiac Wolves forward into the future. I was excited to see what they did next, and pleased to call them my family. And now that they were all free, I hoped they would find their mates too.

As the sky darkened, I easily found Kaden in the crowd,

following our mate bond's steady hum. He took my hand and leaned in to kiss me, while I melted against him.

His hand brushed lightly across my stomach. "How are you feeling?"

"I'm fine." It was cute, how overprotective he was now that I was carrying his child, even when I was arguably the most powerful person at the Convergence. I studied his face, which was more solemn than usual. "How are you doing?"

"It's my first Convergence as a member of the Zodiac Wolves," Kaden said.

I pressed a kiss to his cheek. "Your parents would be proud of you. You brought their dream to life, and made it your own."

Kaden squeezed my hand. "I only succeeded because of you."

I leaned against him. "We did it together."

The last of the alphas joined us, and I looked at all of them, both new and old, all eager for whatever came next. Theo stepped forward, holding the hand of his alpha female, Mae, and the hundreds of shifters gathered around us fell silent. Their mate bond had survived, proving that some of them had always been real.

"The Sagittarius pack welcomes you to the first Convergence of the free, united Zodiac Wolves," he said, his voice carrying across the night.

Kaden and I chanted a few words in ancient Greek, and the black sky lit with a dazzling display of light from a mix of sun and moon magic. We made the lights swirl and dance like the aurora borealis, then spark like fireworks in all different colors, before ending with all the symbols of our packs arranged in a circle overhead. As the magic faded away into the night, the shifters howled and cheered.

Kaden pulled me closer to him as the Sagittarius alpha continued his speech about honoring those we had lost and celebrating all we had gained. As his lips brushed against mine, it reminded me that though this was an ending in some ways, it was a beginning too.

We gazed up at the stars together, and I realized I'd never been cursed by them, as I'd always thought. No, I was blessed. Blessed to have found my destiny in the arms of Kaden and with the Ophiuchus pack. Blessed to have discovered who I really was and uncovered my true family. Blessed to have been able to unite the Zodiac Wolves and to lead them to freedom.

For once, I no longer feared my future. With Kaden, I was ready to face any challenges that might come our way.

Our love was written in the stars, after all.

ABOUT THE AUTHOR

Elizabeth Briggs is a New York Times and Top 5 Amazon bestselling author of paranormal and fantasy romance featuring twisty plots, plenty of spice, and a guaranteed happy ending. She's a cancer survivor who has worked with teens in foster care and volunteered with animal rescue organizations. She lives in Los Angeles with her husband, their daughter, and a pack of fluffy dogs.

Visit Elizabeth's website: www.elizabethbriggs.com

Join Elizabeth's Facebook group for fun book chat and early sneak peeks!

Made in the USA
Las Vegas, NV
22 April 2023

70971394R00198